Something blue flickered in the periphery of Molly's vision. She turned quickly, but there was nothing there. It must have been a bird, or the shadow of a bird. Or maybe it was that turbaned dognaper. Molly quickly twisted around. If he was loitering nearby, she'd catch him creeping up on her.

Again a blue shadow flickered to her left. Molly didn't turn this time. She tried to see what it was without moving. It hovered, then disappeared. Thirty seconds later it appeared to her right. Was it a ghost? A poltergeist was a ghost that was able to move things. Had a poltergeist moved Petula? Molly was determined to find out. Although she was filthy scared, she let the shadow flicker to the left, then again to the right. She stood stock-still. Once more it was there—closer, and then again on the right of her, closer still. Nearer and nearer it got. Right … left … right … There it was to the left … the right … the left. Left, right, left. Her eyes swung from side to side. Molly was so intent upon winkling out the truth that she didn't feel herself falling. Falling into a hypnotic trap.

ALSO BY

Georgia Byng

Molly Moon's Incredible Book of Hypnotism
Molly Moon Stops the World

Georgia Byng

Molly Moon's
Hypnotic Time Travel
Adventure

HarperTrophy®
An Imprint of HarperCollinsPublishers

With a huge thank you to my lovely,
enthusiastic agent, Caradoc King,
and Sarah Dudman, my excellent
and very thoughtful editor

Molly Moon's Hypnotic Time Travel Adventure
Copyright © 2005 by Georgia Byng
Map copyright © 2005 by Fred Van Deelen
Molly Moon logo design by Andrew Biscomb
information address HarperCollins Children's Books, a
division of HarperCollins Publishers, 10 East 53rd
Street, New York, NY 10022.
www.harpercollinschildrens.com

Library of Congress Cataloging-in-Publication Data
Byng, Georgia.
Molly Moon's hypnotic time travel adventure / Georgia
Byng.— 1st American edition.
p.   cm.
Summary: Molly Moon, reunited with her parents, is
hypnotized by a mysterious turbaned gardener and eventually
transported to India, where she meets not only a maharajah
with a speech defect but also former versions of herself.
ISBN-10: 0-06-075034-0
ISBN-13: 978-0-06-075034-3
[1. Hypnotism—Fiction.   2. Time travel—Fiction.
3. India—History—Fiction.]
PZ7.B9887 Mnu 2005   ` 2005014559
[Fic]—dc22   CIP
                                                   AC

Typography by Amy Ryan
❖
First Harper Trophy Edition, 2006
First American edition, 2005
First published in Britain by
Macmillan Children's Books, 2005
12 13 LP/RRDH 10 9 8

For Lucas—
with your magic smile

Molly Moon's
Hypnotic Time Travel
Adventure

One

The old temple priest stooped and slowly filled the metal lily-pad dishes with milk. As he did, sacred rats came scurrying from the shadows to drink. They were, he believed, reborn people. He chuckled as they ran over his feet, and he dropped a handful of sweetmeats on the floor. He nodded to the statue of the many-armed god before him, touched the purple mark on his forehead, then crouched down on his crooked heels.

He thought how pretty the big, flat dishes looked—each was a white moon with twenty dark gray rats around it, sipping at the milk. The rats looked like furry petals, their pink tails flitting about like fronds in the wind.

He glanced through the temple's pillars to the sunny street outside. Three pony dealers were quarreling over some money and, nearby, children were chattering noisily as they watched some piglets snuffling in the gutter. Women in saris stood gossiping as they drew water from a stone well, and nearby a camel groaned as it was loaded. A beggar sat cross-legged playing a flute through his nose. A holy cow whisked flies with its tail and surveyed the scene.

Behind the cow was a rickety wooden paan stall. Here, a man with a pinched rat-like face, a big mustache, and a purple turban dismounted his horse.

Straightening his silk coat, he stood impatiently, tapping the dusty road with a moccasined foot. The paan seller sprinkled some brown betel-nut powder onto a green betel leaf. He added grated coconut and aniseed, and squeezed some red sticky syrup on top. Then he rolled it all up and finally offered the breath freshener up to his customer. Without acknowledging him, the smart man took it and put it in his mouth. He dropped a few coins at the stallholder's feet and, chewing, mounted his horse again.

As the paan seller turned, an incredible thing happened. There was a BOOM, and the horse and its rider vanished into thin air.

The man fell on his knees in fear.

In the temple, the priest waggled his head from side to side. Then he bowed to the rats before him, put his hands together, and said a prayer.

TWO

olly Moon hooked her bony arms over the high back of a green velvet sofa and cupped her face in her hands. She looked out of the high window in front of her at the garden of Briersville Park. The striped lawn stretched away into the distance where pet llamas grazed and a herd of animal-shaped bushes sat in the morning fog. A kangaroo, a rhino, a bear, a horse, and scores of other topiary-hedge animals stood or reclined on the misty grass, menacingly, as if waiting for some magic to bring them to life.

And moving among the beasts, as though searching for a key in the dew, was a woman in a gray cloak. From behind she looked hunched and sad, which made Molly sigh, because she knew the woman was indeed sad.

Molly hadn't known her mother for long. Until a month ago Molly had been an orphan, thinking that her parents were dead. Then she had discovered that she had a mother and father. You would think that a mother who'd found her lost child after *eleven* years would be ecstatically happy, and that is exactly what Molly expected her mother to be. But Molly's mother was not happy. Instead of being pleased, all she could think about was the past and how much had been stolen from her.

It was true that she had been robbed.

For Lucy Logan had been hypnotized, put in a deep trance, and controlled for eleven years by her own twin brother, the very brilliant hypnotist Cornelius Logan. Cornelius had stolen Lucy Logan's daughter, Molly, and put her in a nasty orphanage.

It was Molly who saved Lucy's life. Molly herself released her mother, Lucy, from all of Cornelius's hypnotic commands, because Molly, although only eleven, was a master hypnotist.

Yes, that is a very important point. Molly was a master hypnotist.

Molly hadn't always known that she was a hypnotist. In fact, her first inkling of it had been when she was ten. But she'd learned fast. So far she'd used her hypnotic skills for herself and against people with bad intentions. Now she wanted to use them for something different.

She looked sideways at the wings of the giant building she was in. Briersville Park was massive. Molly wanted to turn part of it into a hypnotic hospital—a place where people with problems could come to be cured. Whether their problem was a fear of heights or spiders or an addiction to doughnuts, Molly's hypnotic hospital would sort them out. Molly looked at Lucy. She found it hard to believe that this woman was a world-class hypnotist. She seemed so limp and useless. Maybe she would even have to be her first patient.

Molly couldn't understand Lucy. She would have thought she should be full of joy. Not only had she been reunited with Molly, she was also about to meet her long-lost husband again, for this was another thing Molly had brought about. Molly had discovered who Lucy's husband (and Molly's father) was. His name was Primo Cell. He had also been hypnotized and controlled by Cornelius Logan for eleven years.

At this point you may be wondering how a girl, even a master hypnotist like Molly, could ever challenge such a brilliantly accomplished adult hypnotist as Cornelius Logan. Well, master hypnotists have the power to make the world stand still. Molly possessed this gift. And in a hypnotic world-stopping battle, she had been able to overcome Cornelius and convince him he was a lamb.

All that had happened in the last chapter of Molly's life—a chapter that Molly was still spinning from. Molly watched her mother stop beside two bushes in the shape of bush babies. Lucy stroked one and sadly put her hand on the other as if it were a gravestone of a person she had loved. Molly sighed. Her mother was so full of regret, it was taking over her life.

Molly picked up a silver-framed photograph from the glass side table and lay down on the floor to look at it. The orphans she had grown up with waved happily from the picture. It had been taken at Christmas. Molly herself smiled out from the picture, too, her curly hair looking crazier than ever, blowing in the wind, her nose its potato self, her closely set green eyes laughing. They were enjoying themselves in warm Los Angeles in America, while Molly was here, far away from them, in cold Briersville, with her sad mother.

Molly chewed the inside of her cheek. Lucy Logan slopping around the house, depressed, in her dressing gown, was beginning to get on her nerves. Her mother's black mood hung in the air like an infectious flu, waiting to be caught. In fact, Molly was already going down with it. She, too, had begun to turn over and over again in her mind the idea that her own life could have been so much better if it hadn't been for that revolting man Cornelius.

There was something else, too. Molly shivered. She fingered the time-stopping crystal that hung like a huge diamond around her neck. She felt apprehensive, as if something weird was about to happen. Perhaps it was just this odd situation she was in with her mother that was making her uneasy.

Molly put two fingers in her mouth and whistled. A second later she heard the scrape of claws on polished oak floorboards as Petula, her black pug, came skidding into the room. With a flying leap she landed on Molly's stomach, dropped a stone that she'd been sucking, and began licking Molly's neck. Petula always made Molly feel whole. She loved her so much that, provided Petula was there, Molly felt everything was all right.

"Training for the circus now? Next time, how about a somersault?" Molly squeezed Petula and rubbed her side vigorously.

"Oooh, you're a good girl. Yes, you are!" Petula licked Molly's nose. "Yes, you are." Molly hugged Petula.

Then, getting up, she carried her over to the window. Pointing at Lucy Logan, she confided, "Look at her, Petula. I've never seen anyone so miserable. Here we are, in this beautiful house, which is all *hers* now, with gardens and fields and horses and everything we need and we've got our whole lives in front of us to enjoy and she's like *that*. Why can't she get over the past? It's starting to make *me* feel bad. What shall we do?" Petula barked. "Sometimes I feel like hypnotizing her to cheer her up, but I can't hypnotize my own mother, Petula, can I?" Petula licked her lips. Molly clapped. "You've got it, Petula! Maybe she's not eating properly."

Petula made a whining noise, as if to agree that this was exactly the problem, and so, deciding that a good breakfast was what her mother needed, Molly left the drawing room. Together they passed along the Bonsai Tree Passage where, in every alcove along the wall, four-hundred-year-old potted miniature Japanese trees stood on elegant tables. Side by side they descended the grand stone Time Staircase, where hundreds of clocks hung ticking cacophonously on the walls.

The window of the staircase was extra tall and January light flooded in. Molly cupped her hand to her forehead as she squinted at the drive outside. A white wheelbarrow that read:

GREENFINGERS
The Gardening Name You Can Trust

along its side was standing on the gravel. One of the Greenfingers workers was there, in his unmistakable yellow company overall, unpacking a bag of shears and tools. The yellow men, as Molly thought of them, were always about, since at Briersville Park there were so many topiary animals to clip and shape, and so many lawns and flower beds to see to. Molly knew most of the gardeners by name but not this elderly man. He was new. She admired his purple turban, his large mustache, and his funny shoes.

Petula barked.

"All right, all right—I'm coming." Molly straddled the banister and slid all the way down to the bottom of the stairs, testing the echo as she went.

"Pe—tuuuu—la."

"Pe—tuuuu—la. Pe—tuuuu—la . . ." the echo swirled about her.

Her ancestor, the original great hypnotist, Dr. Cornelius Logan, smiled down from his portrait. Molly picked up three pebbles that Petula had found in the rock garden, tried to juggle them, dropped them, and then made her way across the grand hall and down to the kitchen.

Petula let Molly go on. She stopped in the hall and sniffed the air. There were strange scents about. Exotic smells. They were coming from the new garden man. She wasn't sure that she trusted him. Under the pepper and spices, he smelled nervous. She'd already tried to communicate her worries to Molly, but with no success. Molly had interpreted her barks and lip-licking as a message that she ought to hurry up and do some cooking.

Petula decided to sit in her basket under the stairs and guard the front door.

She hopped into it, tossed her toy mouse out, and picked up her special stone to suck. Then, finding the cushion too lumpy, she circled five times to flatten it just the way that she liked it.

Finally she sat down to have a good think.

The man outside might be a threat to Molly, she thought. And if he *was* dangerous, who would protect Molly? The woman was no help. The woman reminded Petula of a Labrador she'd once seen who'd fallen into a river and half drowned.

Petula sucked her stone. She'd found it in the big room upstairs, under the bed. It was one of those special stones, like the one that Molly wore around her neck. She knew that Molly could make time stand still when she was holding *her* special stone. She wondered whether she might be able to do that, too. She'd really be able to protect Molly if she could.

Petula had already mastered rudimentary hypnotism. She'd hypnotized some pet mice in Los Angeles. She'd also watched and felt how Molly made time stand still and she didn't think it seemed too difficult. Now, with the suspicious man outside, Petula deemed it her duty to test her skills.

And so, sucking her crystal stone, she began to concentrate.

She stared at her toy mouse as if she was trying to hypnotize it. At once, the warm fusion feeling, the feeling that always went with hypnotism, started to tingle in her paws. But Petula knew this wasn't the right sensation. When Molly hypnotized the world to stand still, there was always a *chilly* feeling in the air. Petula stared at the mouse so hard that her big eyes began to water.

Nothing happened. But Petula wasn't put off. She was a very patient creature. She tried again.

And then it began. The tip of her tail started to grow cold. Petula's ears gave an involuntary twitch. The coldness was now creeping, very slowly, toward her back legs, as though her tail were turning into an icicle. At the same time, it felt as though someone were sprinkling icy water on her fur. Petula kept her eyes fixed on the toy mouse. Now the stone in her mouth was becoming cold. It was making her teeth ache. And yet the clocks in the hall were still ticking. Petula drove her gaze into the red mouse. Her mouth felt like the inside of a freezer—so cold, it was almost hot. But still, the clocks ticked on.

Then the smell of frying sausages drifted up from

downstairs, curling around Petula's nose. She dropped the stone on her cushion and wiped her jaw with her front paw. Stopping time was obviously a little more difficult than she had thought.

She aimed her front legs out of her basket and let them skid forward as she stretched and yawned. She'd go downstairs for some sausage, she decided, and continue with her time-stopping practice a little later.

Cornelius Logan had lived in the house before Molly moved in. He had no interest in cooking; he always employed a chef and he was mean. The kitchen, as a result, had never had money spent on it. Its stove was a heavy, oily furnace with blackened iron plates to cook on and two rusty ovens to bake in. Its porcelain sink was chipped, and its humming, rattling fridge looked and sounded as if it belonged in a museum. Copper pots hung from the ceiling like a multitude of metal fruits, ripe, dust-bloomed, and ready to be plucked.

It was certainly no spaceship kitchen, but it was always warm and cozy, and Molly loved it.

She opened the garden door. After fifteen minutes of tomatoes in the oven and sausages in a pan, it was time to scramble the eggs. Molly laid the table and called her mother inside.

"Muuuuuum," she shouted outside, into the cold morning air. Mum . . . That word always sounded odd to Molly when it came out of her mouth.

"Luuuuuucy. Breakfast," she yelled.

Petula appeared and trotted outside. The sausages, she realized, were far too hot to eat now. She'd come back when they'd cooled down.

Five minutes later, with the room full of smoke because Molly had burned the toast, Lucy was sitting at the table. She was wearing a cloak and, underneath it, her nightie. On her sockless feet she wore a pair of dewy sneakers. A magnificent plate of steaming breakfast lay in front of her. And yet Lucy's sky-blue eyes didn't show any appreciation of it. A small fleeting smile flickered on her lips, but then her depressed expression returned.

"Would you like some ketchup?" Molly asked as she bit into a ketchup sandwich—her favorite thing to eat. Lucy shook her head and put a tiny piece of toast up to her mouth. The tomato on it slipped off and landed in her lap, but Lucy didn't seem to notice. She chewed a mouthful of toast for what seemed like twenty chews, her eyes following a crack on the ceiling.

"You're not feeling very well, are you?" Molly ventured. "Why don't you have some of this?" Molly picked up her glass of concentrated orange juice. "It's just liquid sugar, really, with a bit of a kick. It'll really perk you up. It's my number-one drink." Lucy shook her head. "You know, if you eat some breakfast, it will make you stronger and things won't seem so bad," Molly coaxed. Lucy sniffed and wiped her nose and, as if this gesture was a trigger, Molly found a part of herself beginning to feel cross. Things won't seem so bad? Lucy wasn't the only person around here whose life had been tampered with. *Molly* wasn't complaining. She was moving on. Grasping the world by the horns and moving on. Why couldn't Lucy do the same? Wasn't Molly enough to make her feel happy? Maybe her daughter didn't mean that much to her. Sadness suddenly rained down and drenched Molly, too. This was terrible. Here she was with her mother—a person she *should* feel completely happy and comfortable with—and instead she felt as if she were with a weird stranger whose mood was like a storm on the horizon, just about to break. Molly wished Lucy would break and let all her sadness out of her.

Molly stared at her mother's plate. The two of them sat staring at Lucy's scrambled eggs.

Then, thankfully, Molly's senses snapped to.

Molly knew from experience that the more a person thought a certain way, the more that way of thinking would become a habit.

Molly wouldn't be dragged down by her mother's blackness like this.

"Lucy, you've got to pull yourself together," she said suddenly, feeling more like a mother than a daughter. "What are you going to do—be miserable for the rest of your life? And I'm sorry to bring this up, but you're not exactly much fun for me and Petula. I mean, Petula now avoids you because you always do a sort of sad moan when you stroke her . . . and I . . . well, I just can't handle it. You should be feeling good. *Primo* is coming tomorrow. He knows exactly how you feel. I mean, Cornelius took years of *his* life away, too, so you can talk to him about it. And Forest's coming, remember. He'll help you feel better."

Molly watched as her mother took a sip of tea and dribbled it down her chin. How, she thought, could a person do that? Then she noticed ketchup smeared all down the front of her own sweatshirt. But dribbling tea was a bit different. It was as if the shock of being woken up from the hypnotic trance had made her mother faulty. It was as if her batteries weren't working properly.

Then Molly felt bad. Her mother wasn't a machine. What was she doing relating her to a machine? Her mother was a living, breathing, broken person. It was too much to bear.

Molly got up. She must get some air and get away for

a bit. This fog of Lucy's was suffocating. She couldn't wait for Rocky to arrive. He'd help *her* feel better.

"I'm just going outside to talk to the new gardener," she said awkwardly. "I'll see you later."

Upstairs, Molly went to the porch and opened the front door. Petula stood on the other side of the graveled drive next to the turbaned gardener who was stroking her. Molly smiled because it was a relief to see someone normal, someone who liked animals, doing something friendly.

But then a very peculiar and frightening thing happened. There was a loud BOOM, and Petula and the man vanished into thin air.

Three

"So let's go over this one more time." Primo Cell stood to the side of the library and fidgeted with the cuffs of his tailored blue shirt, trying to be business-like but finding his usual powers of deduction flummoxed. "Petula was on the drive and . . ." He twisted around, his leather-soled shoe pirouetting on the Persian rug. "You're certain it was Petula? I mean, it might have been another dog."

"Yeah, man, that's right," enthused Forest, shaking his shag of gray dreadlocks. Forest was an aging Los Angelean hippie who'd traveled the world. He'd lived with Eskimos and bushmen, Chinese monks and Indian sadhus. Now he lived in Los Angeles, where he grew vegetables, kept chickens, and ate a lot of tofu and turnips. "Sometimes our memories play tricks on us," he said, adjusting his bottle-glass spectacles. "It might have been a different hound or even the guy's back-pack." Forest had odd habits and sometimes he talked rubbish. Molly listened to him now. "Or maybe it was a big bag of dog biscuits with a *picture* of a pug on the front."

"No." Molly stabbed at the fire with a poker as she remembered the horrible moment. "It was definitely Petula. She looked me right in the eye and wagged her tail just before he took her. If *only* she wasn't so friendly. . . . If only she'd run away from him or bitten him. . . ."

"Why don't we telephone the gardening company and find out who the gardener was?" suggested Forest.

"I already have," said Molly. "None of their workers were in yesterday. That man was a fraud. Oh, I hope Petula's all right." Rocky, Molly's best friend, stood beside her. He gently patted her shoulder.

Rocky Scarlet had grown up in the orphanage with Molly—he'd shared a crib with her when they were babies and he knew her better than anyone. He was also an accomplished hypnotist, though nowhere near as good as Molly. His skill was "voice-only hypnosis." He had a lovely voice.

"We'll find her, Molly. It'll just take time. I wouldn't be surprised if we get a blackmail call. Whoever he is probably just wants something. He's just a low-down dirty dognaper, I expect."

Molly looked at Rocky's face. It was a rich, deep black because he'd spent so much time in the Los Angeles sunshine. And his smiling eyes were always reassuring, even though this time, Molly wasn't put at ease.

Rocky went over to the desk and sat down. He picked up a pen and, humming, began doodling on the back of his hand. He drew Petula and a clock. As far as he could see, they just had to wait. He was calm, patient, and logical and was sure that Petula's disappearance would be explained.

Molly slapped her jeans, slumped back in the sofa, and hugged her knobbly knees.

"I don't see how it could have happened. How does a person just disappear like that? I would have felt it if the man made the world stop."

"Yeah, you would have got that chill vibe," agreed Forest from his cross-legged yoga position on the armchair. "You were wearin' your time-stop crystal, weren't you?"

Molly pulled her crystal on its chain out from under her shirt.

Forest poked at the hole in the toe of his orange socks for inspiration. "What do you think, Primo? Rocky and me here, well, we ain't hypnotic world-stopping experts like you and Molly. Do you think the guy in the turban made the world stand still without Molly feelin' it? I mean, she could have been lookin' up that path with Petula waggin' her tail and, BAM, suddenly he could have stopped time and frozen Molly stiff as an icicle. An' then whoever that dude was, he just picked up Petula and walked away. Once he was far away, he started the world again. Well, of course, to Molly, because she was frozen, she wouldn't have seen how he took Petula; it would have looked as if they'd gone in a puff of smoke."

Primo shook his head and picked up a china elephant from the mantel.

"I don't like it," he said, as if speaking to the small sculpture. "I don't like it at all. Theoretically it shouldn't happen. If one hypnotist hypnotizes the world to stand still, other hypnotists wearing their crystals feel it and should be able to resist the freeze. And what was the BOOM sound that Molly heard?"

"Maybe." Forest sighed, lying on the floor and putting his ankles around his ears. "Maybe the gardener was standing on a lea line or something. I mean, you got those way-out druid stone circles in this country, and energy lines are awesome here . . . hmmm . . ." Forest drifted off into his thoughts.

Rocky ignored Forest and instead approached Molly to study her crystal.

"This is the original crystal, isn't it?"

"Yes, look—it's got that icy-looking bit. And I wear it all the time. Even if someone wanted to swap it while I was asleep, they couldn't. I'd wake up. Especially recently. I haven't been able to sleep very well." Molly dropped her voice. "Rocky, it's been like a tomb here, and Lucy's been walking around like a . . . like a *mummy.*" Molly couldn't help smiling. Rocky laughed. After all, Lucy was a mummy—Molly's.

Primo wandered over to the window and looked out at a thin, fair-haired man who was kicking his legs up and running around the lawn leaping over croquet hoops.

"I'd better go out and rescue Lucy before Cornelius starts bleating at her. And in case you're wondering, Lucy's got nothing to do with Petula's disappearance. I know it. I've talked to her. Lucy is only half here, it seems, but she's not under anyone's spell, or hypnotized. She's just wretched and traumatized from what's happened. Poor Lucy. I think I can help her climb out of her misery." Primo watched Cornelius on his hands and knees nibbling the grass. "It's amazing how that lamb man out there was once so powerful. I can still hardly believe that he once hypnotized me to want to be president of America for him. And I would have been, too, if you, Molly, hadn't saved me."

Primo smiled at his daughter.

Primo and Molly had decided to start by pretending that they weren't father and daughter. After all, if you haven't belonged to a father *ever* and suddenly one turns up, you don't really want to keep jumping up and hugging him, shouting, "Daddy." You want to get to know him first. So Molly called him Primo. She liked him. He was positive.

"I'm going to go out and have a walk with Lucy," he said, rubbing his hands together, trying to look as though everything was under control and he was looking forward to it. "See you later. We'll sort out all these problems. It'll be fine, don't you worry." He winked and, making the sort of giddyup, encouraging noise that people make to horses, left the room.

"Just zoning into the Here and Now," said Forest, shutting his eyes and beginning to meditate.

Molly and Rocky walked along the upstairs passage to the stairwell of clocks. The domed ceiling echoed with their tickings.

"I don't like the idea that there's someone out there who can pull the wool over our eyes like this," Molly said as they descended.

"You'd better watch out, Molly," Rocky said, and pursed his lips. "Be on your guard."

Rocky never exaggerated. He was also hard to panic.

So getting a warning like this from him made Molly shudder. She gripped his arm.

"Let's stick together."

"Well, you're going to have to wait for me here; I'm going to the bathroom."

"But how long are you going to be?"

"Oh, three hours?"

"Ro-cky . . ."

The cloakroom door creaked shut. A huge black spider scuttled across the floor.

Molly stood in the front hall picking the dried ketchup off her T-shirt. It was a strange place. The walls were covered with animal trophies. Their glassy eyes stared down at her. And mixed among the heads were antique garden shears—another collection of the mad Cornelius Logan's. A man obsessed with control—controlling people through hypnotism—he'd also created the topiary animal bushes all over his estate.

As she waited for Rocky, Molly walked around the hall table some, inspecting iridescent peacock feathers that stood in a vase. At every corner of the table a different group of animals glared down at her as if she were responsible for their deaths. In a horrible skip, Molly's mind suddenly imagined Petula's head stuffed and staring down, stiff with rigor mortis. She felt faint.

Molly remembered some old wives' tale that peacock feathers in a house brought bad luck. So, seizing the whole bunch, she pulled them out of their pot and marched for the front door and flung it open.

Cold air flooded inside. Molly stepped out into the morning sunshine and down the front steps of the house.

A distant lawn mower droned as it dealt with the winter grass. Light bounced off the place where Molly had last seen Petula, and then, as she walked across the circle of gravel, past the bush sculpture of a flying magpie, a cloud cast a giant shadow over the grounds of Briersville Park.

Something blue flickered in the periphery of Molly's vision. She turned quickly, but there was nothing there. It must have been a bird, or the shadow of a bird. Or maybe it was that turbaned dognaper. Molly quickly twisted around. If he was loitering nearby, she'd catch him creeping up on her. The white columns on the front portico of the house stood like guards and the windows were like watchmen, but Molly knew that out here she was as vulnerable as Petula had been.

Again a blue shadow flickered to her left. Molly didn't turn this time. She tried to see what it was without moving. It hovered, then disappeared. Thirty seconds later it appeared to her right. Was it a ghost? A poltergeist was a ghost that was able to move things. Had a poltergeist moved Petula? Molly was determined to find out. Although she was filthy scared, she let the shadow flicker to the left, then again to the right. She stood stock-still. Once more it was there—closer, and then again on the right of her, closer still. Nearer and nearer it got. *Right . . . left . . . right . . .* There it was to the left . . . the right . . . the left. *Left, right, left.* Her eyes swung from side to side. Molly was so intent upon winkling out the truth that she didn't feel herself falling. Falling into a hypnotic trap.

When the purple-turbaned man was finally standing in front of her, she just gazed straight into his dark eyes. She didn't question his attire: The indigo outfit he had on, tied at the waist with a silken cummerbund and flaring down dresslike to below his knees, the tight white leggings that he wore underneath or the scooped and pointed red moccasins on his feet. She simply drank in his appearance, as calmly as if looking at a picture in a book. She registered the handlebar mustache that swooped up on either side of his dry, wrinkled face, all whiskery below his ears. She noted his crooked orange teeth, and that he was chewing something. She observed the golden chain that hung around his neck with three crystals hanging there: a clear, a green, and a red crystal.

Then she heard his rusty voice. "You, Miss Moon,

are now in a light trance. You will do as I say and come with me. Molly relaxed completely, dropped her peacock feathers, and stood still and silent in a hypnotic daze.

The next thing she knew, the elderly man took her by the arm, there was a distant BOOM and the world around her became a complete blur. Colors rushed past her, then all around her. Even the colors under her feet changed from ochers to browns to yellows to greens to sparkling blues. It was like traveling through a kaleidoscope of color and, as they moved through it, a cool wind brushed Molly's skin and the noise of the lawn mower was replaced by a different sort of humming, a constant noise but of varying volumes and qualities. One moment it sounded like a thunderstorm, the next second like pattering rain and birdsong. And then, all of a sudden, the blurred world became solid again. The ground beneath Molly's feet was a firm green and the sky above, hyacinth blue. The world stopped spinning.

Molly's mind took a few moments to settle. Although she was still in a hypnotic daze, she could understand that the world about her had changed. They weren't in new surroundings; Briersville Park was still there, in all its majesty. But the season was different. Instead of winter, as it had been moments before, it was *summer*. There were huge flower beds to the left and right of her, blooming with roses. There were no topiary bush animals to be seen. What was more, instead of a car parked in the driveway, there was a carriage, with a dappled horse harnessed to it and an old-fashioned groom standing beside the horse. A gardener in woolen shirt and trousers and a brown leather apron was on his hands and knees with a trowel in his hand. A large pile of weeds lay on the ground beside him and the remains of a half-eaten pork pie.

"Damn, wrong time again," muttered Molly's stony-faced escort, looking at a slim silver gadget in his hand. In her hypnotized state, Molly supposed that this device was designed to help him time travel, for time travel, she saw, was exactly what they had just done.

"Excuse me, can I help you?" said the gardener. He frowned and lurched to his feet, straightening his cap.

The turbaned man took Molly by the arm and began striding toward a small arbor of trees, where a burst of laughter rang out.

"Oi!" shouted the gardener, but the mustached man ignored him. "You can't just walk in 'ere. This is private property."

Molly's companion's pace quickened and he pulled her along. The gardener threw down his hoe and began to run after them.

"We'll never get away from that long-legged gardener," Molly found herself calmly thinking. And then, just as they passed the first tree, the turbaned man consulted his silver device. He turned a dial and flicked a switch. Then he pressed his foot on Molly's and clasped the green crystal around his neck.

In a moment the world transformed into a blur of color. When the world became solid again, Molly could see beyond the tree that the gardener was no longer chasing them. He was once more on his knees hoeing his weeds. But only a few weeds lay beside him. What was more, the pork pie sat untouched, wrapped in a piece of yellow waxed paper. Molly's escort had taken them *back in time.*

"Wha—ar—wa—haaa?" Molly tried with all her will to ask why the man had taken her. But her tongue refused to work properly. The man ignored her.

Behind the trees was a grass clearing, and there, on a rug, was a very strange sight. Children dressed in Victorian clothes were playing and laughing. Two girls in pink petticoated dresses sat beside a porcelain tea set, and two boys in tweed breeches and waistcoats were hitting a hoop backward and forward to each other with sticks. In the girls' baby carriage sat a doll in a frilly bonnet. And then Molly noticed that it wasn't a doll at all. As if in some ridiculous dream, Petula, dressed in a frock and with a silly hat on her head, sat panting under the canopy of the carriage.

Four

As soon as Petula smelled Molly she tried to jump out of the carriage and, irritated by whoever the new, distracting arrival was, the young girls turned around. One of them appeared horrified by the apparition of Molly and the turbaned man. The other looked delighted.

"What funny clothes you have on! Have you come from a fancy-dress party?"

The two boys were now staring, too.

Molly knew that it was her jeans and T-shirt with a silhouette of a dancing mouse on it that must look odd to them. In the way that a person completely accepts strange things that happen in dreams, she had already unflinchingly accepted that she was standing in a time different from her own. She was breathing

29

in nineteenth-century air.

The part of her that normally would have run forward and rescued Petula was rigid and hypnotized. Molly instead found herself musing, "Petula is trying to jump out of that carriage, oh, and the old man is walking toward her. He's picked up a purple capsule from the ground and has slipped it into his pocket. That purple thing has led us here. It must send signals to his silver machine." Then she thought, "Those girls are small but their screams are very loud. The man doesn't seem to mind being hit by that boy's stick. Or maybe he does—he's pushed the boy over and winded him. And now the man is bringing Petula over here, and he's taking that dress and bonnet off of her."

At this point the children were making so much noise that they attracted the attention of the gardener. As he rushed into the arbor the turbaned man gave him an angry stare and, with the aid of the clear crystal hanging around his neck, he did something Molly was very familiar with: He froze the world.

Immediately the world was set completely still. It wasn't icy, but it was cool and Molly felt the familiar cold fusion feeling that went with time stopping pulsing through her veins. With Petula under one arm and holding Molly's shoulder, the man sent warmth into Molly to ensure that she was still able to move. He kept

Petula frozen as she was easier to handle this way. Then he led Molly away from the chaotic scene, leaving the shouting people behind them, now silent, stuck in their positions like giant human Popsicles—the boys with raised sticks, the girls with open, wailing mouths, their faces wet with tears and the gardener on one leg as he sped into the clearing.

They walked toward the cabriolet with its motionless horse and groom. Once there, the man gestured to Molly to climb up into the driving seat and he passed her the still Petula. In her trance Molly calmly calculated that when he let go of her arm she must focus upon her own time-stop crystal and resist the frozen world so that her body didn't stiffen and become still like everybody else's. This she did. She noticed that her kidnaper looked impressed.

Once he was up with her he took the whip in his hand and unfroze the world. With a crack, he brought the horse to its senses and they were off. Petula barked. The cabriolet's wheels lurched on the gravel and the knickerbockered groom looked up in surprise. Before he could prevent it, his carriage was away.

The horse cantered whinnying up the drive, leaving another bellowing man behind.

Molly's captor didn't look back. Breathing heavily, he wiped sweat from his wrinkly forehead and began muttering loudly. "Yes, he'll be impressed by the dog. . . . It's one of those strange Chinese dogs. I've done it all right, for once."

Molly didn't know what he was talking about, but in her trance she didn't care.

As they sped along, she recognized where they were heading. They were on the road to Briersville. Of course, it wasn't the Tarmac road she was used to but a rough country lane with daisies growing along the middle of it in a long, grassy tuft. Half a mile on they came to a cart pulled by an ox. The cabriolet had to stop while the oxcart slowly pulled up on the shoulder to let them overtake it. For a moment it was quiet, except for a lark singing in the air above. And then Molly heard the juddering beat of hooves on the road behind. The man looked back to see the angry gardener and groom galloping fast toward them. Cursing, he leaped haphazardly onto the horse that pulled their carriage and forced it to trot on past the oxcart. Now the chasing riders were only yards away. Molly's kidnaper once more froze the world.

Since his body was in contact with the horse beneath him, the creature continued to move forward and away. Molly had focused her mind, so she kept moving, too. Gripping Petula, she glanced behind her and looked with calm interest at their pursuers. They were brilliant statues of charging horsemen on their steeds. Even the dust kicked up by the animals' hooves was stuck, motionless, in a still cloud.

She watched the elderly man bobbing about in front of her as he rode the horse that pulled the cabriolet and she was struck by how remarkably dextrous and nimble he was for his age. And the frozen nineteenth-century world passed by. Molly no longer felt like questioning him. She smiled as if her changed surroundings were just a delightful show for her entertainment. Sweet guitar music could have been playing, the way she smiled.

A motionless woman, dressed in a long brown dress, drew up water from a well. They overtook a scruffy young boy who drove a gaggle of geese along the ditch. All were still as sculptures.

As they reached the outskirts of Briersville, Molly looked up to the hilltop where the orphanage she had grown up in would be. That very building stood all gray and sad-looking, exposed to the elements. She wondered whether it had been an orphanage in 1850, 1860, 1870—whenever it was now.

Her captor drove the horse on into Briersville. They passed the town hall, with its pepper-pot roof. Everywhere was stock-still. The women wore long, bustled dresses and hats. The men's headwear ranged from top hats to caps to floppy woolen hoods. The turbaned man urged the horse on, ignoring its alarm at the immobile world. Grumbling to himself, he weaved the cabriolet through the obstacle course of horse-drawn carriages and wagons.

A busy market was taking place in a side street. There were cake stalls, bread stands, and cages full of live chickens that could be bought and slaughtered on the spot. A meaty-faced butcher held a chicken in position on a chopping board, his other hand raised with a cleaver ready. Petula's sensitive nose picked up the scents in the air of blood and beer and baking and straw and animals and smoke, and she tried to understand why everything smelled so different.

Finally they arrived on the other side of the town, near the common. Molly's kidnaper dismounted and let the world move again. Disheveled from his ride, exhausted from the effort of freezing time, and impatient, he beckoned for Molly and Petula to get down. He held his hand out. In it was another metallic purple capsule that he'd removed from the side of his silver gadget.

"Swallow this," he ordered, his words spiced with a strong Indian accent. Molly paused, tried to refuse, and then did as she was told. The metal pill felt uncomfortable as it made its way down her throat. The man consulted his device, which had a flashing dial on it and a keyboard. He squinted at the tiny buttons and, with a pin from his turban, began tapping in numbers. Molly watched. Finally he pressed a silver button and took her hand.

"You are exhausting me!" he grumbled. Then he raised the silver mechanism up to his neck and with his little finger cupped the *red* crystal that hung there.

His face strained and reddened with concentration. There was the familiar distant BOOM and the world around Molly and Petula began to shift and melt and change again.

A warm wind blew. Molly realized that they were now moving *forward* in time. A rapid succession of noises whizzed past her ears until the silver gadget emitted a bright flash of light. The disgruntled man brought them to a standstill. When the swirling stopped, Molly saw a familiar world. The common was a modern playing field. Two boys in dark blue sweat-suits were kicking a football about, concentrating so intently that they didn't notice the three time travelers popping up.

"Haap!" Molly tried to shout, but her voice was locked in her throat.

The ruffled man ran his hand over his dry, wrin-kled face and walked toward a wooden bench. He retrieved another purple metal pill, which Molly deduced he must have hidden there earlier to help him find the exact place again.

Then he shouted to the boys, "What is the time by your watch and chain?"

One boy stopped with the ball under his foot. "Talkin' to me?"

"Yes, you, boy."

The boy gave his friend a look as if to say, "Cor, we've got a right one here."

"Ten to four," he shouted back. As he did, Molly recognized him. He was from Briersville School. He'd been in the grade above Molly and sometimes he'd played football with Rocky. Yet he looked younger— *much* younger than when Molly had last seen him. They must have landed in a time way before she'd ever found the book about hypnotism, the book from which she'd learned her skills.

Had she not been hypnotized, she might have laughed in amazement or yelped with fear. For Molly was in a time that she herself had already *lived through.*

"Mweal," she grunted, trying to call his name. She glanced over her shoulder at the fields and woods that were the hilly shortcut from Briersville School to Hardwick House Orphanage.

The hill was the route the children from the

orphanage often took. If it had been a school day, they would already have been walking home, as tea was at four o'clock prompt. Sure enough, a group of children was near the top. And, lower down, two small figures emerged from the woods. One had black hair, the other was wearing a brown raincoat with a swirl on the back. They were too far off to be distinguishable. And yet, as she saw how the first one strode on and the other walked sluggishly behind, Molly was distinctly reminded of Rocky and herself. What was more, she had once owned a raincoat with a spiral design on its back.

In her hypnotized state, Molly matter-of-factly concluded that, miraculous as it was, there was a possibility that the person lagging behind on the hillside was herself from *three years before.*

Then she noticed a mechanical whirring that was getting louder and louder.

A helicopter was landing on the playing field. The chopping noise from its blades and engines was deafening.

The footballers covered their ears and watched as it touched down. With the rotor still spinning, her captor ushered Molly in. Her hair blew about as she mounted its metal steps. Petula curled up in her arms, afraid, and burrowed her face into Molly's armpit.

Both wondered where they were going. The hypnotic peacefulness she'd felt before had worn off. Again, Molly attempted to talk. "Wha—ar—yaa—taaaken—ma?"—but her captor ignored her.

As the insect machine swung away and up, Molly tried to see the faces of the children on the slope, but it was impossible. However, over the orphanage she did manage to pick out Adderstone, the orphanage mistress, sitting at a garden table, being served tea by Edna, the orphanage cook. Adderstone looked up sharply at the helicopter and covered her ears while Edna raised her fist and shouted. Molly could just imagine the swear words that were flying out of her mouth.

Below, the fields were a patchwork of green. In twenty minutes they were at the airport. The helicopter landed and, as if all was prearranged, they were met by a white golf buggy, driven across the runway to a private jet, and ushered aboard. Molly, with Petula alert under her arm, walked numbly on.

Five

Nine hours later the jet touched down. Its doors opened and warm air that smelled of bonfires, herbs, and spices rushed in. A hot sun hit their shoulders. Molly squinted as she looked about.

The whole airport, with its control towers and orange windsocks, quivered in the heat. On the runway waited a shiny black car with a flag with a peacock on it.

"Ar—way—an—Andia?" Molly asked, but her words fell on deaf ears.

Soon they were driving, and within a short time Molly knew her guess had been right.

The roads were crammed. Camels and horses pulled wagons and carts. Brightly colored trucks with decorated cabs, hand-painted with pictures of flowers and elephants, were unlike any trucks Molly had seen before. On the back of each was written "Use Your Horn." The driver of their car certainly did. He pressed the horn constantly. And other drivers blew their horns at him. Camels and water buffalo pulling their loads moved close to the edge of the shoulder, where bicycles clattered by, while the noisier, faster traffic was in the main lane. Tiny auto-rickshaw taxis, yellow and black like giant wasps, buzzed past. Women in colorful saris rode their mopeds or traveled on the back of motorbikes.

It was very busy. They passed a huge playing field where hundreds of children played cricket, and then a clearing where gypsies lived. Above their homemade shacks a billboard advertised silk wedding saris. Soon they were in a city.

"Wha—ar—yaa—takan—may?" Molly managed to ask, but her captor stared out of the window at the dusty road and the buildings. Molly felt sticky and hot.

Petula panted. With great effort, Molly took a bottle of mineral water from the pocket of the car seat. She cupped her hands and gave Petula a drink.

She noticed that the roads were getting wider and the buildings grander. They drove down a long avenue with smart embassies on either side. Flags hung outside them in the windless air.

Molly thought how limp she felt, and how this was

what it felt like to be hypnotized. She was tired, too. Time travel was tiring.

"I'm on my own in India with Petula and this complete stranger," she thought. "Why?"

Molly shut her eyes. She urged herself to not be imprisoned by this hypnotism, but it was impossible. Her mind simply couldn't break through the shield that surrounded it. She was reminded of nightmares she'd had of crossing a road, of a big bus coming, but of not being able to move. Of her feet being stuck and her body being paralyzed. Her mind felt paralyzed now.

When she opened her eyes again, they had stopped outside what seemed to be a tourist site. It was a magnificent red fort, crumbling in parts, with tourist shops at its entrance and a taxi stand by its gate.

"Out," the turbaned man said rudely. Molly opened the car door. Petula sniffed about inquisitively and the man picked her up. Again he took out his silver time-traveling device and began fiddling with it. Satisfied that it was programmed correctly, he squeezed Molly's arm.

"Here we go again," Molly thought. "Where is he taking me this time?"

With Petula hooked under his right armpit, the turbaned man felt for his green crystal. The veins in his neck stood out as he concentrated. There was a BOOM, and the world flashed with color. The noise was almost deafening as they shot back in time. A cool wind rushed around them, playing with the ends of Molly's hair and ruffling the man's mustache. The silver box flashed. They stopped.

A painted festival elephant stood beside them. The man growled and stamped his foot crossly. He pressed a button on his silver time gauge and clasped his red stone. With another BOOM and a hot whirl of windy color they moved forward in time. This time when they stopped, it was raining—pouring.

"Aaaahhhhh!" roared the man, now in a terrible rage and soaked. "Why can't I ever get it right? These time winds will send me early to my grave!" He clasped the green crystal.

Molly realized that he obviously wanted to be at the gates on a particular day, at a precise time, and he was finding it extremely difficult. As they lurched forward and backward through time it was as if he was trying to dock a time-travel ship in a particularly tricky space-port. Molly didn't find it amusing. She didn't find it scary, either. She didn't feel much, but her curiosity was still active.

"Plas—tal—may—wha—wa—ar—gawing," she tried again.

The silver box flashed. They stopped. It was a morning. Another fiercely hot sun blazed down.

A look of grateful relief washed over her captor's face. Now ten palm trees were growing by the red fort's walls, and near its entrance, instead of the tourist shops, stood two forbidding, sword-bearing guards. Molly's escort indicated that she should wait. Brushing rain water from his shoulders, he walked over to a large parasol and, from the iron-hard ground, picked up another one of his strange purple pills. Handing a wet Petula to a servant, he took a few moments to straighten his clothes. A bowl of water and a towel were brought for him to wash and dry his face. A servant produced a small pot of something and a mirror in which he checked his appearance very carefully. He rubbed some ointment on the dry skin on his cheek, exclaiming, "Worse, it's worse. I'll rot before I'm young again!"

Then the servant brought him a tray of small green candies. Molly's escort spat on the ground, leaving a gob of red spit there, and he popped one of the candies into his mouth. "Ah! Paan! At least there is *something* good in this world," he muttered. Then, chewing, he gathered up Petula, came back, and tugged at Molly to follow him.

The whiskered guards bowed low as they passed. When they walked through the high arched gates other servants bowed even lower. Molly's escort was, she realized, quite important.

"Not important enough to be *completely* at ease in this fine palace, though," she thought. For as they walked down the cool marble passages, it struck her that her companion was getting more and more nervous.

When they climbed some pale green steps to a giant amber and gold entrance, Molly noticed that his hands were shaking. He twitched nervously on the top step, as if trying to make his mind up about something, and then he thrust Petula into Molly's arms. Petula, sensing the tense situation, dived under Molly's baggy T-shirt and wriggled up inside to hide.

A turbaned footman dressed in white bowed, with his hands in a praying position. Then, silently, he opened the door.

Trembling, the mustached man led Molly in.

They were in a long, golden chamber with thousands of silver spikes set in the ceiling. The gilded walls were decorated with colored glass in the shape of elephants, and the floors were covered with thick, sumptuous rugs and huge velvet cushions. The air was musky with incense. Molly's eyes skipped past low, mosaic tables to the room's end. Here was a scarlet bed with a purple bolster behind it and, reclining on it, a man in a shiny red coat.

For a moment, Molly thought her hypnotized judgment was playing tricks on her, because the reclining man looked enormous. He seemed to have been magnified. His dark, turtlelike head and huge body seemed twice the size of the servant behind him, who stood fanning him with a wide, flat bunch of peacock feathers. Was the servant a midget?

The giant man clicked his long fingers, and the chamber echoed with the noise. Molly's companion hurried forward, pulling her with him. The closer they got, the larger the man on the bed appeared. Molly had never seen a man so big, or someone so reptilian. The skin on his face was dry and scaly like a tortoise's. His large, dry nose was as rough as a pumice stone. If Molly hadn't been hypnotized, she would have been horrified by his monstrous looks. When they were ten paces away he lifted a round piece of glass to his right eye. And then he let out a deafening roar.

"YOU FOOL," he thundered. "YOU IDIOT, ZACKYA! IT'S THE MONG WROLLY. YOU'VE FETCHED THE MONG WROLLY WROON!"

Six

Petula, terrified, tightened into a ball inside Molly's T-shirt and tried to pretend she wasn't there. Molly's time-travel escort gave her a look of shock and then of complete repulsion.

"Oh, my peacock dropping! I've done it wrong . . . again," he cursed. The whites of his eyes glistened with fear. He turned quaking to his master.

"The wrong Molly, sahib, but that cannot be. Maharaja, I went forward to precisely the right time and fetched her. She was at Briersville Park."

"Briersville Park? BRIERSVILLE PARK? You FOOOOL," boomed the giant man in a deep, curdling voice. He grabbed the peacock-feather fan from the punkah man beside him and hurled it toward them so that Molly's escort had to dodge. "Zackya, do you *theally rink* she would *ever* have been at Briersville Park *before* she found the hypnotism book? I wanted the Molly Moon from a time before that—*I wanted Molly Moon from the time when she lived at the orphanage,* you imbecile. Cornelius Logan kept his residence *sop tecret.* He would never have let her come to Briersville Park *before* she found the hypnotism book."

"Cornelius might have wanted to train her up before she found the book, Your High—"

"Don't answer me back. So STUUUUUUPID!" The dreadful roar that came out of the man's mouth as he stood up practically sent a breeze to ruffle Molly's hair. Molly's eyes were not deceiving her—the man *was* ginormous, but now she was finding that there was something wrong with her ears.

"Of course it's the mong Wrolly Wroon. Are you blind? This one is wearing a stycral." He jabbed a large finger in the direction of Molly's neck. "She's already a world stopper, you inconsequential piece of camel dung. *Only hypnotists are world stoppers.* Why else would she be wearing a STYCRAL?"

"Stycral?" Molly thought. "Oh, he means my time-stopping crystal." The giant's voice rumbled angrily, bouncing off the walls of the golden chamber.

"You have fetched me a Molly Moon from too far in the future, you useless cockroach. I told you. I explained it *tree thimes.*" The giant took four huge steps toward them, getting bigger the closer he got. He leaned his tree-like form down and, as if his subordinate were just a schoolboy, clasped his ear and gave his head a good shake. "Or did it go in one ear and out the other?"

"I thoughtttt . . . I thought this was the riiiiiii . . ." The man could hardly get his words out for the jangling.

"*You* thought. What a joke," said the giant, dropping him disgustedly. "As usual, I'll have to soo it mydelf." Then, with the sharpest of deliveries, he spat, "This is how it works, you idiot. I have to remove Molly Moon from the time *before* she found the hypnotism book. Before she found it. Stunderhand? Then, when I *kill* her, she won't be able to become a hypnotist and make the trouble that she did, will she? She won't ever risdupt my plans and stop Primo Cell from becoming president of America, like she did . . . and Cornelius from ruling the whole world for me. And why? Because she will have *died* before she found out how to hypnotize anyone at all." He cupped the escort's head in his slab hands again and began to squeeze.

"HAVE YOU THOT GAT?" he shouted.

Molly found quite a few thoughts jostling for attention in her head, even though all were very hazy since she was still hypnotized. The first was that it seemed this colossus of a man from the past had once controlled Cornelius Logan. This time-traveling giant had evidently traveled forward in time, from *this* time, and hypnotized Cornelius to carry out his master plan. Cornelius, whom Molly had hypnotized to be a bleating lamb! It was almost unbelievable. This giant man clearly wanted to be powerful in Molly's time. Molly wondered why.

Her mind sipped at this thought as if it were a nice cup of brain-wave tea. Molly realized that she had unwittingly upset his plans. She had taken Cornelius off course. So this giant, quite logically, Molly thought, wanted to catch Molly at the time *before* she'd found the hypnotism book, so he could *kill her* before she could make trouble.

This made complete sense. Molly swished this thought about in her head and blinked as she digested the situation. And finally, she observed, there was nothing wrong with her ears. The leathery-skinned giant (who seemed to have the same skin disorder as the shaking turbaned escort) had something wrong with the way he talked. He got his words back to front— frack to bunt. He spoke in "spoonerisms."

The giant dropped the escort, who now stood beside Molly adjusting his neck where it had cricked slightly. The red juice from the paan he had been chewing dribbled down his chin. He wiped it with a handkerchief.

"You *also* took far too long," the huge man complained. "Too nervous of fenty-twifth-century travel, I suppose, you wimp."

"Your Highness . . . Maharaja. I thought it was better to guarantee her arrival. I am not confidant riding those superfast-beam jets of the twenty-fifth century. I will practice on my own, and improve my skills, I assure you, but I didn't want to lose Miss Moon at a jet-beam port." The man exposed his red-stained teeth in an ingratiating smile.

The maharaja wasn't listening. He was now studying Molly. His huge, bloodshot eyes darted about as he registered her scruffy looks, her size, and her closely set eyes.

"Who would have thought that someone smo sall . . . look! The time winds are affecting her already. Zackya, release her from her trance."

"Are you . . . sure, Your Highness?"

"Do as I say, you fool."

Zackya, Molly's captor, obediently stepped in front of her. He brought his dry, knobbly fingers to her forehead and snapped them together.

"You are released." The hypnotism was broken. The veil of mist covering Molly's feelings lifted and she felt utterly present. She now knew how Petula felt, buried under her T-shirt; Molly's immediate burning wish was that she could disappear, too.

Now the full weight of her situation tumbled down on her. She was caught in a terrible trap. Stuck in another country and another time. Even if she managed to escape the giant maharaja and his assistant, she would still be imprisoned in a time that wasn't her own, because Molly had absolutely no idea how to time travel. She felt as vulnerable as a worm in the beak of a peacock, as hopeless as a prisoner facing execution. The palm of her hand grew clammy as fear overwhelmed her. Molly had never, ever felt this helpless before, and it took immense self-control not to break down in tears.

But Molly was experienced with unkind, heartless people, and she knew from the giant's cold, immobile face that no amount of pleading would help her. She possessed enough knowledge of sadism to know that if she cried now, he would enjoy the spectacle for a while and then he'd lose interest in her. From the way he was leaning down, looking fascinated into the sides of her eyes, she was certain that her best chance of survival was to be as cool and mysterious as possible. She ignored his damp, garlic breath and his rhinoceros skin. She ignored her own fear. She crossed her arms over Petula, badly hidden beneath her baggy top, and she managed to calm her mind and make some calculations.

The first was that this man and his assistant were obviously both very fine hypnotists, as was Molly.

The second was that they were both also world stoppers. They could both stop time, just as she could.

Molly suspected that they might be better hypnotists than she was (after all, they were both time travelers) and, for this reason, she decided not to use her crystal to stop time. However, she was sure that, as far as time traveling went, one of them wasn't very good at it. It struck Molly that if the best assistant that this rich and powerful giant could find was this man Zackya, who was crouching in the corner, then good time travelers were rare.

Molly stared straight ahead and ignored the maharaja as his sticklike, heavy finger poked at her forehead. She felt very alone and really scared, but she knew she mustn't look it. To protect herself, she feigned a look of haughty pride, as if she was deeply insulted to have been so rudely dragged back in time.

Molly remembered a pompous character in an old film she'd watched on video over and over again at the orphanage. The general in it had been captured by the opposite side and, instead of being wide-eyed and subservient, he was loudly objecting. Molly knew she should try to be like him, which meant putting on a huge act. She wasn't too confident of her acting, but she could remember the general's lines since she and Rocky had so often said them to each other. The adrenaline pumping through her gave her courage, and Molly surprised herself as some of the general's pompous words suddenly flew from her mouth.

"I find this imposition most inconvenient and degrading. In fact, it is downright impertinent!" she blustered.

She shivered as the final "impertinent" left her mouth, because she knew that behaving like this was a complete gamble.

Her tall captor narrowed his eyes and glared at her. Molly gritted her teeth.

"Do you?" he said slowly.

"*Yes.*" She pushed her mind to remember and imagine the general in the film, and she continued. "Yes. To be sneaked up on in such an underhanded way by your subordinate." Molly wasn't sure whether she knew what "subordinate" meant, but she carried on, anyway. "I should have been challenged properly in a *hypnotic duel*. It's downright rude. *Then* to be escorted through time by someone so . . . so unexperienced and uncapable." As she heard her own words Molly remembered that she should have said "*in*experienced and *in*capable." She steamed on. "It is not the sort of treatment that *I*, a world-class hypnotist, *expect* from you, another world-class hypnotist. If *I* were in your position, *I* would have found a much worthier escort. I would have shown more respect."

Molly could hardly believe that these sentences were tumbling out of her mouth. She was either digging herself a grave with them, or airlifting herself out of trouble—she had no idea which. But knowing she must act the part entirely, she now summoned up some very precise hypnotic energy and turned her eyes to the giant's. He already had his eyes glaring hypnotically. His large, bulbous eyes, set in their dark sockets, were horrible. Around the tannin-brown pupils, the whites were veined and bloodshot. Molly had never faced such huge or such repulsive eyes, yet her green eyes dealt with them. She leveled her gaze at his and felt his power. Steadily she looked straight into the eyes of the withered, walrus-skinned, tortoise-faced man.

Fascinated to be up against eyes the caliber of Molly's, the giant enjoyed the unusual sensation of the challenge. Now he could see how this scrawny, potato-nosed girl had tipped over his neatly organized plans. Her power was like that of no other hypnotist he'd come across. She was experienced, too, he could sense. For every time he refocused, to catch her out and knock her hypnotically, she predicted his move and rebuffed his look. She was good, very good, especially for her age. But she knew nothing of the rules of time travel, so that put him leagues ahead of her. He admired her talent and her boldness, too. It was almost a pleasure to meet her. Although she was a little too big for her boots, he thought. Perhaps she would be some sport. Perhaps he ought to knock her down to size. Maybe he would. He dropped his gaze.

"Hmmm," he mused. "So you see yourself as a flutterby princess." He clapped his huge hands. "Perhaps the princess would tike some lea."

Seven

At once the far doors swung open and eight turbaned servants came scurrying in with trays. These bore silver teapots, jugs, porcelain plates, cups, and glasses and, in the time that it took Molly and the giant to walk down the chamber, a low walnut table was laid. Molly's chair faced a painted wall, where a mural of a hunting scene depicted in very fine detail the giant maharaja on an elephant, a rifle in his hand, shooting a tiger dead. It was a beautiful painting, though Molly didn't like the subject matter. The green woodland showed Molly something of the country that surrounded the fort.

"It's a refreshing change," the giant admitted, reaching for an oversized muffin that a half-starved servant offered him, "to meet someone who doesn't cower in front of me like a beaten dog." He gave a cursory glance in Zackya's direction. "I apologize for the walf-hit who brought you here. He is actually an 'Untouchable.'"

"An untouchable?" Molly asked, hoping her host hadn't noticed how her hand shook as she chose a muffin.

"Yes. He was born into the lowest caste, the lowest rank of Hindus. Most Hindu Indians would think he was no better than a sewage rat. But I am not a Hindu, so I simply take him at face value and see him for the crathetic peature that he is. Because of me, he is free. I FREED him." The giant raised his voice slightly, charging the air with menace. Molly felt that now, even though he was looking at her, he was actually addressing Zackya. "I FREED him and LOOK how he repays me. BY NOT CARRYING OUT MY INSTRUCTIONS!" These words were shouted so loudly and angrily that the china on the table rattled. And suddenly, the giant's temper flared up madly and out of control.

"USELESS, AREN'T YOU? ALWAYS HAVE BEEN, LITTLE ZACKYA. WATCH OUT, WATCH OUT. I'll HAVE YOU CHOPPED UP WITH SHARP KNIVES. FEED YOU TO THE CEAPOCKS." His voice dropped to a purr. "Or maybe I'll just hypnotize you. You wouldn't like that, would you? Avoided it for so long. Wouldn't like to be HYPNOTIZED!"

Molly was shocked by the giant's violent mood swing, and even more so by what he was saying. Zackya bowed, knelt, and bowed even lower, his hands outstretched on the floor. Then, as quickly as it had risen, the giant's temper disappeared. "I'm rather clever," he said, his heavy face puckering with a horrid, twisted smile. "You see, I have to have thumsing done in the future. Thumsing done that cannot be done in these times."

Molly tried to pretend that his fit hadn't bothered her in the least. "What?" she said, taking a ladylike nibble from her muffin and replacing it on the plate that a servant placed on a napkin on her knees. Inside, she quaked. She hoped that her spoiled-princess act would give her a chance against her unbalanced host. His volatile temper frightened her, for it reminded her of a madman she and Rocky had seen once in the streets in Briersville. The man had escaped from the local psychiatric hospital. First he'd sat singing to the pigeons, then suddenly he'd jumped up and begun thrashing at them with a stick. The giant had the same unpredictable temper. She must be extremely careful or she would be peacock meat. Petula squirmed, starting to get very hot. Molly squeezed her to be still.

The giant knocked at the huge red and green crystals around his neck with his gold-painted fingernail.

"I have to mine some more of these stycrals. Time-travel crystals. They come from deep down, biles melow the surface of the earth. I need them." The maharaja put a large piece of cake in his mouth.

"Why?" asked Molly, trying to sip her drink casually. She gagged. It was water flavored with lime and salt.

"Because"—crumbs flew out of the giant's mouth as he explained—"when I have traveled back to the beginning of time with a single crystal, if I have *large quantities* of stycrals with me, I can be levitated to the 'Bubble of Light.' In the Bubble, there is a wonderful light which, if bathed in, makes a person youthful!" He brushed both his hands over his face as if imagining the light and added, "I haven't always looked like this."

Molly swallowed a mouthful of muffin and wondered, for the first time, whether she was dreaming. "A wonderful light that made a person look younger, that shone in a place called the 'Bubble of Light' at the beginning of time?" Who'd ever heard of sunbathing to get a youthful glow? The giant was madder than she'd thought. For a moment she wondered whether, if she were to have a hospital where she used hypnotism to cure people and if this giant were a patient, whether

Rocky and she could work out how to cure him. In a flash she wished Rocky were with her. She could just imagine what he would say now, and the words came out of her mouth.

"I thought the beginning of time was full of fire and explosions. Wouldn't you be burned alive if you landed in it?"

"No. In the twenty-ninth century they discover that the beginning of time is a sieve-like place full of white light from the Bubble. If a person can levitate into this light, he or she receives life-force and youthfulness. Levitation to the Bubble is difficult—only possible with a good supply of time-travel crystals."

"Oh . . . right." Molly lifted her eyebrows. "And you say you need to mine the crystals in *my* time . . . in the twenty-*first* century. . . ."

"Yes, because now, in the 1870s, it is impossible. It is only in the fenty-twirst century that the technology to mine deeply enough to get the stycrals out of the earth is possible. It is very, very expensive to do. It is only with the resources of many countries that it is possible. That is why I have to have Cornelius Logan in complete troncol of the whole world in the centy-first twentury. He will hypnotize all the world leaders." Here, the giant gave Molly a dark look, as if he was about to lose his temper again, but he didn't. "You have got in my way, but I will put my plans back on track," he said. "Then, once Cornelius is in troncol, I will have the power and wealth of many, many countries at my tingerfips. The mining can begin and I will get mountains of stycrals. Armed with tons and tons of stycrals, I can get to the beginning of time and attain *youthfulness.* Simple, you see. And it would have been done by now, too, if it weren't for a problem that occurred: You, Miss Moon, were the mevious donkey that escaped the laboratory." The giant snorted impatiently. "I am put out, I must say. It has taken me years to work out how to mine the stycrals. Then I came up with the ingenious plan of using hypnotists from your time to do the work for me. I went to the future, to your time, to the time when you were just born, and I hypnotized Cornelius. I put the whole plan into action. Primo Cell and Lucy Logan's baby was put in an orphanage. That was you, of course. Primo Cell and your mother were split apart. Everything was wet up to serk. It took a lot of effort to set things up so that Cornelius's life would end in him ruling the world for me. It was exhausting work. Time travel is exhausting. But I knew it would be worth the effort." He glared at Molly.

"I time traveled to modern India and phoned the Hite Whouse, in America, expecting to speak to Primo

Cell and Cornelius, expecting to hear about *rooms* full of mined stycrals. But, instead, another man was president. My plans had been wrecked."

Molly again tried to look unshaken. She put on an uncaring, hard expression and sipped at a yellow drink. She was so scared that the sugar in the drink felt electric on her tongue.

"After more exhausting detective work," the giant continued, "I realized that *you* were responsible. Hmm. I stupidly gave in to my fatigue and sent that imbecile Yackza to fetch you. And he fetched the *wrong* you. Don't you agree? He should have gone back in time and fetched the ten-year-old Molly Moon, who hadn't yet learned to hypnotize. For me to kill. Then my plans would have gone smoothly—as Molly Moon would have been too dead to ruin them. *Do you understand?*"

Molly, still acting her part, lifted her nose and shrugged. "Of course I understand. Time travel isn't rocket science."

And then something awful happened.

Petula, who had stayed invisible under Molly's T-shirt for so long, got the fidgets. She was roasting under there. She began to wriggle and push her face out. And at once the giant saw her.

"WHAT IN NOT'S RAME IS THAT?" he boomed. He leaned forward, and his cranelike arm shot out and ripped Petula from her hiding place. "HOW DID

THIS ANIMAL GET THROUGH THE NET, YACKZA? *YOU WANTED THIS LUMP OF MEAT AS A PET FOR YOURSELF, DIDN'T YOU, YOU STUPID MAN?"*

Held upside down by her back legs, Petula let out a yelp and started whining loudly. In the giant's hands she looked more the size of a guinea pig than a dog. Molly's first impulse was to scream, but she just managed to hold it in and transform her cry.

"How DARE YOU!" she shouted angrily, slamming her glass down on the table. "Put her down at once. If you treat that dog badly, I certainly won't help you."

This made the maharaja look up. He turned Petula the right way up and began to laugh.

"Melp he . . . ha ha ha . . . Melp he? HA HA HA. I must say, HA, I never thought you would be such an amusement!" The giant grinned. His teeth were horrible. All stained orange. "I tell you what, my dear, why don't we have a gittle lame?"

"A game?"

"Yes. This dog will be the stakes. What happens is this: I will show you the rudiments of trime tavel. And then you will go back in time and fetch something for me. If you manage to fetch the thing, well then the dog . . . I assume it is a dog, it's so ugly—which end is its rear end?—then the dog lives. If you fail, the dog dies. Curried pug might become a delicacy born today!"

Eight

Molly followed the giant maharaja past the still-cowering Zackya and through a tall, golden door. They ascended a flight of narrow steps.

"These steps were built two drunhed and thirty years ago," the maharaja complained, squeezing his large body up the tight stairwell. "I keep meaning to go back to 1638 to hypnotize the Mughal architect of that time to design them bigger, but I'm too busy."

They stepped outside into a large, open-topped court-yard with dark red sandstone walls punctuated by arched, glassless windows. Pointed domes of sandstone and white marble crowned the walls, and a flag with a peacock on it flew on a pole that reached high into the blue sky. It was a roasting day, but at this height a cool breeze blew in from the countryside around. Molly could see the simple old city outside, with its flower-filled gardens, and the brown, bushy hills nearby. To the west was another red stone building with minarets and domes like onions. In the distance were towers and white gherkin-shaped buildings, as well as smaller, hutlike houses. And in between were palm trees and paved areas, and sunbaked roads where people and animals walked. Sounds drifted up from the city—cries of stallholders selling their wares, shouts of drivers directing their horses or buffalo or camels or elephants. Over this came the hum and buzz of a hive of bees that hung outside one of the rooftop windows, and water splashing as it ran into a pool in the center of the courtyard. Molly noticed a chain of Indian servants quietly passing buckets to one another, the top man pouring the water into some hole up high so that it streamed down the pretty water channel into the central pool. It was arduous work for them.

"So," said the maharaja, stroking his scaly chin and placing Petula on the top of a stone plinth. "Here is your challenge to save your dog from becoming curried pug. This morning before my bath a ceapock got into this yourtcard and was removed. I want you to go back in time and fetch that ceapock for me." The giant clicked his fingers and spoke to a servant, who nodded and scurried away.

"But I don't know how to handle peacocks," Molly protested. "How do I catch it? Will it bite?"

"Ha! What diriculousness! To be worried about how to net a ceapock! I think you'll find that the trime taveling is the thing that will stump you. HA!" He slapped his red silk coat with immense amusement.

Molly glared at him, for she knew this was not funny. Zackya slithered out from the narrow stairwell onto the roof courtyard.

"Yackza, pick up the dog and rut a pope around its neck."

Zackya slid slyly forward and picked up Petula.

"By the way, Yackza, don't think your incompetence has gone unnoticed by me. I realize that this smelly aminal is here because of you. The only reason I am not punishing you is that you have unwittingly brought me some entertainment."

Zackya bowed low and gave Molly a hateful sideways look.

The giant clapped his hands and the servant who had rushed off now came back. He was carrying a black velvet cushion on which sat a selection of red and green crystals. Rubies, emeralds—Molly wasn't sure what they were.

"Green is for traveling backward. Red is for going forward. Pake your tick."

Molly took a quick look, as though choosing a chocolate. Each colored crystal was a slightly different shade of green or red, and each bore a slightly different fault. A fault like a tiny scar, as if it had once been cut open. None was perfect. Molly decided upon the two brightest crystals. As she picked them up she noticed a faint surge of energy coming from each. She tried not to react. "Now what?"

"Ha! So confident! You just wait. HA!"

Molly was sick of the giant patronizing her. "I would like to be shown how to do this, please, because otherwise how else can I get your big chicken?"

The giant frowned. Lifting his lip in a sneer, he began. "It's simple, but it takes practice. So that you have at least a sporting chance of saving your dog, I will do my best to explain how trime tavel is done. But *just once*—I am not the patient sort, so listen. Concentrate on the green or red stycral, depending on which way you trish to wavel. Then put your mind into a semitrance—as you do when you stop the world. Stare into the space of now, and summon the cool fusion feeling of world stopping. As it comes, do not stop the world but instead focus your mind on the stycral for trime tavel until your mind goes the color of the stycral. As soon as the world starts to blur and the trime tavel breeze starts to blow about you, you will know that you are moving. You will also hear a distant BOOM behind you. For anyone in the room *watching* you disappear, this BOOM will be lery voud, unless you have a de-BOOM device, of course. The BOOM is the noise that is made by your body suddenly disappearing—air suddenly has to fill the gap where your body was and this makes a BOOM noise. Simple physics. That is the easy part. The fiddicult part is stopping at the correct time. That takes instinct and practice. Are you ready?"

"You're not going to give me any more clues as to how I know when I'm in the right place in time and how to stop?" Molly asked worriedly. "Don't I get a gadget like Zackya has?"

"That gadget is for complete idiots," the maharaja replied.

Molly looked across at Petula, who was now wearing a homemade rope lead. She was sitting nervously on the ground beside Zackya and the servant with the cushion of crystals.

"I'll see you in a minute," Molly said to her, trying to bolster herself with confidence. Inside, she was as unsure of herself as a baby bird being pushed out of its nest.

Molly gripped the green crystal in her right hand. She stared at the ground. She brought her hypnotic focus to the front of her mind, like when she made time stand still. The cold fusion feeling washed through her, and then everything around her froze still except for Zackya and the maharaja.

"WRONG!" the giant thundered. Molly ignored him and had another go. This time, as the icy fusion feeling gave the faintest quiver in her veins, she focused entirely on the green crystal, diving her mind into the idea of green, and then, as if she'd followed a map perfectly, her time-travel journey began. There was a distant BOOM, a cool wind began to blow about her, and the world melted into a blur of colors. Sounds dipped and changed and rang in her ears.

And then the red-robed giant was there beside her, taunting her, time traveling at the *exact* speed she was, with the colors of the changing world swirling around him.

"Where are you going to, Molly?" he mocked. "You haven't the faintest idea, have you? Can't you toncrol your journey?" The huge man popped out of Molly's vision. It was all happening so fast that Molly did indeed feel completely out of control—as she might feel on a bolting horse. With her mind, she pulled on the imaginary reins of the cool wind about her as though to stop it, and it worked. She stopped. It was cold. She had no idea how far back in time she had traveled.

A woman in an orange sari holding a broom pointed at her and shrieked. Molly realized it must have looked like she'd sprung from thin air. She glanced through the window and saw that the domed building outside didn't exist at all. She must have traveled much too far back in time.

Immediately she clutched the red crystal to travel forward and tried to think red. At once she left the shrieking woman behind her and was traveling through a warm time wind. She stopped again. This time, a moon hung over the courtyard. In front of her sat a very tall Indian boy, reading.

"Cetch me a fandle. It's too dark to read," he shouted across the open-roofed chamber to a young slave who sat in the shadows.

The slave saw Molly, and his mouth dropped open. "Sahib, sahib!" he cried, pointing at Molly. The student slammed his book and turned angrily on him.

Molly gripped her red crystal and removed herself. She was amazed. She knew she had just seen the maharaja and Zackya *as children.* She'd recognized them.

Now, a hot geyser of panic rose inside her. If she didn't master this time travel, she would be stuck in time and Petula would be at the mercy of the giant. Molly was reminded of another time she'd panicked. She'd cut her thumb on a salad-dressing bottle and blood had spurted all over her lettuce and cucumber. Rocky had told her to breathe out very slowly to ease the pain and stop the panic. Molly wished he were here now, and tears filled her eyes. Then she took a deep breath in and exhaled very, very slowly, humming as her nostrils expelled air and calmness came to her.

Above Molly's head the sky flashed day, night, day, night. For an instant, rain was all about. For another nanosecond, sun blazed down. The elements were all about her—wind, fire, water—but in her time capsule Molly was shielded from them.

Molly tried to remember how long it had taken her to go back in time from Petula in 1870 to the time of the shrieking woman. If she simply went forward by the same amount of time, she would return to the courtyard with Petula. She stopped. Unfortunately she had now arrived in a time when *lots* of people were in the courtyard. It was wet. Three people saw her and pointed in alarm. But Molly paid no attention. She saw a small hive hanging from the arch of the window and she knew she was close. She gripped the red crystal again and this time looked up at the sky to make a judgment. Blacks and blues flared above her head. Molly tried to think how long a year took to pass. Was it a second? How long would those wild bees take to build their hive? She stopped. The hive was the right size. But the surroundings didn't feel right. This time, Molly shut her eyes. The only thing left was for her to rely on her instinct. She went deep into her feelings and tried to picture when the room felt peacock-y. She went forward for an instant and once more opened her eyes. An alarmed bird let out a cry. It was a peacock, but was it the *right* peacock? Molly looked at the pool and saw that the water was covered with pink rose petals. On a chair were silk clothes. Giant clothes. Molly didn't know how she'd done it, but she'd landed in the correct time. The maharaja's bath time.

Petula lay with her head on her front paws and tried not to shake. She was very scared because she could sense that the giant man striding up and down the courtyard didn't like animals *at all*. He smelled faintly of roses, but he also smelled of garlic and bad temper. Bad temper was a horrid scent. It smelled of burned hair and hot tar. The stench oozed from every pore of the giant's body. Petula put her paws over her nose and tried to ignore it.

She thought about how Molly had just vanished into thin air.

In Briersville the turbaned man had vanished in the same way after leaving her with those children who'd put her in the pram. Every time she and Molly and their kidnaper had traveled through the colored, windy tunnels, Petula supposed that *they* had disappeared, too.

Was Molly in a wind tunnel now?

A piece of dried meat dropped onto the floor beside her, and a moccasin prodded it toward Petula's mouth.

"Eat," Zackya hissed.

Petula stared at the ground. She couldn't eat a thing. She was far too worried about Molly and about what the giant might do next. Her back leg still hurt where he'd so roughly held her upside down. Petula watched as he studied the bees' nest hanging by the window. She wished the bees would swarm and sting him.

Now all Molly had to do was catch the peacock. What was the phrase the giant had used? "Net a peacock." Molly put the crystals in her pocket. The bird was roosting on the branch of a tree, twitching nervously, its green feathered tail hanging down behind it. Molly approached it, making a friendly chucking noise that she knew budgies liked. When she was a few feet away from it, she jumped and tried to grasp its body. But the bird wasn't fooled by her trick. It screeched and shot away from her arms, the mucky ends of its tail whipping her in the face as it went. Her nose was filled with a rank, dusty, dirty-chicken smell. Molly coughed. She needed a net. Then she realized there was a far simpler way of sorting this out. All she needed to do was stop the world.

The peacock stood on a small column in the corner of the courtyard, planning its next step. Its tiny brain was finding it difficult to both balance on the column and decide what to do about Molly. Molly picked up a large pair of shorts from the chair and, with her own clear crystal, stopped the world. Everything went completely still. All the bells in the town outside ceased ringing, and the noisy cows and the grumbling camels went quiet. The peacock went as still as a beautifully painted sculpture set on a plinth. Molly marched over to it and put the leg hole of the shorts over its head. Then she tightly wrapped the rest of the material around its wings and legs so that it couldn't flap or scratch. It was well and truly caught. For a moment, Molly relaxed. She rubbed her cheek. It was feeling very dry. She walked through the chilly, frozen world to the flower-filled pool, cupped water in her hands, and splashed her face.

It was then that she realized she was busting to have a pee. She glanced about for a place she could go. Her eyes fell again on the giant's tub. It would have to be her huge toilet. A pity it wouldn't be flushed before his bath.

Molly felt much better after that. As she walked back to the peacock it struck her that with these gems she could now escape the maharaja. She could even, she calculated, go back in time, travel to Briersville, and have Zackya wrestled to the ground by another gardener before he even took Petula. It would be difficult, but she could do it, couldn't she? But the problem wasn't Zackya. It was the maharaja. If Zackya went missing—if he never turned up at the fort with a hypnotized Molly—then the giant, furious, would come himself to get Molly. He might shoot back to Briersville to when Molly was eight, and kill her then and there. Molly didn't like the situation she was in, but at least she understood it a bit, and her gamble at playing the part of an uppity, cross prima donna was working. Molly decided to stick with the predicament as it was. She picked up the peacock. She unfroze the world, and the bird went stiff with fear in her arms.

This time, she didn't hold the red crystal. She had a heavy bird to deal with. But she thought about it and, because it was in her pocket, this worked. It was difficult to concentrate enough to bring the peacock with her, but finally she found they were both moving through time.

A small spurt of travel was all that was needed, she knew. She opened her eyes. The courtyard was still empty. A jot more. The giant was in his bath, with attendants pouring large jugs of hot water over his scaly shoulders. He really did have a terrible skin condition,

Molly thought. The peacock struggled. A slip more. There they were. The giant was dressed, Zackya stood beside the servant with the cushion of crystals, and Petula, scared, lay curled up on the ground.

"Am I late?" Molly asked, placing the frightened peacock in Zackya's arms. The bird began to squawk, and pecked at his chest.

Zackya dropped it, his mouth agape. He'd never expected Molly to complete the challenge. And he was shocked to see the peacock unwrapping itself from his master's underpants, dragging them about the court-yard.

"Take it away!" shouted the maharaja irritably, choosing to ignore the sight of his underclothes. Zackya grabbed the giant's pants before the bird escaped them. He hauled it squawking toward the courtyard door.

"So," said Molly, as the bird's cries became more distant, "I hope you are a man of your word."

"Hmm. Not usually." The giant was not amused by Molly's success. In fact, he found her achievements in time travel very annoying. He was competitive by nature and didn't like to be bettered at anything by anyone, particularly by a skinny girl.

"I was better than you when I stirst farted," he boasted. "You think that you're good—you are. But not *that* good. Give me back the stycrals and you may have your dog." Molly handed the two gems over. "Now come with me."

"Where to?" asked Molly, her fear returning like an uninvited guest.

"I have to go and get thumsing to show you."

"What?"

"Oh, you just sait and wee."

"I just have, thanks," Molly thought.

The Maharaja put his hands on his giant hips and laughed a belly laugh that echoed around the courtyard and up into the air above the fort.

"I'll show you *real* talent, your shadylip!" he boomed.

Then he strode toward Molly and grabbed her. Petula crouched, barking, preparing to attack. But the maharaja ignored her. As though Molly were as light as a pillow, the maharaja pulled her out of the courtyard and along a narrow passage. Petula followed, barking, nipping at his heels. Molly struggled and tripped behind the stooping man. The maharaja was far too big for the passage and found the journey through it very taxing. Finally he pushed her into a small, ornate room and stood his full height again.

"Get your dog to shut up or, I'm warning you, *I'll* shut her up." Molly scooped Petula into her arms and held her close.

The windowless room was high with a domed ceiling. From its beams were suspended glass lamps and two large hanging beds. The beds were wooden and exquisitely carved. The heavy silver chains on which they hung had links shaped like elephants and horses. Silver caskets and boxes lined the lowest parts of the walls, and higher up were shelves packed with silk cushions and bright, soft blankets. The floor was covered in a patterned carpet, and the walls were decorated with thick, silver, bracelet-sized rings. The maharaja lifted Molly and Petula like toys and dumped them onto one of the swing beds.

"You will wait here," he ordered. "Now I'm going to show you real trime-tavel talent."

With that, he shut and locked the heavy, carved door behind him.

Nine

Molly lay down on the brocaded daybed. It swung slightly. She looked up at the ceiling, which was decorated with hundreds of small mirrors. She could see multiple images of herself lying on the daybed. She covered her eyes with her hands and, now that she was alone with Petula, let out a miserable cry. She curled herself up in a ball and wished that she could disappear. Petula snuggled into her, nudging her with her wet nose, as if to say, "Don't worry Molly, it'll be all right. I'll help you out, I promise."

Molly was too scared and apprehensive even to stroke Petula. She knew from the way the maharaja was behaving that what he really wanted to do was frighten her.

"Of course, he'll be able to frighten me," she whimpered, half to Petula and half to the many Mollys reflected on the ceiling. "I'm only Molly and he's a time-traveling, hypnotizing, heartless, cruel, smelly, huge, lizardy . . ." She couldn't go on. She knew that if she let herself dwell on the maharaja's character, and on what he might have planned for her, she would soon be too scared to breathe.

She thought of Rocky and all the people she loved, and wished with all her heart that she was with them. Then, exhausted, she fell asleep.

While she was asleep, Molly dreamed very strange dreams.

The first was set in Hardwick House Orphanage, where Molly had grown up. In the dream it was a summer's day but she, her *ten-year-old self*, was on her knees in Miss Adderstone's downstairs study. She was in the middle of doing a horrible punishment set by Adderstone. Molly was fluffing up the mangy carpet with her own hairbrush, trying to make it look new. Suddenly, in her dream, the window was pushed wide open and a terrifying, tall, scaly man in flowing robes, who looked as though he had stepped out of a pantomime, reached into the room and pulled her out of it. Fear cut through her as, in her dream, the man held her head in his vast hands and made her look into his eyes. She was hypnotized. Then, everything became slightly blurred. Colors washed around her.

Molly's next dream was set even earlier in her life. She was about six, and the dream was not as clear as the first one. It was more like a distant memory. She was sitting in the brambly garden at the orphanage. In her dream, Molly was suddenly really scared because, instead of her six-year-old friend Rocky emerging from the building with the Frisbee that he'd promised to fetch, a giant man, dressed like someone in a fairy tale, materialized. He appeared out of the air, as if by magic. Adderstone's puppy, Petula, was under his arm. Molly screamed, until, again, the man glared at her and the dream faded into flashing colors.

The last parts of the dream were very faint and very distant. Molly was playing with a toy train. A big man picked her up and all the colors of the rainbow came flushing down over her.

As she writhed and turned in her uncomfortable sleep, Molly knew who the man in red was. He was the maharaja. In her dreams, he took her away from Hardwick House Orphanage, far away. They traveled in a very fast, flying-saucer-shaped machine. And an eleven-year-old Rocky was in the dream, as well as Forest the hippie. Both were hypnotized.

Molly opened her eyes and wondered how long she had been asleep. Petula lay snoring beside her. Molly shook her head, hoping that *this* room and this reality were a dream as well. But they weren't. She felt very muddled. And then she thought about her dreams. Peculiarly, they now felt like memories. Molly realized, with slow-growing horror, that the stories revealed in her head weren't fantasies at all. They were *real* memories. *Memories just put there by the giant.*

And, instead of fading, like dreams do, these memories were moving and *growing*. She could now remember coming to this very palace when she was ten. Molly put her hands to her head and shook it. Was she going mad? What was happening? Her mind was re-creating her past. New memories were growing in her head every second! It was as if parts of her life when she'd been ten, six, and even three were being *relived* so that she was getting *new memories*. She remembered a very distant memory, from when she was absolutely tiny, of arriving at a big red castle and having to walk up a long flight of stairs and of a kind big girl with scruffy hair helping her.

Molly *also* remembered arriving at a red fort when she was ten and helping a three-year-old upstairs.

She remembered wondering, as a ten-year-old, who this huge man was as he herded everyone along a passageway that was far too narrow for him. But Molly wasn't just remembering this as a ten-year-old. Molly was remembering coming down the passage as a six-year-old, and as a three-year-old, too. She remembered how she'd thought that the man looked like a big baboon stuffed down a tight rabbit hole, and she remembered feeling like a little rabbit being dragged along. A hypnotized rabbit.

"MOVE!" Molly looked up. She could hear the giant maharaja coming. He was coming back! What was more, she knew exactly whom he was coming back with.

Molly winced and screwed up her eyes. She breathed short, terrified gasps, and whimpered. She couldn't bear this. This was real, but it was scarier than any nightmare.

Then there was a knock at the door.

"Good evening, Lommy," came the maharaja's cruel, twisted voice. "Do you mind if I come in? I have some visitors for you."

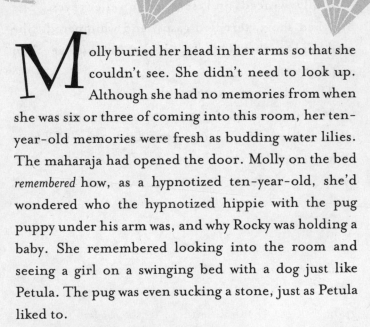

Ten

Molly buried her head in her arms so that she couldn't see. She didn't need to look up. Although she had no memories from when she was six or three of coming into this room, her ten-year-old memories were fresh as budding water lilies. The maharaja had opened the door. Molly on the bed *remembered* how, as a hypnotized ten-year-old, she'd wondered who the hypnotized hippie with the pug puppy under his arm was, and why Rocky was holding a baby. She remembered looking into the room and seeing a girl on a swinging bed with a dog just like Petula. The pug was even sucking a stone, just as Petula liked to.

"Ah, so you are still here!" The maharaja chuckled meanly. Petula sat up and whined. She cocked her head and sniffed the air, extremely confused. Three walking Mollys had just entered the chamber, and Rocky and Forest, both usually so full of life, were standing there like zombies, one holding a baby and the other a puppy—a puppy that smelled oddly *like herself.*

On the bed, Molly locked her arms and peered through a crack at Rocky and Forest. Was it really them? They were in exactly the same clothes as they'd been wearing that cold morning in Briersville Park. Had the maharaja really managed to travel to the future, fetch them, and bring them to 1870s India? Why not? That toad Zackya brought *her* here. But why had the maharaja brought Rocky and Forest here? To show off, Molly supposed. She dreaded to think what horrid plans he had for them. She hated him for messing with her friends' lives as well as her own.

Molly refused to look up. She knew that if she did, everything would get much more complicated as everyone recognized her and she would have the shock of seeing the younger versions of herselves at the same time as she got their memories. And Molly felt that this would be so frightening, she might scream or faint.

And she mustn't react. That was exactly what the giant wanted. If she screamed, he would feel that he'd won—he'd know that he'd impressed her. She didn't want him to see her weak. She must pretend to be as tough as a hardened warrior. If she could con him into thinking that she were steelier than anyone he'd ever met, then she might buy herself more time—more time to think of how to overcome him, to destroy him, even.

As Molly stared into the V of light between her clenched arms, she knew that she had never felt so violent toward someone. And then the maharaja did something that made the situation worse. He clapped his hands.

At once, fierce, scared feelings rose up through Molly, columns of tenseness, as fear broke out among the younger Mollys in the room. As the giant snapped them out of their trances the reality of their situation hit them. Molly's mind was full of horrible memories.

The ten-year-old Molly looked about herself in alarm and she dropped the hairbrush that she'd been clutching. She wondered whether she was dreaming, but only for a split second. Her fear was wide-awake fear. She understood that for the past few hours she had been hypnotized and now she'd been released. She also knew that she'd traveled back in time. But how or why all this was happening was a complete mystery. She glanced toward Rocky, shocked to see that he looked older.

"Is that you?" she whispered.

Rocky's brow was furrowed with intense thought as

he stared at the baby in his arms. "Yes," he said slowly.

The ten-year-old Molly looked down at the six-year-old crying beside her and at the three-year-old holding her hand. "And these children . . . They look like me—are they *me*, Rocky?"

Rocky nodded.

The ten-year-old went cold. "Why? And *how*?"

"I don't really know. This is Forest, and that girl on the bed is an older version of you. She's an eleven-year-old Molly."

For Molly on the bed, these memories were so vivid and so deeply disturbing that she found her stomach cramping convulsively.

The giant maharaja surveyed the scene cruelly.

"Ha. Amazing, Molly, isn't it?" he commented drily, preening himself. "Do you stunderhand how I've done this?"

Molly shut her eyes. She knew she must calm her emotions and ignore these newly built memories and feelings that were flooding into her mind and her muscles. She lifted her thoughts to concentrate on her breath. She breathed in and very slowly out. "I am me, now," she thought. "*I* am me, and they are my past. They are here, but I am me now. I am the latest Molly, the fullest Molly. I am me. They are me, but *I* am in control. I have lived the longest. I am the oldest. *I* am in control. Their minds, that are making my memories, are full of fear, but I will not freak out, I do not need to be afraid, because I *understand* what is happening, so I am in control. They don't understand, but I do. *I* am in control." Molly breathed deeply, breathing out slowly and deliberately, and she focused her mind. Then she looked up.

Her ten-year-old self recognized the Molly on the bed and cried out. But Molly blocked out the thoughts that were coming from herself as a ten-year-old. She refused to let the memories affect her.

"Of course I understand how you've done this," she said, drawing herself upright, seeming as unruffled as the sea on a windless day. "The moment your servant escorted me here, on that little time-travel trip, I was already aware that this sort of trick could be played. What do you take me for? Brainless? I suppose you've never met someone with your abilities before. You seem to be unaware that I am just as cunning as you, Mr.—? Ah, it strikes me that we were never formally introduced. How rude of you." Molly pulled an iron curtain down on her memories. They were squealing to be heard, but she shut the memories of her earlier selves out of her mind.

The maharaja was shocked, and he showed it. His competitive spirit was bruised. *He* judged the mind-warping feat that he had just performed to be brilliant, unsurpassable. The same trick made sniveling wrecks of the greatest, most powerful maharajas and their princesses. Some went quite mad from the experience. All were reduced to shadows of their former selves. And here was this child of eleven, utterly unimpressed, saying that she could do it, too, unaffected by the experience of seeing herself in various younger forms. He could hardly believe it. He searched Molly's face. Was she lying? Pretending?

"Why are your younger selves crying so pathetically? Your hardness is an act," he concluded.

"Mr. Maharaja, if you don't even have the decency to introduce yourself properly, I shall be forced to call you Mr. M. In answer to your question, they are upset, of course, because they don't understand what is happening to them. I am an accomplished hypnotist. They know nothing of hypnotism, world stopping, time traveling. What do you expect? I am a different person to these Mollys. They are me before I learned hypnotism— before I hardened. You forget that I have been through a lot in New York and Los Angeles. You have no idea. I am fearless because I understand. They are afraid because they don't. What is more, I think it is somewhat over-egging the pudding to have snatched Petula as a puppy."

Molly gulped. Her hands were getting sweaty, which was always a bad sign. She had never spoken like this before and she thought she sounded like a character from a space-station soap opera addressing an alien. The ten-year-old Molly looked at her eleven-year-old self in awe. The girl seemed so strong and confident. She couldn't imagine that she would ever talk in such a pompous way—the manner reminded her of the way a captured general talked in a film she'd often watched with Rocky.

The maharaja, meanwhile, was amazed. And a new thought that had born its seed in his head was growing and winding its way into his plans. He glanced at the baby that the black boy was holding. Until now, he'd never entertained the desire to have an heir. This was partly because he didn't think he needed one. His aim was to travel to the Bubble of Light at the beginning of time and rejuvenate himself repeatedly. He might live for thousands of years. He also had never wanted a child because he hated the idea of having a child that wasn't as brilliant as he was. But here was a baby who was obviously going to grow into a child prodigy, a genius hypnotist, with a hardened, sophisticated character. He didn't need an heir, but it might be good to have a companion.

So far, Zackya was all he had. As a child, the maharaja

had had problems. He had a chemical imbalance in his brain that meant he often flew off the handle. He was too bad-tempered, overgrown, and dangerous to be the sort of a son his parents wanted to show off. In fact, they'd found him an embarrassment, and so, cruelly, inhumanely, had locked him up. He'd lived out of the sight of people except for the servants who brought him food, a trail of different nannies and tutors, and Zackya.

His mother and father had shunned him as though he were diseased. People avoided him, and so he learned to despise all people. But this baby was different. She had huge potential. He could model her on himself and, when she grew up, she would understand and love him. For the first time in a long time, the giant felt warmth toward another human being. And at once he knew exactly what he was going to do next.

"My name," he said politely, "is the Waharaja of Maqt . . . the Maharaja of Waqt." At this point, the three-year-old Molly began to wail uncontrollably. "Shut up. I'm spying to treak," he blustered. And he pushed the small girl toward the Molly on the bed. Molly found herself in the strangest position she had ever been in. She had to pick herself up.

She was holding herself, and the small girl stopped crying. And as if some warmth replaced the fear, Molly felt a memory of a feeling, ever so faint, in herself, of being young and being cuddled. It was lovely. Her cuddle was very faintly making herself feel better. Molly could hardly believe it. She hugged the little Molly.

"Don't worry," she whispered. "Don't worry any-more."

Rocky watched in disbelief. He didn't notice Waqt's great hands coming toward him. In a flash, the maharaja seized the baby Molly and moved away to the other side of the room.

"Give her back," Rocky cried, rushing toward him.

"I wouldn't attempt to get her off me," Waqt spat, the words machine-gunning out of his mouth. He put his foot up to prevent Rocky from coming closer. "If you do, I'll be forced to drop her in a different time zone where you won't be able to see her *ever* again." Rocky stopped dead in his tracks, and the six-year-old Molly ran to Molly. She didn't understand how she'd been transported here, but she did know that the best place in the room was away from the giant and beside the big girl on the bed. More waves of warmth and security flooded through the oldest Molly as she held her younger selves.

Rocky began talking slowly and deliberately.

"Please give her back, won't you—give her back? It would—be so—much—better—"

"Ha! Do you really think, boy, that you can hypnotize me using your pathetic voice? Ha!"

Rocky blushed angrily.

"What are you gonna do with that baby?" said Forest, slightly recovered, handing the puppy to the ten-year-old Molly. This Molly studied the long-haired man in front of her. She'd never met a hippie before.

"Who is that baby, anyways?" he was saying, his round glasses slipping down his nose. "And, hey, why are we here? Man, it's bad karma to steal people and, like, take them to different time zones. I mean, we like our home zones. Can we go home?"

The maharaja ignored Forest. He tapped the baby's head with his bony finger.

Molly couldn't bear it. One slip, one squeeze, and the giant could kill the baby he was holding. That baby was *her*. If he killed her as a baby, then she *now* couldn't exist. All the Mollys in the room would cease to exist. Would they just go up in smoke? What would happen? Molly didn't want to find out. She *must* get herself back. She concentrated on her clear crystal and somersaulted her mind, bringing the world to a flashing halt. She stopped the world.

But, of course, the giant was fast on the draw, as fast as a beam of light. His skill was beyond any she'd ever encountered. Everyone in the room froze stiff as an icicle, except for the Maharaja of Waqt and the sleeping baby in his arms.

"CAUGHT you," he said in a singsong way, whipping his head around to face Molly full on. He glared at her hypnotically, and she resisted his gaze. If the energy between their eyes had been visible, it would have looked like two electric bolts of light—Molly's green, and the maharaja's brown with a red bloodshot blot in it.

"Don't bother trying to outdo me," said Waqt. "I'm invincible. Always alert. You won't catch me off guard. Never. I expect attack from every ridection. From the pesent, the prast, and even the future. That's why I carry this gun." He patted the leather sheath on his belt that, until then, Molly had assumed was a knife. "Who knows who will, sometime in the future, want to come back and wipe me out? Just think how they could pop up and surprise me! They don't realize that I always expect them. I expect attack erevy moment of erevy day. And that is why I am always prepared, so, Molly, you haven't the slightest chance." Around them, everyone was as still as rock. "You should find yourself more talented friends. That boy's attempt to hypnotize me was useless! He leeds nessons in voice-only hypnosis."

The air was chilly. Molly felt scared and lonely here

on her own with Waqt, but she didn't show it.

"Now that your friends are quiet, I'm going to tell you what I'm going to do." He put the sleeping baby on a cushion on the floor. It went still. Then he moved toward Molly. He pushed her against the wall, put her left hand through one of the silver metal loops, and clicked it shut. Then he took a key—the key to the handcuffs—off a hook on the wall by the door and slipped it into his pocket. He gathered up the ten-year-old Molly, holding the puppy, the six-year-old, and the toddler Molly as if they were shop mannequins and, choosing not to put movement into their frozen bodies, he placed them in the passage outside the chamber.

He pulled the frozen Rocky over to the wall. Even Forest was reasonably easy for him to move, as Waqt was so big. Soon, they were all handcuffed. Molly didn't show any emotion, but inside she was boiling.

"What are you going to do with the baby and the other Mollys?" she demanded. Waqt ignored her and picked up the baby.

"WHERE ARE YOU TAKING ME?" shouted Molly.

"Oh, you? Why, you're staying here, of course." The maharaja trembled with laughter.

"The OTHER ME's," Molly growled angrily.

"Oh . . . oh, I *see*. Going to keep them, of course. Going to rear the baby as my own. This is the consolation for you, you see, Lommy. At least you will survive in a new form. Of course, as the years go by, all the other you's will lose their past orphanage memories. The three-year-old Lommy Loon here will be the first to lose all her memories of being an orphanage child. As this baby relives your life here, and reaches three years of age, her *new* life will replace the first three years that you had before. And as she grows, all your hild-chood memories will be replaced, because this baby will relive your past with me, here. For instance, the child that I rear will have no memories of that fat old woman I noticed doing the ironing when I went there, nor of the orphanage mistress." The giant paused and made a sour face. "Of course, I will have five Lommy Loons here, which is probably far too many, so after I have learned something about your character from the child Mollys—I might test them a bit—and after I have used them as nannies, I will probably kill them. I will have a cobra bite the toddler and, when she dies, the six-year-old here and the ten-year-old, and *you, too,* believe it or not, will all die as well. Because if you have died when you were a toddler, you cannot be alive today. I'm sure you understand." Now the giant's voice dropped to a kindly tone, which was deeply creepy because he didn't have a drop of kindness in his poisonous nature. "But, Molly," he purred, "remember, there is a consolation. You *will* live on, in a way, because I will let this maby Bolly live, and so your life will be *re-formed*. *My* baby, whom I will rename Waqta, will have a lorious glife. A life lived in palaces, with everything she desires!" Waqt shut the door and shouted from the corridor, "She'll have elepants as phets!"

Eleven

Molly unfroze the world.

As she did, Rocky and Forest came to, shocked that their left hands were locked in handcuffs attached to the wall.

"Man, this is ba-ad," moaned Forest. The children outside began to cry noisily. Then they went quiet, and Molly felt numbness and she knew that the Mollys outside were hypnotized again.

Rocky tugged at the handcuffing loop around his wrist.

"Is he coming back soon?" asked Forest. "What's the plan?"

"I'm not sure," said Molly. She explained what had just happened.

"I wish I could have hypnotized him," Rocky said. "He

was so alert. He knew what I was up to as soon as I started. The trouble with voice-only hypnosis is that you need a good minute of talking to get the subject into a trance."

"Don't worry," said Molly. "I couldn't get him, either. He's good, Rocky."

"And how long does he plan to keep us hangin' here like unused puppets?" asked Forest. "I can't do my sun salutations like this."

"Forest," said Rocky sternly, "get a grip."

Molly winced. Only a few minutes had passed and already her wrist hurt where the metal handcuff cut into it. Petula sniffed at Molly's knee and whined as if to say that she wished she could help. But seeing that there was nothing she could do, she went back to lie down under the hammock to suck her stones.

Molly watched Petula, wishing desperately that she was as free as she was.

"You know, he's such a freak, he'll probably leave us here to die of thirst!"

"Unless we could pull these things out of the walls," said Rocky. "We'd be left with big silver bracelets, but at least we'd be free."

"'Free Bird'—man, I love that song." Forest turned and began pulling at his wrist iron, trying to release it from the wall.

"We need something sharp," Rocky said, glancing

about the room at the cushions, "to dig the attachments out of the plaster."

Molly glanced over at Petula.

"Petula's stones!" she cried. "Heel, Petula! Let's see what you've got." Petula trotted obediently over.

"Drop!" said Molly. And Petula dropped two pieces of colored glass at Molly's feet. They made a CHINK noise as they landed.

"Man, you shouldn't suck glass, you'll cut your mouth!" said Forest. It took a few seconds for Molly to realize what Petula had been a guardian of.

"WOW! Petula! Where did you get these? I can't believe you!"

"It's going to take a lot of scraping," said Rocky. "Those are hardly sharp at all."

"We're not going to need to scrape!" Molly brushed the gems toward her with her sneaker. "Rocky, look! These are time-travel crystals. I can't believe it! Petula must have taken them off the cushion next door. It was covered in them. You see, Waqt was showing me how time travel works and so he made his servant bring a whole load of them in!"

Petula was very pleased to be making Molly so happy. She sat up wagging her tail.

Quickly, for she knew time was of the essence, Molly explained to Forest and Rocky how hypnotic time travel worked and how she had fetched the peacock.

"So, if I go back in time, the cuff around my wrist will just disappear."

"But Forest and me will still be handcuffed."

"Not when I get the key and bring it forward in time to unlock you."

"Wow, just like the peacock . . ."

"Yes, except, unlike the peacock, I'll have to take the key back in time again and hang it on the hook where it belongs. Otherwise, it will be missing when that old tyrannosaurus needs it to lock us up like he did. It has to be put back or else he'll get suspicious."

"Do you think you're up to it, Molly?"

"I have to be." Molly slid her sneakers off and wriggled her feet out of their socks. Then she clenched a crystal under the toes of each foot. She took a deep breath and concentrated her mind.

"I'll see you later," she said. In a moment there was a small BOOM, and she vanished.

Molly was swirling backward through a cool time wind, focusing her mind on the green crystal under her right foot. Because she was in the *same* room, with no changing sky above her, the colors around her hardly changed. She tried to remember the feeling she'd got when fetching the peacock. The timing instinct that had worked for her then was what she needed now. She felt herself passing through the moment before—when the maharaja had been taunting her. Fear shook her, as she thought of his gun. But she knew she mustn't think of this because if she did, she would never receive the right instinct about stopping. The room changed color. Molly stopped. The first thing she noticed was that her hands were free. The room smelled of mold.

The walls were terra-cotta-colored and completely undecorated. Molly quickly bent down and gathered up the crystals from under her feet. She went to the door where the key hook would be. Then she aimed to go forward in time. She remembered how Zackya had gone red in the face as he tried to park in the correct time zone, and she now understood how he felt. She decided to relax. Perhaps if she relaxed deeply, she would get the correct instinct. Molly clasped the red stone.

A swirl of color took her forward in time. Again, she stopped. The maharaja was standing in the room! His back was to her and all the younger Mollys were standing beside him, their gaze on the bed in front of them. Rocky was in the room and Forest, too. They were all hypnotized. None of them saw her. There, lying on the bed, was her eleven-year-old self, with her hands over her head and face. The maharaja began to chuckle in a mean, rumbling way.

"Ah, so you are still here!" he said to the Molly on the bed, not noticing the one behind him. Molly could hardly believe it. *She was visiting a moment she had just lived through!* She backed out of the room, her heart cantering. Halfway down the staircase she concentrated on the green stone, and at once she disappeared with a small BOOM.

She put her invisible time-travel antennae out and tried to feel her way. She wanted a very short trip *back* in time. She stopped and ran up the stairs toward the chamber. This time the room was completely empty, and there, on the wall, was the key. Molly ran forward and unhooked it.

Now concentrating on the red stone, she was soon flying forward again. She tried to sense her way back to the time she'd come from. This was going to be a close call. She didn't want to arrive in the room while the maharaja was still in it. She thought lightly, tuning her senses, balancing the past and the future, trying to get to exactly the moment she had left her friends.

Then Molly stopped. And there in front of her were Rocky and Forest, imprisoned in the irons. She rushed forward. Petula bounded up to her.

"How long have I been?" she asked.

"About three minutes!" said Rocky. "But you look different. Your skin is . . ."

Molly unlocked their handcuffs. Three minutes? So she'd arrived three minutes after she'd left them. She'd wanted to land three *seconds* after she'd left them! But three minutes was pretty good. Better than good.

"What do you mean, I look different? Actually, tell me in a minute." Before Molly lost the antennae feeling, she gripped the green stone and the world was spinning backward again.

She shot through minutes and hours to the time that she had felt before. She opened her eyes. There was the empty hook on the wall. She placed the key where it belonged and shut her eyes. Would she be able to arrive exactly in the right moment beside Rocky and Forest?

With a blur of color she was moving again. A certain sensation in her invisible antennae directed her. But there was more than this, this time. The closer Molly got to the time where the maharaja and her younger selves were, the more she could feel them. When the feeling reached a peak, Molly knew she was in time with the six-year-old, the ten-year-old, the toddler, and the baby Molly just as she had been before. Like different notes played on some sensation instrument, the four younger Mollys made an intense harmony that reverberated in her. Molly also thought she could sense exactly where she herself had come from. The combination helped her know when to stop.

Rocky and Forest looked surprised to see her. Both were out of handcuffs.

"Man, it's so cool how you do that! You kinda pop up!"

"How long ago was it that I undid your handcuffs?" Molly asked, quickly slipping her socks and sneakers back on.

"About an hour," said Rocky. He looked upset and worried and very relieved that Molly was back.

"We thought maybe you got lost. But, Molly, there's something else," said Rocky. "Your skin. Your face has started to wrinkle or something—in patches, it's so dry that it's almost scaly. Look!" Rocky led Molly to the wall that was decorated with small chips of mirror. She shrank back in horror when she saw her reflection.

"You probably just need to drink some water." Forest peered at Molly's cheek and poked it. "Or maybe it's some scaly skin condition that is comin' out because you're stressed."

"Or maybe it's the time travel," suggested Molly, touching the dry, crusty skin near her ear. Then a noise in the courtyard outside broke their discussion.

"Let's cut the medical and get out of here," suggested Rocky.

Twelve

The jeweled corridor outside was dark and silent, except for the occasional *meow* of a peacock from the palace gardens. They crept out and down the stairs, pausing at the bottom to look left and right, uncertain which way to go. Rocky went to the other end of the corridor and frantically tried that handle. It gave way and Petula darted through.

They found themselves in a musty-smelling room with a wax-covered candelabra hanging from its ceiling. On the right were two wooden latticework screens through which shone thousands of spots of light. A door with a curtain hanging across it stood half hidden to the left. They tiptoed quickly across the room toward it. As Molly's eyes adjusted, she could see that the lotus-patterned wallpaper was punctuated with the heads of dead animals—stag with magnificent antlers, wild boar with fierce tusks, and leopards, their faces snarling stiffly. Lined up on the floor against the wall were tiger skins with their heads attached. A shaft of sunlight fell upon a Victorian daguerreotype photograph of a hunting party. In the picture, the giant Waqt leaned proudly against a dead elephant, his rifle slung over his shoulder.

"Come on, let's get out of here," Molly said.

As if in answer, a grunt came from the corner of the room, making everyone jump. They turned to see what horrible beast might be there.

But it wasn't a beast. There, sitting cross-legged on the floor, was a thin man in a knee-length outfit—a cream shirt, with pleats around the bottom, and orange leggings. He wore a pashmina shawl and a faded turban with green and gold stripes running through it. A tired black feather sat feebly in the silk.

The odd thing was that directly above the man's head was a large portrait of an Indian prince dressed in *exactly* the same clothes. Each man wore a green, gem-encrusted brooch in his turban. Both were covered in precious jewelry. The difference was that the living breathing man was dirty and disheveled. His unkempt black beard bushed down his chest, and his mustache fell about his jaw like hairy black seaweed. From the glazed look in his eyes, Molly knew he was hypnotized and when her eyes quickly scanned the plaque under the portrait that read:

The Maharaja of the Red Fort

she knew he was the true owner of the palace they were in.

"Don't stop," said Rocky, hovering by the curtained door. "We've got to get out of here, Molly."

"But this man's the real maharaja!" Molly bent toward the zombielike man. "Hello, can you hear me?" Petula sniffed at his silk-soled feet. "It's awful. Looks like he's spilled a hundred curries down his shirt."

"Hurry up, Molly, someone's coming."

The maharaja on the ground grunted.

"Oh, I wish I could undo your hypnosis," said Molly apologetically, "but it will be locked in with some sort of time-stop lock or a time-travel lock, *with* a password. And I'm afraid I just don't know what that is."

"Molly, man, you better move," said Forest, wiggling about as though he had a snake down his shirt. "I got this vibe that people are, like, comin' soon."

Sounds in the passage echoed his warning. Copper doors clanked against walls as they were roughly opened. In a moment their escape would be known. There was nothing for it but to leave the hypnotized maharaja. Molly leaped up and followed her friends through the curtained doorway.

Now they were in a white and blue corridor. This had *six* doors along the sides of it.

"Which way?" Molly asked frantically. "There's so many flippin' doors!"

"The main entrance must be to our left," insisted Rocky, opening one.

A large garden lay before them, with a green lawn and borders full of flowers. Inside the building they heard a shout. It was Zackya's rusty voice. "Sound the alarm. The prisoners have escaped!"

Molly, Rocky, and Forest dashed across the grass, with Petula behind them. They could see the entrance of the fort through a colonnade at the end of the garden. Drums sounded and peacocks roosting in the trees began to screech.

Four turbaned guards emerged from behind the columns ahead and unsheathed their swords.

Molly grabbed the red crystal from her pocket.

"Okay, quickly—Forest, hold my shoulder; Rocky, hold Petula, and put your hand on my shoulder, too.

Whatever you do, *don't let go!*"

"Hurry up, man!" urged Forest, hopping from one foot to the other, starting to giggle hysterically. "Those guys are coming and they don't exactly look as if they're gonna ask us to dance."

"Forest, just shh, okay?" Molly pleaded. "Try to pull yourself together. I've never taken off with other people before, so if you want to get out of here alive, just be quiet a minute."

Just then, the door from the white and blue corridor burst open and Zackya emerged.

Taking a sudden U-turn decision, Molly felt for the clear crystal that hung around her neck and, with swift expertise, froze the world.

Zackya felt the moment and resisted the freeze. In a second, the two of them were standing in a still landscape. The soldiers looked like giant toys, stiff and immobile. Forest's and Rocky's expressions were set, flushed with panic. The screeching of the peacocks ceased and silence reigned.

Zackya avoided Molly's eyes. Molly hid the red crystal from him. She realized that he had no idea that she had some time-travel crystals. She also saw that he was nervous of her hypnotic powers.

"You can't escape me," he said.

"But I can delay you, Zackya."

"Oh, yes? And for how long? Time stopping is

exhausting, even for a seasoned hypnotist like myself. So for you, it won't be long before you collapse from the cold." He kicked a stone and it bounced toward Molly. She shrugged. She didn't disagree, even though Zackya had completely misjudged her capabilities. Instead, she lied.

"I *am* feeling tired and cold. But I'd rather faint than give in to you."

Zackya laughed and kicked another stone. Inside, he felt uneasy. He didn't want a competition to see who could bear the cold, still world the longest—already he could feel his rheumatic knee aching. Nor did he want to try hypnotizing Molly.

"What's the password to free the hypnotized maharaja?" Molly demanded.

Zackya shook his head. He really didn't like this. He wondered what would make Molly give in and stop the freeze. Then, an idea dawned on him.

"I don't know the password, but I will strike a deal with you," he said. "If you unfreeze the world, I will tell you something about the hypnotized maharaja."

Molly pretended to look unsure. "Why would I agree to that?"

"Because, Miss Moon, you will have to give up, eventually. This way, at least when you are caught and imprisoned again you will have something new to think about."

Molly made a sour face and then she nodded.

And so Zackya, extremely pleased to have caught Molly, and very relieved not to have to tell Waqt that he'd lost her, started to spill the beans about the lonely man inside. His first impulse, though, was to put the record straight about himself.

"Before I start, I want to explain my relationship with Waqt," he began. "You may think that Waqt hates me. He may call me a dog and spit on me, but you should understand that *I* am the closest thing he's ever had to a friend. And, although I was once an untouchable from the lowest caste, at least I was never an *outcast* like him. You see, Miss Moon, Waqt's royal parents chose to cast him out and to lock him up like a mad person." Zackya pointed to the building behind him. "That man in there is Waqt's younger brother. When he was a boy he lived the life of a prince while his elder brother, the giant, was left to rot." Zackya's face went strangely soft, and then his mouth twisted as though he'd tasted something bitter. "Waqt's father and mother thought that if they locked their monstrous child up they could pretend that he and his fits of temper didn't exist. All those childhood years I spent with him, I saw him spurned and I saw his hatred grow. He went through fifty-seven nannies and even more tutors. He was impossible. No adult could cope with him."

"Where did Waqt learn about hypnotism?" asked Molly. Zackya answered as though his thoughts were far away.

"He found a book. He was always reading. Then we escaped. We went to China, where he learned about time travel from an old warrior. Eventually we returned." He paused. "Some people say that revenge is a dish best tasted cold. Well, by the time we returned, the past was cold, but Waqt never forgot how his parents had treated him. His hate still burned like a furnace inside him. That is why he hypnotized his brother and seized all his power."

"What about you? Do you hate his brother and his parents?"

Zackya's eyes narrowed. The cold, still world was getting to him now. The tip of his nose felt numb. "You're getting a little more explanation than you deserve, Molly Moon. I think it is time for you to honor your side of the bargain and unfreeze the world."

"No, tell me more first. Do you hate his brother and parents?"

Zackya growled. "Very well. One more slice then, Miss Moon. His parents are dead, but I still hate them. Because of the monster they created, I live in fear every day of my life of Waqt hypnotizing me. And I am chained to helping him source his precious crystals because, as you can see, if we don't get to the Bubble at the beginning of time, our skins will drop off us. Time travel makes the skin go scaly.

"Of course, one day Waqt will reward me with my freedom. By then, I will have traveled to the Bubble of Light. My skin will be glowing and youthful. And, by that time, Waqt will own every fort and every palace in India. He will give some to me. So, I will be young *and* I will be powerful. *This* is what I wait for." Zackya spat on the ground. "And now, Moon, you must let the world move."

Molly felt Rocky's and Forest's still hands on her shoulders. She checked that Petula was under Rocky's arm.

"I don't like to break promises," she said to Zackya, "but I do like to be free." With that, Molly simultaneously focused on the red crystal and let the world defreeze.

As their surroundings sprang into action, she sank her mind into the red crystal.

"Whoa, okay, I'll be quiet," said Forest.

Molly willed warm time winds to envelop them. In a second there was a BOOM and they were moving.

Thirteen

"So," said Waqt. "I am letting you out of your trances for an hour or so. I hope you are pleased."

The *ten*-year-old Molly blinked up at the huge, scaly man in front of her and cast her eyes over his equally reptilian assistant, who had just arrived with a notebook and a pen.

"You're *late*, Yackza," the giant snapped. Molly tried to work out whether she was dreaming. Had she really just met an eleven-year-old version of herself? And an older Rocky? The small girls beside her huddled close, hiding their eyes in the silk of the strange new dress she had on. Were they younger versions of herself? All this was impossible. She must, she concluded, be dreaming. And yet she felt so wide awake. As though the moment was real. Molly looked around the room. It was a beautiful room, with colored marble embedded in the walls and golden chairs to sit on.

"Who are you?" she asked. "And why are we here?"

"The only reason you are here is to show me thumsing of what this baby's character will be when it grows up."

The ten-year-old Molly decided not to argue with him. "Why are we dressed in these Indian clothes?"

The giant ignored her question.

Molly shook her head. She felt completely disoriented and confused. Was she mad? Maybe she was actually sitting in Hardwick House imagining all this. Perhaps the giant in front of her was a distorted Adderstone, the orphanage mistress.

"Is this another one of your punishments, Miss Adderstone?"

At this, the huge man in front of her let out a demented laugh. "Ooooooohhhhhhh, how amuuuuusing," he declared. "You really are entertainment, Miss Moon!"

Molly shook her head. "It wasn't me who overflowed the bath, Miss Adderstone. This isn't fair. Whatever you're doing, please stop."

"Overflowed the bath! Overflowed the bath! HA! Ha ha ha!" Waqt wailed with laughter.

"Let me put you out of your misery. I am not Miss

Adderstone. Ha! I am the Maharaja of Waqt. Born 1835. Prone to fits. Tall, hark, and dandsome—don't you think? Cooped up by my own parents for fifteen years. Imagine that! Well traveled, to put it mildly. Europe, Africa, China, the future, the past! But enough of myself. We are here today to analyze you. You will now show me thumsing about yourself. We want to see what sorts of talents the maby Bolly has inside her." He put his hands on his hips and nodded to a servant at the door.

Six men came in with an assortment of apparatus. One placed a Chinese abacus at the side of the room, others set up a low table and put a large pad of heavy paper on it as well as a long black box and some big paintbrushes.

The maharaja sat down cross-legged by the table and bid Molly sit, too. Nervously she obeyed, deciding that if this was a dream she might as well go along with it.

Waqt picked up a paintbrush and opened the box. Inside was a pot of water and a block of dry black ink.

"The art of Chinese painting," he said, wetting his brush and dabbing it on the block to absorb ink, "is something that comes naturally to people with artistic talent." With a flourish and with a swishing left and right of his brush, he painted the outline of a scene—

craggy mountains and a stormy sky, with a spiky pine tree and a wolf in the foreground. "I have always had the raw talent. I refined it with years of practice in China. Now it is your turn to show me your talent."

The ten-year-old Molly felt a knot in her stomach. She hated being tested. She knew she wasn't talented at anything.

"I am not good at art."

"Oh, pick up the blasted brush," said Waqt.

Molly leaned forward and tremulously began a picture. She tried to paint a mountain, but it just looked like a lump. Her sun looked like a tennis ball, and her pine tree was like a Christmas tree that a small child had drawn. Instead of a wolf, she painted a stick person.

"Oh!" sighed Waqt disgustedly. "I see the baby won't have artistic talent." Then he shouted, "WRITE THAT DOWN, YACKZA."

Next they moved to the abacus. Here, Waqt tested the ten-year-old Molly's mathematical skills. Molly wasn't very good at sums, and because she'd never used an abacus before, it made everything worse. She fumbled with the beads.

"USELESS AT MATHS!" bellowed Waqt. "Write that down, Yackza."

And so the testing continued. A sitar player was

ushered in to try to teach Molly to play on the stringed instrument, but she could hardly play one note correctly. An Indian dancer was called in to give her a lesson. Molly's attempts at being graceful were disastrous, and Waqt cut her short.

"USELESS!" he exclaimed.

Finally he clapped his hands and two men placed a large, embroidered sack full of colored crystals in front of Molly.

"Do you feel anything for these stycrals?" asked the giant. "You may touch them if you wish."

Out of breath, Molly picked up a scarred red crystal. "Very nice," she said, nervously replacing it.

"Is that all you feel for them?" Molly shrugged a yes. "Write that down, Yackza. Before she learns to hypnotize, the stycrals mean nothing to her." Then he asked, "Is trime tavel something you have ever thought about?"

Molly frowned at the man in front of her and suddenly felt very antagonistic toward him. Who was he to quiz her like this? Angrily, she replied, "*Why* should I tell you what I have thought about or not thought about? I don't know you."

"Hmm. Spirited and cautious. Got that, Yackza?" Then he turned to Molly. He bent toward her, expectant of her answer. "You may be a fiery one, but I still want to know—is time travel something you've ever thought about?" He was so close, she could see residues of makeup that he wore to disguise his walrus skin.

"I think . . ." Molly racked her brains for what to say. She didn't want to say this man was mad, she didn't want to say how frightened she was. She found herself thinking of her friend Rocky and wishing he were with her. She wanted to say that if he was here he'd know what to say. And then, the words of a song he'd once made up sang through her head and, echoing them, the ten-year-old Molly said, "I think . . . there's no time like the present."

The giant squinted at her and smirked. "HA! Poetic. At last, some talent. Write that down, Yackza." Then he clicked his fingers and Molly was hypnotized. A memory of Rocky's voice gently rang in her head.

There's no time like the present,
No present like time
And life can be over in the space of a rhyme.
There's no gift like friendship
And no love like mine.
Give me your love to treasure through time.

The *eleven*-year-old Molly opened her eyes to check that the others were with her. They were traveling forward in time. Rocky to her right, with his eyes shut, while Forest's eyes bulged with pleasure and his mouth glooped open like a surprised goldfish as he watched the swirling colors around him. Zackya's guards didn't seem to be chasing them. Molly relaxed and she wondered what they should do next. She decided that stopping for a while at some point in the future would be good, as that would give them time to formulate a plan.

She let her invisible measuring antennae become her leaders, and she judged what she felt might be a hundred years in the future. Then she made them stop.

The sun had moved across the sky. It was a hot morning. The Red Fort's walls cast short shadows. The garden about them was no longer finely kept and populated with peacocks. Instead, it was dried out, and brown municipal park benches were positioned along its walls. A small Indian child in red dungarees, who was standing with his parents, pointed at Molly and her friends and began to shout.

"Mama. Those people and that dog came from nowhere! Maaaammmmma!"

"Yes, yes," said his father as he turned around. He patted the boy fondly on the head and laughed as if marveling at his son's imagination.

"And look at her big diamond, Daddy."

"This is so cool!" said Forest. "Next time, we could go back and meet the ancient yogis of India!"

"We're not out of the woods yet," said Molly, removing her crystal from around her neck and putting it in her pocket. Rocky gave her Petula. "Remember, Zackya is a time traveler, too. And there's something I didn't tell you about. When I was hypnotized he made me swallow this metallic purple pill thing. It's still in my tummy. Zackya's got this special machine that can locate his purple pills—a tracking device. He isn't that good with it, but he's not completely useless. I wouldn't be surprised if he's following us right now. The machine can tell him what time we're in."

"Does it show him exactly what street you're on, too?" Rocky asked. Molly shrugged and wiped her hair from her eyes. It was swelteringly hot.

"There's a whole load of stuff I did back there," she said hurriedly. "I stopped the world. Zackya told me all these things about Waqt and that hypnotized man. He's Waqt's *brother* and, oh, there's another thing. Time travel makes you age!"

"Whoa, it's the time travel making you wrinkly."

"Don't say it as if I've won the lottery, Forest!" said Molly. "I don't want to start looking like an old woman!"

"Shh." Rocky eyed Molly's cheek. "I'm sure it doesn't happen that quickly. I expect Zackya and Waqt have been time traveling for years."

"Around China," agreed Molly.

"You're only going to pop about in time a bit," said Rocky optimistically, "so it shouldn't get worse. At the moment it's only by your ear and it doesn't really show."

Molly eyed the Red Fort. It was now a fully fledged tourist attraction, with stallholders outside the gates selling balloons, postcards, souvenirs, drinks, *batasha*— cotton candy, nuts, and sweets. She was a little at a loss as to what they should do next. But she did know that they ought to at least get away from the fort.

"I'll tell you more about what Zackya told me in a minute. First, let's move."

And so they walked on. To the side of the road two cows stood minding their own business.

"Cows are allowed to wander around freely here," Forest pointed out as Molly and Rocky led him quickly away from the gates, past the curvaceous white Ambassador taxis that were waiting for customers. "Hindu Indians consider cows holy. Their owners let them meander about and then bring 'em food. Everyone loves cows. On the whole, they don't eat 'em here."

"The best thing we can do is get lost in a crowd," said Rocky, ignoring Forest and tugging at Molly's sleeve. "Let's go over there to where it looks like the shops are. The more people around us, the safer we'll be from Zackya."

They hurried under an arch where a sign proclaimed "Chandni Chowk. Old Delhi." Here the crowds thickened and the wide streets were as busy as the inside of a beehive. There were swarms of rickshaws and hordes of carts pulled by strong men. These carts were piled high with things to sell—like firewood, or water canisters, or scrap metal.

People stared at Molly and Rocky in their Western clothes. Even though it was modern India (Molly wasn't sure what year), the clothes that people wore here in Old Delhi were anything but modern. Some men were in *lungis*—baggy, wrap-around shorts made from a simple piece of material, a few were in plain trousers and shirts. Others wore long sarongs. The women all wore saris or *salwar kameez*—a long dress with trousers underneath. A rickshaw man pedaled three children in ill-fitting uniforms, ringing his bell as he passed by. His young passengers pointed at Petula and then giggled madly at Forest.

"This is making me feel really nervous," Molly moaned. "If Zackya *does* chase us to this time, he'll easily be able to track us down as so many people are noticing us."

Just then there was a scream from the street behind them, a scream followed by shouting and a low, baying noise.

Fourteen

"Move!" Forest cried. He pushed Molly and Rocky backward until they were wedged up against a shop wall covered with tin saucepans. In front of them, the crowd surged away from the center of the street where the baying noises were multiplying and becoming louder.

"Is it Waqt?" Molly asked Forest. "Shouldn't we run? I've got that purple pill inside me. He'll track us down here."

"It's not Waqt. Stand on that ledge. Look!"

Molly and Rocky, clinging onto Petula, stepped up. In front of them was a sea of heads and, like water magically parting, the crowd made a long clearing. Six black cows were running down this gap, causing mayhem. They'd already knocked over two rickshaws and a stall selling fruit. They seemed to be dangerously stampeding, but not out of malice; they were frightened—something farther up the street had scared them. Men tried to calm them. One managed to flap a sheet in front of the mooing leader and so divert her down an alley. The others followed her. And, as quickly as it had been stirred up, the busy, scruffy street returned to its normal state.

"Man, that's India for ya!" Forest exclaimed. "You wouldn't get a sight like that in an American or European city. Cows stampeding the shopping district! That's action for you. I love those holy cows."

Zackya stood at the entrance to the Chandni Chowk. He'd been given permission to leave the maharaja and so was now intent on catching up with Molly Moon. He had to lock the escapees up again before Waqt realized they'd gone, but he was having problems. The hypnotized guards he'd brought with him from the 1870s had already caused trouble. Their swords and old-fashioned attire had frightened some tourists. Two screaming women had frightened a group of cows that had in turn taken off and galloped into the busy market streets. Now, a fearless old Indian woman was lecturing him, her hands on her hips, and this was making it impossible to read his silver tracking device.

"You should be ashamed of yourself, upsetting the holy cows like that," she heckled him, in Hindi. "Just look at the trouble you and your band have caused. Look at the crowds. People could get hurt." As she waggled her finger, Zackya looked up. He gave her a filthy hypnotic stare.

"Wapplyglupglup glaap," the woman said, still wagging her finger, and fell silent.

Zackya turned away and concentrated on his silver box. It refused to work properly. It was showing that the girl, Molly, was in this time, but when he asked it in what direction she was to be found, the gadget merely blinked at him. He switched it off and called his guards over.

The cool alleyways of Chandni Chowk were much more peaceful than the streets. Forest led Molly and Rocky through an alley only wide enough to let one rickshaw along it at a time. The crumbling walls of dilapidated three-story buildings rose up on either side of them. Black electricity wires swirled above in a spaghetti-like tangle. They echoed Molly's feelings. For she was very confused and muddled as to what to do next.

"Shouldn't we go back now?" she suggested.

"What, in these clothes?" said Rocky. "We'll stick out like aliens. Before we go back to Waqt's time we should get some Indian outfits."

They glanced along the alley. On either side of it, every available space was a narrow shop. Molly had never seen such narrow shops! They were often only the width of a person sitting down with their legs stretched out. Some shops were wider with lovely padded-cloth floors. And shoppers took their shoes off before going in.

"That's real sensible," said Forest, smiling. "No floors to clean. Hey, isn't India cool!"

"Do you think we'll find a clothes shop?" Molly asked as they passed one that sold costume jewelry and red and gold scarves.

"Sure, just keep walkin' and you bet we will."

And so they continued up the alley. Petula stayed close to Molly. As they walked, Molly told the others what she'd learned about Waqt's past.

"Sad guy," said Forest.

"Mad guy, you mean," said Rocky. Then he stopped. "Wow, what's that? Smells like sugar and doughnuts!" Molly walked nervously on, but Rocky hovered at a bakery shop where trays of pastry shapes were laid out under white mesh.

Beside the biscuits was a large silver pot in which was a white milky liquid. In the center of this pot floated a slimmer pot with ice in it, keeping the milky substance around it cold. At the other end of the counter was a miniature wood-burning stove with a copper vat on top.

A lilac-shirted shopkeeper watched Rocky and smiled.

"We don't have much electricity here in Old Delhi," he explained. "So that's how we keep liquids cool and fresh. And we use old-fashioned fire to cook with. Have you ever eaten Indian sweets?" Rocky shook his head.

"You speak very good English," he observed.

"Of course!" The baker laughed. "Many Indians do."

Rocky watched as the man took a scoop of doughy mixture and rolled it into a ball. He tossed this into the vat, which contained hot oil. The man then fished the ball out and dropped it into a bowl full of syrup along with fifteen or so more of the golden dumplings.

"My customers like these sweets the best. They're called 'gulab jamun.' Here, taste one."

Rocky shook his head. "I haven't got any money."

"Not everything in life costs money!"

The dumpling was delicious and Rocky could have stood for a long time tasting the man's wares, but Molly pulled him on.

"Thank you," said Rocky as they moved away down the alleyway. "That man was so nice."

"So was the guy who makes noodles," Forest agreed, still chewing what he'd been given to taste. "Wasn't that delicious, Petula?"

"But we've got to hurry," said Molly. "Come on, you

two. We're not on vacation." While Rocky crouched down to tie his shoelace, she approached a sturdy, bald man who owned a mask shop. "Excuse me. What year are we in?" Papier-mâché faces of tigers and lions, birds and elephants peered down at her.

"It's 1974, of course!" he chuckled. "Would you like to try on a mask?" He held a mirror up to her face. Molly glanced into it and saw the scaly time-travel skin by her ear. She was just about to look away when she noticed an inch-long scar on the side of her neck. She gasped, touching it and wondering how and when it had got there.

In that instant, Molly was struck by a thought. If this was 1974, and Waqt was in 1870 with her younger selves, by now her own history in 1870 would have played out. Surely she should now have *all* the memories from her ten-year-old self in 1870 because that time had passed. And yet she couldn't remember any more of her time as a ten-year-old in India. She couldn't remember how it had gone—*how it had finished*. It was as if the memories were lagging behind, still traveling from 1870 to this modern time, and they hadn't arrived yet. Was this scar from her time in 1870s India?

The man held an elephant mask up to her.

"Try one?"

"No thanks."

Molly was suddenly filled with cutting fear. She didn't like this at all. Her younger selves were stuck in the past, their memories hidden from her, and now there was this mysterious pink scar on her neck. Molly realized that she must get straight back to the 1870s and find Waqt. She knew she wouldn't relax until she'd saved her younger selves and somehow caught him.

How she should catch Waqt was a terrifying prospect. It would be worse than trapping a vicious wild animal. A papier-mâché tiger face snarled down at her, reminding her of Waqt's hunting trophies and his gun.

The answer lay in the crystals, Molly thought. If they could just steal all of Waqt's time-travel crystals, and his time-stop crystals, then they'd have a chance. Without the crystals, Waqt would be reduced to being simply a very powerful hypnotist. Just a maharaja with power over hundreds of guards. Molly gulped and touched her scar.

"Hey, you two," she called. The others had been distracted again. They were watching a man in a cog shop fix something with a blowtorch. "I really think we should go back." Molly tried not to sound too nervous. "Now," she said more frantically, picking up Petula.

"Fine, fine," said Forest, ambling over. He wiped

some sweat from his forehead. "I dig those time winds."

Molly found a nice, clear area at the side of the alley, and soon they were flashing through the decades again. Molly extended her invisible antennae and tried to sense *when* her other selves were. She felt their vibrations and stopped. The time winds subsided.

A holy cow was standing right beside them. It let out a *moo*. The air was cooler than before, but it was still hot. Molly had arrived in exactly the same time that her young selves were in. Because of this, she was able to get their memories. Right away she remembered being ten and being tested by Waqt. She winced, and told the others how he'd made her paint, use an abacus, and dance and play the sitar.

"Waqt's on some kind of headmaster's trip!" said Forest.

Molly glanced up and down the alleyway about her. All the electricity spaghetti was gone, but the shops were roughly the same size and the smells were similar, too. Even the mask shop was there. Molly realized that the man who was standing inside it painting a leopard mask might be the great-great-great-grandfather of the sturdy little man she'd spoken to in modern-day India. She decided to check what time they were in, so she walked over to him. He put down his paintbrush and, pressing his hands together, bowed his head slightly.

"*Namaskar,*" he said.

Molly assumed that this was a way of saying hello. She did exactly the same.

"*Namaskar.*" Then she added, "Excuse me, what year are we in?"

Zackya stood impatiently in the middle of the road. The small silver tracking device hidden inside his clothes let out a *bleep.* Irritated, he plunged his hand into his pocket to retrieve it.

"So you've moved to another time again, Moon," he muttered, reading the dial. He looked about him for his guards, indicating to the nearest that he wanted them to gather quickly. The fourth guard was over by a newspaper stand, asking its keeper questions. Zackya didn't have time to wait. He bid the three hypnotized guards beside him to get into a time-travel position. This they did, their hands on each other's shoulders. And with a BOOM Zackya lifted them out of the year 1974 and back to 1870.

He felt no compassion for the guard whom he'd left stranded in a time that wasn't his. This guard was only lightly hypnotized, so he would, in a few weeks, come out of his trance and think he had gone mad. He would be an 1870s person marooned in the 1970s. No one would believe him when he told them that he belonged to a

buzzing about them. The second alley was the resting spot of a small, skinny monkey eating a piece of bread. The last alley led to what seemed like a place full of shops. Rocky started out down this leg of the alley. But after a few strides he realized that the pickpocket's footsteps had *stopped*. With wily instinct, he looked up.

As he did, Molly, Petula, and Forest caught up with him. Rocky stood with his hands on his hips, his lungs heaving, and stared upward.

"Are you all right, Rocky?" Molly asked. She hoped he wasn't about to have one of his asthma attacks.

Rocky nodded.

"What are you going to do to me?" said a silky voice from above. The brown-faced urchin edged his way farther up the banyan tree. Petula barked.

"Nothing," wheezed Rocky. "We just want the red and clear stones back." He began talking slowly, for if he could just wind his hypnotic voice around the pickpocket for long enough he'd be able to persuade him to climb down. "Why don't you just bring the stones dow—"

The boy interrupted him. "You mean the gems?"

"The crystals." Molly pushed her hair out of her eyes. She'd noticed that the boy was shifting himself higher up his branch—in fact, to the level of the windows of the nearest building. There was no time to try to hypnotize him down with Rocky's voice or even her eyes. He was moving away too fast and he refused to make eye contact. "You speak our language very well," she said, trying to stop his ascent.

The thief looked suspiciously down, wondering why the person he'd just stolen from was flattering him. "Maybe I do. Why do you care?"

Molly realized that the only option left to them was bribery.

"If you give those crystals back, you will be far better off than if you run away with them," she said. "With the red crystal, I can take you to a different time—to the future, if you like. How about that?"

The boy frowned and glared down at them. That was the most ridiculous lie he'd ever heard.

Rocky butted in. "Molly's telling you the truth. Molly can time travel because she's a master hypnotist. And with the clear crystal, she can stop time. Honestly. Me and Forest here can't make them work. We really need the red crystal back, because we're from the future."

The boy up the tree looked at the odd party below with their strange dog and he began to laugh. "Well, I've heard a lot of lies, but I've never heard one as wild as that!"

Forest started laughing, too.

"Forest, this isn't funny," said Molly. "If we don't get the crystals back, we're as good as—"

"It's okay," said Forest, and he delved into his jacket

pocket. Pulling out a small black object, he said, "Ever seen one of these?"

He switched a button, and the tape recorder in his hand started playing groovy Los Angelean music.

"Magpie Man! He'll steal your heart and your soul . . . OOOOOh aahhh," sang the pop star Billy Bob Bimble. The boy up the tree nearly fell down with fright.

Just then there was a low shout. Everyone turned to see an official in a brown uniform marching toward them. He was wielding a baton. The boy in the tree began to scramble up the branch to the high window. He made a deft leap, but his tunic caught on a stubby twig, so he half tripped, falling onto the branch below. Molly gasped. The official was now beside her, roaring at the boy.

"I told you I'd catch you," he shouted in Hindi. "Tonight you're sleeping in a cell, you rotten thief."

"Man, go easy on the kid," said Forest, but the short, muscly official ignored him and continued waving his nightstick and shouting.

Molly knew this noise would soon attract attention, so she summoned the warm fusion feeling and at once her body hummed with the familiar heat of hypnotism. She tapped the policeman on the shoulder. He glanced irritably at her and at once he fell prey to Molly's powers. He was hypnotized—silent as the cud-chewing cows down the alley. Because Molly didn't speak Hindi, she pressed her finger to her lips. "Shh."

The boy up the tree dangled from a branch, fascinated by what Molly had just done. Then she spoke to him.

"I'm going to need your help. I can't speak this man's language and I need to leave him some hypnotic instructions."

"This is a trick, isn't it?" said the boy. "You're on his side. Make him do something really stupid that he wouldn't normally do. Then I'll believe you."

"I told you, you have to tell him what to do. I can't speak his language."

A naughty glint flashed in the boy's eyes. "I will, then."

Molly patted the man on his shoulder. She put her hand to her ear and pointed up the tree, indicating that he should listen to the boy.

"Remove your trousers," the boy said in Hindi so that no one there except the official could understand him. The man nodded and at once began unbuttoning his trousers. Soon they were halfway down his legs, revealing orange underpants. The boy let out a whoop of laughter, but then another look of suspicion crossed his face.

"Cry like a baby elephant!" he ordered, again in Hindi.

"Waaaoohaah!" the policeman trumpeted.

The boy smiled. "Hop about like a crow!" Now the man was hopping around with his trousers around his ankles. Molly had to admit this did look funny. She glanced at Rocky and tried not to laugh.

"Man, give the guy a break," said Forest. "Don't humiliate him. What if someone sees him? He's going to trip on his pants in a minute." The boy clambered slowly down the tree, his eyes full of delight.

"You can pull your trousers up and stop hopping," he said to the policeman. At once the man stood still and pulled his trousers up.

The boy eyed Forest's pocket. "What was that machine that sings?" he asked, now on the ground.

Molly looked at him. He had green eyes like hers, except his were set in a handsome brown face, so they sparkled more, and his nose was straight and attractive, unlike her potato nose. He wore a paint-covered, ragged tunic that revealed a thin chest and ladderlike ribs. She wondered why he had been reduced to stealing things from people in the street.

"It's called a handheld tape recorder," explained Forest, offering it to him. "Really commonplace in the twenty-first century."

The boy eyed Molly's T-shirt and Rocky's jeans. "So, you're saying you're from the future?" He narrowed his eyes and gave them a sideways stare as if reconsidering whether this was a trick. The policeman burped.

"I don't believe you're from the future." He paused. "But I do believe you are a hypnotist."

"Tell the policeman that from now on he will think of you as a good, law-abiding person," suggested Molly.

The boy's eyebrows arched. "I see." Again, he spoke in Hindi. "From now on you will think of me as a god and tell the other officials that I am the best child in Delhi. You will also give me a few rupees whenever you see me. Now you can go."

The official nodded and bowed very low. Then he stood up, reached his hand into his pocket, and gave the boy a handful of coins. The boy stared at the money in his palm.

"My goodness, you certainly are a hypnotist!" And, as if the coins in his hand were the key to his trust, he said, "Are you really from the future?"

"Yup," said Molly. The policeman walked away.

"And you'll take me with you to your time?" The boy still wasn't sure whether he believed this was possible, but he saw that a friendship with these people would probably be helpful to him.

"I'll take you on a trip, yes, and then I'll put you back here again. But I can't do it without the crystals."

Molly put her hand out coaxingly. "Ever wonder what the world will be like in a hundred years?"

The boy hesitated. Then he took the tape recorder from Forest and handed the red and clear crystals over. Molly took them gratefully. She put the red crystal in her pocket and hung the clear one back around her neck.

"Don't worry," she said. "I don't break promises."

Zackya snarled at his tracking gadget. He knew the readings telling him he was in exactly the same time as Molly were correct, but the device seemed to be suggesting that she was to the East of him as well as to the West.

"Stupid twenty-fifth-century instrument!" he snapped, shoving it into his pocket. "I'll get you, Miss Moon. You haven't escaped me. I'll search every well, every cobra pot. I won't sleep until I've found you."

Sixteen

The boy twiddled the button on the tape recorder and smiled. Then he looked at Molly's and Rocky's sneakers.

"Horrible shoes you have to wear in the future!" He laughed.

"Actually they're state-of-the-art sneakers," said Molly, "but I suppose they do look crazy."

"Don't you cut your feet going barefoot?" asked Rocky.

"Oh, no! The soles of my feet are as hard as cow hooves. Come," the boy said. "You must be thirsty after all that running. I will take you to my friend's tea stall."

Molly nodded.

"That would be lovely, but we're in a bit of a hurry. In fact, we're being chased."

The boy raised his eyebrows. "It was lucky I stole your precious crystals, because now you have met me. I can help you." With a wry smile he added, "My services are not expensive. Let us go for some chai. On the way you can tell me who is after you and what your plans are."

And so their friendship started. They began to walk down through the maze of alleys, through dusty, dappled light, deeper and deeper into the heart of Chandni Chowk. Petula was more relaxed now. Her nerves gave in to her curiosity and she darted around excitedly, deciphering smells. This place was like nowhere she'd ever smelled before. The odors were complicated and rich and told hundreds of stories.

The boy's name was Ojas, which, he said, was a Hindi name meaning "brilliance" or "shine" or "glow." To begin with, he wanted to address Rocky and Forest as "sahib" and Molly as "memsahib," because he said this was the polite way for him to address people of higher rank than himself. But Forest, Molly, and Rocky wouldn't hear of this and insisted he use their first names. As they walked, Molly and Rocky learned more about the caste system.

"Ah, don't you know about it?" Ojas laughed. "Well, let me tell you. It's existed among the Hindu people since ancient times. It divides us up into ranks of importance. A person can never change the caste that they're born into. The highest rank is that of the Brahmins or priests, then come the rulers and warriors. Below them are the farmers and traders, and lastly come the servants and laborers. That's my caste. Each level is divided up again, and the lowest of the lowest castes does the dirtiest jobs, like shoveling sewage. Not very nice." Ojas made a face. "The lowest of the lowest are called the 'untouchables.'" Ojas took a left turn past a pile of boxes. "Someone from the highest caste won't even walk on the *shadow* of an untouchable because they are considered so lowly." Waqt, Molly remembered, had said that Zackya was an untouchable before he had freed him.

"The caste system is going to weaken in the future," Forest said as they squeezed past another sacred cow.

"Oh, I am pleased!" Ojas exclaimed. "Now follow me through this building. It is a shortcut."

Ojas had no parents. He used to live with his father, who was one of the maharaja's *mahouts*, or elephant keepers, in the Red Fort.

"My father died from a poisonous growth in his stomach," Ojas explained.

"That's real bad luck," said Forest as they followed the boy through a dark corridor filled with hanging washing.

"Yes."

Everyone was quiet for a moment. Molly broke the silence. "Did your father speak to you in English?"

"Yes," said Ojas. "The Maharaja of the Red Fort was a kind man, who enjoyed educating his servants. Whatever caste they came from, they were taught to speak English. My father taught me. Life was good before my father died. Then, everything went upside down. The kind maharaja went mad, and his brother, who for some reason calls himself the Maharaja of Waqt—'Waqt' means 'Time' in Hindi, you know—took his place as ruler."

"The Maharaja of Time!" said Rocky. "Talk about giving himself airs and graces."

"So you know of him?"

"His sidekick is chasing us," said Molly. "And Waqt has stolen something of mine"—Molly wondered whether to explain to Ojas how Waqt had taken her younger selves, but decided he would never believe her—"so we are chasing Waqt."

"Are we?" said Forest, scratching his head.

"Yes. Or at least I am. I have to somehow steal all his crystals and then get Waqt."

"You make it sound as easy as catching a rabbit," said Rocky.

"The Maharaja of Waqt is known to be very bad-tempered," warned Ojas. "Are you sure you want to pursue him? Perhaps it would be better to wait for the Maharaja of the Red Fort to get better. Perhaps he would help you."

"The original maharaja didn't go mad," Rocky said. "He was hypnotized and imprisoned in the Red Fort. We saw him."

"Hypnotized?"

"Yes, by Waqt."

"That certainly is news," Ojas commented, picking his way over a pile of bricks and through a hole in a wall out into another alley.

A tea stall was suddenly before them.

It was like an open cupboard at the side of the walkway with a wood-burning stove set into it. An iron kettle stood upon this with steam blowing out of its spout, and a row of cans lined the back of the worktop. Beside a pot of sugar a big sieve sat in a ceramic bowl, and in the open cupboard underneath were stacks of terra-cotta plates, teacups, and teapots. A small boy played on the ground with a broken cup and some stones. He looked delighted when he saw Petula. His mother stood above him in a yellow sari. On her arms and ankles she wore scores of golden bangles, while gold jewelry hung from her ears and nose, too, and a *bindi*, a red holy dot, was painted on her forehead. A dark, bangled baby sat on her hip. The woman smiled at Ojas as they approached, and her small boy waved. Ojas bowed with his hands pressed together and asked her something in Hindi. The woman waggled her head from side to side and laughed. Then she began busying herself with tea making.

"We don't have any money," said Molly. "Perhaps we could borrow some of yours, Ojas."

"Do not worry," said Ojas. "Last month I stopped her little boy from running in front of a British horse-drawn carriage, so now she always gives me free chai."

"Are there British people here in India *now*, in 1870?"

"Oh, yes. They've been here for a long time . . . since about 1600. Before that, the Muslim Mughals invaded India. Everyone wants India, it seems! The Mughals were here for five hundred years! They built some lovely mosques. But still, you know, most Indians are Hindus, not Muslims. And now we have the British here. They die like flies from the heat and stomach sickness. The Portuguese, French, and Dutch are here, too, but the British have managed to take control the most. India has so much for them to take for trade, you see. The British make much money from India. We are a huge country, and wheat, cotton, tea, and coffee grow very well here. And we have wonderful precious stones and marble and hardwood. You have a fat queen called Queen Victoria. She always looks so cross in her pictures. She should come to India; then maybe she would look happier!"

The tea lady poured out cups of chai—tea sweetened with sugar, cinnamon, ginger, cloves, and cardamom. Ojas took a slurp from his and continued.

"Queen Victoria has lots of Raj officials who keep India under her command. They have built many buildings here, too. Some are really quite impressive, but not as beautiful as our temples and palaces. Oh, but the railways they have built—*they* are amazing!"

"But if this country is now ruled by the British, how come the Indian maharajas are here?" asked Molly.

"The maharajas have their princely states. India is a very, very large place, so there is plenty to go around. Everyone can have a slice!"

The lady in the yellow sari offered everyone a piece of cake and a glass of a sweet drink. She put a dish of water on the ground for Petula.

"Ah, sugar-cane juice," sighed Forest. "I haven't had this for years, man! And I've got some good news for you, Ojas. In the twentieth century, India's gonna get this real cool peace-lovin' guy called Gandhi and he is gonna free India. In 1947, India will rule itself."

"That's seventy-seven years away," said Ojas,

squinting as he did the sum in his head. "I'll be an old man by then. Or dead."

"That's a bummer, man!" said Forest.

Not knowing what Forest meant, Ojas just waggled his head from side to side, in the way the tea lady had, and Molly and Rocky laughed.

"This is so nice of your friend," said Rocky. "I wish I had something I could give her. He reached in his pocket and found a pen. "Maybe she could sell this to a rich person here—I mean, a pen is an amazing thing if you're from 1870." He showed Ojas and the woman how the pen worked by drawing on his already doodle-covered arm.

While the woman giggled, drawing a line on Ojas's arm, Molly was suddenly overcome by a new memory. It came so suddenly that she found herself involuntarily shaking her head as if an earwig were in her ear.

"What is it?" asked Rocky. Molly opened her eyes.

"I have memories of getting on a steam train. It is a very luxurious carriage. It's a royal train or something. I was carrying a baby."

"Is Waqt on the train?"

"Yes. That's one of the strongest parts of the memory. He looks so stupid, all stuffed into the train. He's so tall, he can hardly fit. Like a giraffe getting into a train. The train is leaving. I'm remembering its noise and the steam."

"And, Molly, are we in exactly the same time as them?"

"Yes." She nodded

"So they're leaving now. What shall we do? We have to get to the station."

Molly and Rocky both turned to Ojas.

"We've got to get on a train," said Molly. "We don't speak Hindi. Will you help us?"

"How do you know the Maharaja of Waqt is on a train? Are you a magician?" Ojas asked.

"I'll explain how I know later. I'm not a magician, but we are in a hurry. Will you help us?"

Ojas tilted his head and shut one eye. "Because you hypnotized that officer for me, I will help you board a train—as long as you remember that trip you promised me to the future. On the way to the station you can tell me what Waqt has taken from you and how you know where he is. If I think I can help you, I will tell you my price. You might employ me as your guide."

"That sounds good," said Molly, "except we haven't got any money to pay you."

Ojas rubbed his hands together, cleaning them of crumbs. "I am sure, Mollee, that with your skills money won't be too hard to come by."

* * *

Fifteen alleys away, Zackya and his men were making progress. He and his guards had stumbled across a uniformed official sitting on a step counting his fingers. The man's head nodded and his eyes quivered in their sockets. Zackya recognized these signs as the aftereffects of hypnotism and so set to interrogating him.

Seventeen

Ojas guided Molly, Rocky, Forest, and Petula swiftly down a different set of alleyways. As they hurried along, Molly explained to him how the Maharaja of Waqt had kidnaped her younger selves. Ojas listened, half suspicious that Molly and her friends were mad.

"So you want to follow Waqt secretly?" he said, grasping that at least this much of their situation was true.

"Yes."

"In *those* clothes?" Ojas let out a puff of disbelieving air.

Molly looked down at the dancing mouse on her sweatshirt. Her mind switched into top gear.

"Tell me, Ojas. Are there any really *horrible* keepers of clothes shops here?"

"There is one, but there are far more friendly shop-keepers—don't worry."

"What has the nasty one done that makes him so horrible?" Molly persisted.

"Oh, you ask such strange questions! But I will answer. There is one very rich, cruel man who has a shop near the bazaar. He has a very short temper and he beats his wife and his children. I don't like him at all because once he boxed my ears when I was simply sitting on his doorstep taking a thorn out of my foot!"

"Does he speak English?"

"Yes, but he is not a kind man, Mollee. You don't understand."

"I do. Trust me. Will you take us there?"

"As a special gift I will," said Ojas. "But you have to remember, Mollee, after that my extra services will cost."

"Fine," said Molly, "but let's get there quickly."

Soon they were inside a large shop surrounded by shelves of folded clothes. Forest shut the silk curtain over the shop entrance behind them. Petula sniffed at the carpeted floor.

"Hello, is anyone here?" Molly called.

A brawny man with a potbelly emerged sleepily from behind the counter. As if to introduce himself he made a snotty, guttural noise and cleared the phlegm from the back of his throat.

"Good afternoon," said Molly. "We would like some clothes."

The doughy-faced shopkeeper surveyed Molly's jeans and mouse top and sneered. He lazily drew himself up and then he saw Ojas. For a moment he leered forward, but reminding himself that there might be business at stake, he resisted booting Ojas out.

Molly was onto him before he knew it. She tapped him on the chest and stared into his puffy eyes. His nose twitched irritatedly as he prepared to object to her prodding, but actually he was easy meat. In a second, her incredible eyes had delivered their blow straight to the core of his brain, reducing him to a nodding idiot.

"Now you are completely under my power," Molly said. "I want clothes for us all. And after that, we would like some money. Quite a lot of it." Ojas nodded. He'd already decided that, if he helped Molly, a lot of money was what he'd be charging.

The somnambulant man stepped forward and nodded to the girl, who now, in his eyes, seemed a goddess. He understood Molly's language fairly well. In his trance he began selecting clothes from the shelves. Ojas watched with amazement as he found a long, box-collared, burgundy shirt for Rocky, with a pair of pajama-like trousers to match.

"Will this *kurta churinder* be all right for you, sir?"

He found a similar outfit in gray for Ojas. Ojas put it in a bag.

"I will save it for best," he said. Forest chose a white *kurta churinder*, while Molly was given a steel-blue sari.

"This is no good," she said, eyeing the miles of material that was being presented to her. "I'll never be able to tie one of those things on my own."

"What are you doing Mr. Shopkeeper!" interrupted Ojas. "Girls don't wear saris in India; only women wear saris."

The hypnotized man offered Molly a long, tunic-like outfit with trousers underneath.

"This *salwar kameez*?"

Soon, everyone was ready. Molly had a veil to throw over her head, and the boys all had mini turbans. On their feet they wore Indian moccasins, except for Ojas, who was more comfortable barefoot. Molly was given a purse filled with coins, and she also took a cotton bag that was strong enough to carry Petula, should she need to disappear suddenly.

As they left, Molly turned to the shopkeeper. She had been so busy that she hadn't had time to think what pearls of instructions to leave the man with. So, pulling ideas from the air, she began.

"From now on, you will never say an unkind word

to anyone. You will be like a saint—"

"They don't have saints here," interrupted Forest.

"Like an angel?"

"No angels, either. How about a Jain?"

"What's that?"

"Jains are a sort of Hindu who believe in peace and nonviolence. They try not to step on insects and they even wear white masks over their mouths so that they don't by accident swallow a bug or flies. That's considerate."

The shopkeeper awaited his instructions.

"So, you will be like a Jain. And you will be extra kind to your wife and children, to make up for all the times you've hit them. And you will sing much more than you do now, and you will learn to play the . . . the . . ."

"The *shehnai*," suggested Forest. "That's a really cool Indian wind instrument. Like an oboe. You blow it."

"The *shehnai*," Molly finished. Then, without anyone knowing, she concentrated on her clear crystal, froze the world, and said, "And this instruction is locked in with the word 'Singsong.'" Now she knew her instructions would stick. She let the world move again.

As they walked down the alley away from the shop the man broke into song.

"He was very lucky to be hypnotized by you!" said

Ojas. "To be given a new lease of life like that is worth far more than all that you took from him."

"Yes, I think so, too," Molly agreed, jingling the heavy gold coins in her new purse.

Zackya and his men found themselves at a tea stand. They were parched and thirsty from their search.

"You, woman," Zackya said rudely, in Hindi, "tell me now. Have you seen a girl with a strange dog?"

The yellow-saried woman threw a stick down the alley for her young boy to retrieve. She didn't want him talking about Ojas and his friends. As he ran off laughing, she shook her head.

"Would you like some tea and cake?" she asked, turning to push the pen Rocky had given her behind the sugar tin. There, too, was a small clay pot full of powders. The mixture was a traditional medicinal recipe of crushed herbs that gave whoever ate them a "purging of the bowels"—in other words, diarrhea. The tea lady surreptitiously sprinkled a good dose into the rude man's tea. With luck, this would cause a delay in his journey and so help her friends.

Zackya drank his tea. As the woman threw her puppylike son another stick, a horrible thought struck him. Molly Moon's escape was now a matter that he should report to Waqt.

* * *

Half a mile away, Ojas led Molly and her friends to the station. It was a long walk along dry, grimy roads heavy with animal traffic. Buffalo pulling carts, camels drawing wagons, and elephants, too, with canopied seats tied to their backs. In her new clothes Molly didn't feel so conspicuous. She enjoyed watching women walk by with large brass water pots on their heads, and barefoot children tearing down the streets. The smell of burning incense, herbs, and cooking fires hung in the air, and the hot March sun shone down. They passed a snake charmer who sat before a large round basket playing a pipe so sweetly that his pet cobra danced. Molly wished that she could just enjoy her surroundings, but she knew that they had to hurry. The memories that were growing in her head from the younger Mollys told her that Waqt was already well away from Delhi.

They arrived at the Delhi train station and Molly put her veil over her head.

"Stay here, out of sight, at the back of the platform," said Ojas, and he slipped away into the crowd.

Parties of British people thronged the station. The women were clad in cumbersome Victorian dresses, tight at the waist and full to the ground. They wore large, uncomfortable hats with nets over their faces. The men

159

with them were in white suits and heavy, helmet-shaped "topi" hats. Soldiers in breeches and high leather boots stood around chatting. Here and there sat children wearing starched clothes and white topis, stiflingly hot.

"This is an outrage!" complained an elderly Englishwoman to her withered husband. "That giant just *stole* our engine!" Molly noticed a sad set of coaches sitting engine-less on some spare track behind the main line.

"He's so bally *tall*," replied her husband in a clipped croaky voice, "that no one dare contradict him."

"If I had been here," said the woman in a very hushed voice, "I would have poked him with my parasol where it jolly well hurts!"

"My dear, don't let it upset you. It will only make your varicose veins throb. Another train is on its way. And it goes in exactly the same direction. To Jaipur."

Just then, there was a loud cry.

"Thief! Stop, thief!" A tall man was pointing through the crowd to a ragamuffin boy darting away from him.

"I don't believe it," Rocky said. "It's Ojas!"

Molly at once focused on her clear crystal, and the platform life was brought to an immediate standstill, frozen into a tableau. The Victorian man's hat was tumbling from his head as he rushed after Ojas, and the people about him were as still as wooden carvings, their expressions of wide-eyed excitement stuck on their faces.

It took a few minutes for Molly to find Ojas. He was bending low as he ran and, so, well hidden. In his hand was a crocodile-skin wallet. Molly grabbed his arm, sending movement into him. As he shot away from her in full flight, she tugged him back. At once he saw the still world about him.

"What . . . what's happened to everyone?" he asked, gaping in amazement. Molly was furious.

"Why did you do that, Ojas? You *knew* we didn't want to draw attention to ourselves. This isn't a game, you know. We told you we needed your help. This isn't helping us. You could have been caught. You know we can pay you. You didn't need to steal a stinking wallet. And you shouldn't steal—it's bad."

"Bad? BAD?" shouted Ojas. "You just stole off that shopkeeper. You just helped me steal from that police officer. Don't be so high and mighty. You're as bad as me. The difference is that I have no one in this world and I have to look after myself. It is not easy living on the street. I have to grasp opportunities when I see them!"

Molly was taken aback. She hadn't tried to put herself

wide iron berth full of coal and the driver's cabin. A fireman shoveled coal into the firebox, heating up the water in the tank. The driver brought the train to a halt and pulled the whistle again, releasing excess steam into the station. The waiting passengers burst into animation. Everyone began pushing and jostling to get on board.

"Why don't we just go backward in time and catch the one Waqt caught?" asked Rocky.

"Too risky," Molly replied. "I thought about it. If he catches us following him, that's it. We're as good as barbecued. Mind you, this train is filling up so quickly, I don't know how we're ever going to find a space." Indeed, the Victorians, feeling they owned the train, had greedily filled the four best, fan-carrying carriages at the front of the train while Indians, whom the Victorians refused to sit next to, were already spilling out of the last two, hotter, carriages.

"Look at that! Segregation! Wow, disgusting, isn't it?" said Forest. "You'll be pleased to hear, Ojas, that in modern times, people of all races sit together! Citizens of the globe, man!"

"But there's *nowhere* for us to sit," Molly pointed out. "The carriages are bursting."

"No problem." Ojas laughed. "We ride on top."

Molly looked at him. "On top of the train?"

"Most absolutely certainly, Mollee. On top is closer to the gods."

"We could always go to the future and catch a *jet* train, or whatever they'll have then," Rocky reminded Molly. Then he shook his head. "But you know, Molly, on top sounds good."

Eighteen

Waqt's train was super-luxurious. He kept his own special coaches at Delhi station. Whenever he needed to go anywhere, all he had to do was have a pulling engine taken from another train, which is what he'd done today.

Waqt lay back on a bolster and thought how entertaining the angry, stuffy people at Delhi station had been.

It was lovely and cool. This was because in the center of the carriage was a large box with a huge lump of ice in it. A "punkah boy" sat on the floor in the corner operating a rope that swung a fan over this icebox, producing a cool breeze that wafted over Waqt and his fellow passengers.

Opposite him, the ten-year-old Molly sat with

the puppy Petula on her lap. The six-year-old and the three-year-old sat beside her, and the baby Molly lay in a crib gurgling. All except the puppy were hypnotized.

The door of the compartment opened and three servants walked in. They quietly threw a white linen cloth over a table and began laying out plates of Indian food. A plate of tandoori chicken tikka and another of *seekh* kebabs. There were lentil *papad* wafers and *raita* (whipped yogurt with herbs) to dip the *papad* into. There were delicate puddings flavored with saffron.

Smelling the food, the puppy Petula opened her eyes. She jumped off the ten-year-old Molly's lap and began barking at the table. The maharaja threw a cushion at her.

"SHUT UP, YOU THILFY AMINAL!" he shouted. Tersely, he ordered the punkah boy to play with the puppy.

The skinny boy jumped to his feet and pulled the puppy over to him. He reached into his pocket and pulled out a small stone that he threw a short way across the floor for her. She retrieved it and, happy to be occupied, began sucking the stone.

Waqt cast his bloodshot eyes over his hypnotized guests. His gaze came to rest on the three-year-old Molly.

"Hmm. Testing you on this journey will pass the time." He pulled a pair of chopsticks out of his pocket. Then, heaving himself upright, he crawled (because he was too big to walk in the train) toward the young Molly and clicked his fingers in front of her eyes.

The three-year-old Molly was at once present. For the previous few hours she'd been hypnotized, of course, but all that time she had watched the maharaja. She'd come to the conclusion that the giant was very like a tortoise she'd once seen on television. Now, able to speak, she said, "You're gonna have to get a very, *very*, VERY big box to get into when you hivernate."

The maharaja looked perplexed. He decided he wasn't in the mood for a three-year-old today. He clicked his fingers, and the child was again in a trance. He turned to the six-year-old and, clapping sharply, released her.

The six-year-old Molly at once came to. The last time she'd been let out of her trance had been in the swing-bed chamber, and she'd cried her eyes puffy. Now she was more composed. The giant man didn't seem as frightening as he had before. "Who are you? Have you 'dopted me? 'Cos I don't want to be 'dopted by you. Can you take me back to Briersville? I don't want to live in Africa."

"I see your logic," said Waqt. "Don't worry, I haven't adopted you. I'm just borrowing you to see how talented you are."

Molly looked at the hypnotized Mollys, struck by how like her they looked.

"Why are they all half asleep? You woke the big one up before, an' she's called Molly, too, isn't she?"

"Observant, I see," said Waqt, pointing the chopsticks at her. "Now, are you hungry? Because you are going to show me how dextrous you are. These are stopchicks. Everyone eats with them in China."

"Are we in China?"

"No, but I spent fifteen years in China learning how to trime tavel."

"Fifteen years! Weren't you very good at it?" Molly asked innocently.

Waqt bristled. "Let's see how good *you* are with these. You use them like so." He crawled to the table and demonstrated how to pick up a piece of chicken tikka. "Now you can eat all you want, but only if you use the stopchicks."

The little Molly took the chopsticks and looked at the food-laden table. She wrinkled her nose. "Got any ketchup?"

"No ketchup."

"Are we in Africa?"

"Use the stopchicks."

"Australia?"

"Use the stopchicks."

"Never heard of a country called Usethestopchicks," grumbled Molly under her breath. She frowned up at the tall man above her and said slowly, "An'—I—don't—like—that—food, *so I won't use the chopsticks!*" She turned and walked back to the velvet cushion by the wall, picking up the black puppy as she went. "Didn't even say please," she muttered.

Waqt was shocked. He wasn't used to people disobeying him. He wasn't used to the company of children.

"Don't you dare . . ." Then it struck him that he wanted the baby Molly to grow up bold. "Good," he finished. "Stubbornness is good. Now the next thing you are going to show me is whether you have an aptitude for languages. Repeat after me: *'Elvaleah maleleia ey nuli.'*"

The young Molly held the puppy to her chest and shut her eyes. They did French at school and she wasn't very good at it. Just like she wasn't good at sums or writing. She didn't like being tested, and this man was starting to frighten her again.

"Good puppy," she whispered in its ear. The puppy helped her feel safer. It reminded her of Rocky and

Mrs. Trinklebury, the cleaner at the orphanage.

"Come on, repeat after me, *'Elvaleah maleleia ey nuli,'*" ordered Waqt. The small girl looked up at him.

"I won't do your silly talking. An' I want to go home," she said.

Waqt growled and clicked his fingers. "Oh, go back into your trance." He glanced down at the sleeping baby.

"Not a great beauty, are you?" he said to it. "A potato nose, closely set eyes, and it doesn't look as if you're going to be a child genius, either. Nor an artist, musician, dancer, or mathematician." Waqt's mouth puckered as he saw that the baby he'd hoped to rear wasn't going to be brilliant in every department. Then his lips parted in a grimacelike smile.

"But your talent at hypnosis will make up for your defects. Little Waqta, ugly as you are, you will be a genius hypnotist. Now. I will take you to Jaipur and begin the moon ceremonies to inaugurate you into my world—the crystal-fountain ceremonies! I have a feeling, my little Waqta, that you are going to be a huge magnet for the crystals." The baby Molly gurgled.

The crystal fountains. How Waqt loved them. Few hypnotists knew of the sources of the crystals, but he did; he'd been initiated into the world of the crystal fountains in China. It never ceased to amaze him that they existed. For all over the world could be found very special, ordinary-looking cracked rocks, from which, on certain full-moon nights, the clear, red, and green crystals would emerge. Master hypnotists could draw them from the earth. Waqt was sure and very excited to think that this small baby would. "Does that sound good, Waqta?" he said, tickling the child's chin. "Of course, it does."

The puppy Petula watched the giant. She didn't like the look or the smell of the huge man, and her instinct told her that it wasn't good that he was breathing all over the baby. She walked over and sat down beside the tiny Molly and barked protectively.

"Not yours," her small bark meant.

Miles behind Waqt's train, and with Petula under her arm, the eleven-year-old Molly clambered up the iron stepladder at the very back of the *Delhi Rocket*. She faltered as new memories filled her head, but she brushed them away, determined not to dwell on them. She took Ojas's hand and he hauled her up. The train's sides dropped away like sheer cliffs, but there was a section in the middle with more iron bars to hold on to. Already people were sitting here. As they walked past them Petula sniffed at a chicken that was tucked under a boy's arm and a goat that was sitting very quietly beside its owner. Petula could sense that these animals knew something about the journey ahead. With her canine reckoning, she deduced that up here the journey was going to be ten times as windy as when she'd ever stuck her head out of a car window while driving along. She licked her lips and began to snuffle her way under Molly's veil.

As she did, a nervous scent that she recognized caught the very edges of her smelling vision. It conjured up pictures of the turbaned man. He was getting closer by the second. Petula barked at Molly to warn her.

"We won't fall off, Petula. I'll hold you tight," Molly said.

They found some space on the third carriage of the train and settled down. The engine at the front let out a whistle and covered them in steam. An Indian girl beside them let out a shriek of laughter, but Molly suddenly became apprehensive.

"Don't worry," Ojas assured them all. "Hold on and duck whenever we go under bridges. You'll be fine." He shut his eyes, put his hands together, and began mumbling prayers.

On the platform the stationmaster blew his whistle, and the engine made its much louder reply with a piercing screech. Then an arduous *chuff-chuffing* began. The long metal coupling rods that moved the wheels 'started to slowly turn, and the train began to move.

They edged out of the station and Molly surveyed the scene behind them. For a moment she thought she saw Zackya arriving in a wheel-less, stretcherlike litter carried by four servants, but the train was accelerating fast now and as it turned a corner she lost sight of him. She wondered whether fear had made her imagine it.

Soon the journey blew Zackya from her mind. She watched the landscape about her turn golden as they moved southwest toward Jaipur. Molly thought of Waqt up the track ahead of them. She hadn't the foggiest clue what he was planning. She only hoped that his plans didn't include killing any of the Mollys he had taken traveling with him. Molly's fingers involuntarily shot to her mouth and she bit them as she questioned what would happen to her now if he *did* kill one of her former selves. As the veil on her head flapped in the wind, her imagination began to whirl. If Waqt chopped a finger off the six-year-old, she wondered, would she now suddenly have a long-healed stump? She touched the scar on her neck. What had caused it? It was obviously from a cut that had originally been fairly deep. Why had her memories disappeared when she'd traveled forward to the next century, but this scar had appeared? Where were the memories that went with the scar?

And, as the hours passed, a new question germinated in Molly's mind. Why was Waqt so keen to keep the baby Molly as a child for himself? Why wouldn't the three-year-old, the six-year-old, or even the ten-year-old do? Maybe it was because the baby would have absolutely no memories of her life at Hardwick House. But the suspicion that ate at her was that the reason he didn't want to adopt the older Mollys was that there was something *wrong* with them. Ever since Lucy Logan had been so unenthusiastic about being reunited with her long-lost daughter, Molly had begun to feel that it must be because she, Molly, wasn't good enough. And now Waqt was sending her the same message—that Molly wasn't the sort of person you'd want to discover was your daughter or, in Waqt's case, adopt. This made Molly feel bad.

As the sun shone down in her face, furnace hot, Molly was comforted by new memories of her trip to Jaipur as a ten-year-old. So she knew that, at least so far, Waqt was treating her other selves reasonably well.

The train snaked across the dry Indian landscape. Smoke from the locomotive trailed above their heads. The wind threatened to blow everyone off, and Petula's ears flapped like wings. Forest's dreadlocks thudded against his cheeks. He smiled, looking out through his lashes at the beautiful, sun-baked hilly countryside around them.

They saw wild boar scrabbling among bushes. They even caught a glimpse of a leopard as it streaked across a hillside for cover. Ojas had to shout over the wind for his voice to be heard.

"If you look carefully, you may see a tiger! Or a rhinoceros! And look at that herd of elephants at that watering hole! I told you this was the best way to ride."

The countryside was teeming with animals. Herds of deer took off in fright as the train roared past. A bear nodded at them from a hilltop, his forelegs against a tree where a bees' nest hung.

The train came to a small rural station and stopped, its mission to pick up parcels and sacks. On the platform were people waiting to sell food to whoever could pay. Molly could smell curries and warm bread. Ojas took some of their money and jumped down to fetch them a meal and fresh water.

Petula shook her head and wiped a paw across her dusty muzzle. She watched Ojas picking a path across the platform toward the stall that smelled of onions and bread. She deduced that the train was going to be stopped for a while and saw an opportunity to stretch her legs.

She stood up, shook herself off, and yawned. Then she headed up the train.

She walked by a cage full of chickens that panicked and clucked. Petula gave one of them a hypnotic stare. As she went past the passengers squashed together on the roof, hands shot out to stroke her. One old lady gave her a succulent piece of lamb. Petula nodded and took it gratefully. A small boy offered her a slice of mango. Petula declined, but barked a thank-you.

At the end of the train, Petula took a quick look at the top of the engine and sniffed. She could just make out the driver's packed lunch. He seemed to be having something with cheese.

Then she made her way back down the train. People were just as friendly as they had been on the way up. The people here were wonderful, Petula thought. If it wasn't for the giant and his helper, this would really be one of the nicest places she'd ever visited. She could see Molly now, standing up, looking for her. She barked and Molly saw her.

Just then a sudden strong smell hit Petula's nose. It was a dreadful stink. Petula recognized who it came from. It was the nervous, impatient odor of their kidnaper—but with the smell of bad eggs on top. It was coming from the carriage directly below Molly.

Petula began to run. She must warn Molly.

Molly looked for Petula and spotted her heading off up the train. Just then, it dawned on her that her memories had changed.

Forest and Rocky both glanced at her.

"Hey, man," said Forest. "Have you just had your mind rearranged? I just remembered that old Zackya got on this train, too."

"So did I," said Rocky.

"And me," agreed Molly. "I remember seeing him get into the carriage below us. And we all ducked so he wouldn't see us. As we left Delhi I thought I saw him arrive at the station. He obviously missed the train . . ."

". . . and he has orders to catch up with Waqt . . ." added Rocky.

". . . so he went back in time to jump on this train before it left. And that's why we are suddenly seeing him in our memories. He's changed our past as well as his own."

"That's amazing, man. My brain does a loop-the-loop just thinkin' about it." Forest went cross-eyed as he tried to understand.

"Luckily Zackya doesn't know that Ojas is our friend." Molly put her hand on her stomach as she remembered Zackya's purple metal capsule. "I hope his tracker can find only the time that a person is in, not the place. Otherwise, if he switches it on, he'll realize we're right above him."

Molly watched Petula running along the train roof toward her.

"Slow down, Petula," she said under her breath. "You don't want to fall off."

Petula arrived, panting, and at once began pawing the train.

"Ojas is getting some water," Molly said. "And food."

Petula sighed. She stared down at the metal roof and wished she could see through it.

In the carriage below them, Zackya was lying flat out on the train banquette, asleep. The powder that the tea lady had sprinkled in his chai had already begun to work, and his stomach bubbled. In his pocket his slim, futuristic gadget lay switched off. He had given up on it as it seemed to have overheated. Two red-faced women in crinolines sat opposite, looking extremely cross and cooling themselves with ivory fans. They were disgusted both by this man's rudeness and at their husbands' timid behavior. Their waistcoated husbands stood at the door smiling stupidly, looking as though they'd been hypnotized, which of course they had.

"I must say," one woman managed to say from under her netted hat, "you have the manners of a wild boar."

As if in agreement, Zackya farted, gave a snort, and then continued snoring. An absolutely rotten pong filled the air.

"This is too much!" The ladies held handkerchiefs to their noses and, coughing, they left.

Ojas came back with water, some roti breads, and a simple mixed-vegetable curry. They ate quickly, as eating on top of the moving train would definitely be a see-if-you-can-eat-in-the-wind experiment. And then, with a whistle, the train started again.

From the top of the train they saw avenues of trees and distant compounds of bungalows where the British lived, and simple Indian villages. They saw grand palaces belonging to rich Indians and ancient Hindu temples that looked like those sandcastles that are made by dripping watery sand onto one spot in a lumpy pile. They saw Indian soldiers dressed in Victorian uniforms, and occasionally British officers and cavalrymen on horseback. They passed colorful crowds performing religious puja ceremonies outside temples and they went by hundreds of fields where Indian farming families worked. Finally, after seven long, hot hours, they arrived in Jaipur.

Molly and her friends sat still as everyone else disembarked. Their ears were still ringing from the wind, and their faces were sunburned, as well as dry and dirty from dust and engine smoke. Molly watched carefully until finally she saw Zackya emerge into the crowd. He was walking in an odd way—as if he had something wrong with his trousers. Indeed he did. While he'd been asleep, the tea lady's powder had caused an unfortunate explosion from his rear end. The crowd parted as he passed and Molly noticed three Indian children holding their noses and pointing at him, giggling. Zackya wove his way to a taxi stand and barged to the front of the long line. Two smart British officials and their overdressed wives objected loudly, but were soon quelled by a dose of hypnotism. Zackya climbed into a carriage and pointed in the direction he wanted to go.

However, before his man-drawn carriage set off, three teenage boys approached it. They raised their hands and threw what looked like packets of flour at Zackya. These exploded on impact, drenching him in colored dye—crimson, orange, and blue. The teenagers hopped around laughing as Zackya stood up and swore at them.

"What was that all about?" asked Rocky as the carriage left.

Ojas laughed. "In March India celebrates the festival of Holi. A lot of colored ink is thrown about. How do you think my tunic that I was wearing before was stained so bright? In Delhi, the celebrations are nearly over, but it seems that here they are still having fun."

Finally, wet with blue, red, and yellow dyes that had been thrown at them while they were waiting in the line for a carriage, everyone piled into a buffalo-pulled wagon. Ojas had discovered that Zackya was headed in the direction of a place called the Amber Palace, so he instructed the old farmer driving them to follow him there.

As they left the station they saw the Holi festival in full swing. Dancing girls entertained a crowd. Others sang happy Holi songs. People chased and spattered one another, or fired colored dye through odd nineteenth-century water pistols. They were all whooping and laughing.

The wagon rolled out of the town to where the roads were banked with plumed grass and the fields were full of sugarcane. They passed through groves of trees where big fat pods hung from branches and tethered goats grazed. Forest pointed out mango trees and pistachio-nut trees and a snake that no one else saw, then dropped into silence. Everyone was exhausted—partly from the long train journey but mostly, for

Molly, Rocky, and Forest, because time traveling was in itself very tiring. So they made themselves comfortable on the farmer's jute sacks and soon, with the rocking motion of the wagon and the distant chanting from a temple, they were asleep.

When Molly woke, the sun was very low in the sky. Rocky was already up. He smiled at her. The cart was trundling along a rough road that dropped on its left to an arid valley floor. Up ahead was a vast gray palace. A winding, walled road climbed from a small village at the bottom of the hill to its hilltop entrance.

Molly found that while she'd been asleep her head had filled with new memories from her hypnotized ten-year-old self. She remembered that Waqt took them up by elephant to this hilltop palace and that he left them in a chamber decorated with shells and took the baby Molly outside.

Rocky winced when she told him.

"This is so freaky," he said.

"It's horrible. My life now depends on Waqt's whims. If he has a fit of temper and decides to finish me off, I'm dead. Me here now? Well, I'd just disappear. And you know, if that happens, if he kills me as a toddler, so that I never grew up at the orphanage, all *your* past will change, too. We wouldn't have been friends, you wouldn't have had to stick up for me all those years, we would never have gone to New York or Los Angeles together. Who knows where you'd be now?"

"On the run in America," said Rocky. "I would have been adopted by that family and run away."

"I wish we could work out a way to get Waqt." Molly frowned. "Just chasing him feels so out of control." Petula licked her hand and pricked up her ears as she tried to sense why Molly was so tense.

"You're going to have to think about it like this," reasoned Rocky. "If he does kill you as a toddler, you won't feel it. You'll just suddenly not be here."

Molly's eyes opened as if she'd seen a monster.

"Even if it hurts, you won't feel it *now*. Because it will be in your past. You would have the memory of him being *about* to kill you, I suppose—which would a horrid memory—and then you'd be dead. At that point, you and I and Petula and Forest won't be here in India, because the past will have taken you out of the picture. Everything will adjust to you having died as a toddler and none of us will have the remotest idea of what might have been. That is what would happen. So you mustn't worry, Molly. There's no point in worrying."

"But look at this, Rocky." Molly showed him the scar on her neck.

"When did that happen?"

"When we went to the future."

"But didn't it come with a memory of how it got there?"

"No."

"Odd."

"I know. Rocky, you know if he does kill the younger me, before I found the hypnotism book, well, then Cornelius would have done everything that Waqt wanted. And that's very bad for the people of the world. So there is a bigger reason for stopping Waqt killing the younger me's. But, anyway, I don't want to die. I've still got so much to do. I wanted to start that hypnotic hospital, not chase this horrid man around India. That was my plan."

Rocky grinned. "Maybe he'll be your first patient."

"And you, Rocky, can write a song about all of this when it's over." Molly felt better. She woke up Ojas and asked him to tell the wrinkly driver to look in her eyes so that she could hypnotize him.

The old man's cataract-covered eyes soon glazed over, and Ojas gave him instructions to drive up to the palace and say that he had to collect some rugs for mending.

Molly, Rocky, Forest, and Petula hid under the mass of jute sacks in the back of the wagon and Ojas sat beside the driver. He'd taken his fancy new jacket off, so that his chest was bare, and he wore his old trousers.

The wagon began its journey up the stone-slabbed road, up to the Amber Palace.

Nineteen

Zackya was pacing up and down his private chamber. He'd rid himself of his dirty trousers and now, fresh from his bath, smelled of cloves and orange oil. Never before had he had an accident like that. He poured himself a honey and chamomile draft in the hope that it would calm his jangling nerves. But that was impossible, because in the courtyard below his private rooms he could see Waqt in a long cloak, gesticulating and noisily instructing a circle of elderly male priests who huddled around him.

They were standing beside the Amber Palace's crystal fountain. It didn't look like much—it was an ordinary rock with a long crack in it—but its worth was tremendous. For like all crystal fountains, this cracked rock produced crystals once every few years. Zackya had visited hundreds of crystal fountains. For in China Waqt had become the owner of an ancient map of the world that located crystal fountains and predicted when they would bloom. And so Waqt had traveled like a maniac, from one fountain to the next, arriving in time to harvest the precious gems.

The Jaipur palace crystal fountain produced gems every March full moon. Waqt's hypnotic presence helped to draw them from the earth. Zackya was never invited to join him during these ceremonies, as Waqt didn't consider Zackya a good enough hypnotist to magnetize the crystals. Zackya scoffed. He watched as his master explained to the priests how the ceremony was to proceed. He knew that the maharaja was particularly excited about tonight, for he calculated that with the *four* Mollys present, especially the baby Molly, the crystals would come pouring out of the earth as never before. He was obsessed with that baby, Zackya thought.

"It will all end in tears," he predicted, glancing out of the window and watching as Waqt took a handful of crystals from his special bag and spread them out on the rock. Zackya always steered clear of his master's strange ceremonies. During their fifteen years in China he'd seen his master cobbling together his own homemade religion—one that revolved around the crystals. He'd observed as Waqt had taken a slice of one religion, a pinch of another, a spoonful of a third, and mixed them together.

What chilled Zackya now was the prospect that he was going to have to spoil his master's special ceremonial day by telling him that the eleven-year-old Molly was missing. This might be the last straw. Today might be the day that Waqt *finally* hypnotized Zackya. He twitched. Being hypnotized by Waqt was his deepest fear. He didn't want to end up a hypnotized zombie. Zackya despised Molly Moon for escaping. He hated her for causing this situation. Zackya shook as he sipped his honey drink and prepared to go down to the courtyard.

Through a hole in the sacks Molly could see the high walls of the steep road and various arches that spanned it. At the top of the slope the wagon stopped and their driver explained in Hindi to the guards that he was there to pick up some rugs that needed mending. The guards let him by without question.

Now the wagon's wooden wheels rattled over the final threshold of the palace into its lower grounds. Molly dared to take a peep through her sacking and what she saw made her jump. For all about were elephants with painted faces and yellow silk headpieces.

Their mahouts sat on top of them, with their legs wrapped behind the elephants' ears. They were chatting to one another, and so didn't notice the shapes in the back of the wagon. One elephant did investigate, though, and Molly felt its trunk prod and sniff her leg. Its owner gave it a sharp order, and the trunk quickly recoiled. As they passed, another elephant peed, splashing a guard on the ground. The guard was furious and began waving his sword at the naughty elephant, and the mahouts laughed as though this were the funniest thing they'd ever seen. This distraction was perfect for the wagon's entry to the inner sanctum.

Molly, Rocky, Forest, and Petula lay quietly under the jute cloth, tense and still. Molly could sense that she was very near to her younger selves. There was a certain warmth, a comfortable sensation inside her, just under her rib cage. She wondered whether they could feel her, too.

Beneath this warm feeling, however, was a very distant shrill alarm. She knew instinctively that this fear was coming from her baby self. Her baby self was crying. Molly wanted to jump out of the wagon and tear up the path to wherever Waqt was. She wanted to pull the baby away from him. She wanted to make him disappear. But this was impossible. She knew she must be patient.

The wagon drew into a clearing beside the tradesmen's

entrance to the palace. Molly heard the driver explain something to someone. Ojas also gave an instruction and then the wagon was moved to a quiet, covered place. There was a sound of footsteps receding. Ojas prodded Molly.

"Come on your own with me now," he hissed urgently. "We will find where Waqt is."

Molly threw back her hot coverings and climbed out. Petula gave a little whine.

"See you later," Molly whispered, and she and Ojas hurried up a reed-roofed walkway. At the end of it was a small side entrance to the palace. Ojas quietly pushed the door open and listened. Then he beckoned Molly in. Molly's head was once more filling with memories.

The *ten*-year-old Molly sat on a bench looking on to a raised courtyard. The giant maharaja stood in front of her beside a rock. He had a baby in his arms. The infant looked like a tiny doll in his oversized hands. Low balconies about them thronged with servants of the palace. And chanting in a circle around the giant were fifteen weird, wizened men with long white beards and mustaches and flowing purple robes. The maharaja began to pass the baby around. Each elderly man bowed as he took the infant and then stepped toward the rock to sprinkle it with water, then flower petals, then dust. The baby was crying, but no one seemed to care.

Ojas led the way up a winding staircase.

"They're very high up," Molly explained. "You see, I have clear memories of them being at the top of the palace."

"Well, this is probably as high up as the palace goes," said Ojas, puffing. "I just hope we don't meet any guards."

"I can hypnotize guards, remember," Molly reassured him.

Finally there was a door. It was locked. Ojas looked shiftily about and then took a piece of wire from his pocket.

"My time spent thieving has given me useful skills," he said, picking the lock.

They found themselves in a turret room hung with faded red tapestries. To Molly's disappointment, it did not lead to the place of her memories. But it gave them a bird's-eye view of it. For through the turret's high window, Ojas and she could see across and down to the large central royal courtyard. The weird priests' chanting voices echoed around the palace.

"OOOhhhdlllllyaaaaa! OOOOOhhhhdhhhyyllllyyyaaaaaaa!" Two of them were swooping around like strange, hopping vultures. Above, a faint full moon hung in the dusk sky, like a shy actor afraid to perform. Waqt held the baby Molly above his head and turned her around and around as if luring the moon out with her. Then he laid her on a blanket on a rock behind the other Mollys. They sat hypnotized, unaware (as was the watching Molly) of the marvelous properties of the cracked rock behind them. The old priests danced. Their robes flared as they spun like tops.

And then, near to the baby Molly, the special rock gave birth. One by one, nine crystals—three red, three green, three clear—emerged like huge glistening beetles from the crack in it. Waqt sprang upon them and roared with delight.

From their high vantage point, Molly and Ojas heard Waqt's walruslike roars but had no idea what had caused them. They nervously watched as he bent over by the baby Molly. Then they saw Zackya stepping gingerly out of the crowd. He wound his way through the leaping priests to Waqt's side and beckoned him closer.

Molly could see Zackya pulling the silver gadget out of his pocket and showing it to Waqt. He seemed to be pleading. Waqt's yellow eyes narrowed, and he sneered at his servant.

"What is it, Yackza? It better be important. Very important."

Zackya stood on tiptoe to mumble in Waqt's ear. "I

might have expected as much from you, you incompetent fool," Waqt growled furiously. "It's not the machine that needs mending, it's your brain. Why I bother with you, I don't know." Then, as if something inside him had snapped, he screamed, "I OUGHT TO PUT AN END TO YOU NOW, YOU USELESS EXCUSE OF A PERSON!" His shouting echoed around the courtyard and up into the heavy air. The drumming stopped. The priests bowed down until they were cloak-covered humps. The crowd was fearfully quiet. Four saber-bearing guards jumped to attention and the metal scraping as they unsheathed their swords filled the air. Zackya measured the intensity of the outburst and tried to gauge whether he was indeed about to be executed. Was this the end? Then Waqt turned away from him and began muttering. Zackya breathed a sigh of relief.

"She's clever, this Molly Moon," Waqt observed, talking to himself, stimulated by the idea of this young, brilliant hypnotist. "Clever enough to follow me by using her own memories probably. Ha! Perhaps she'll provide some sport. I do so adore funting and hishing." He stepped toward the hypnotized ten-, six-, and three-year-old Mollys and said to them, "From now on, you will forget everything that happens to you here in India, unless I tell you to remember." He gave a sickly, throaty chuckle.

"You see," he went on, tossing his words to Zackya behind him, "I can now play darrot and conkey with the escaped Molly Moon. If I want to let her know where I am, I can. I can let one of these three here *remember* something, as a clue for her. But if I *want,* I can *stop* them remembering and she won't know where we are. Ha! Ha ha ha! She will just have to follow whatever clues I choose to *leave* her. Ah, what fun!"

Waqt had never played games when he was young. Now he was like a spoiled, monstrous child making up unfair rules to a game he intended to win.

Up in the turret, Molly and Ojas watched and tried to decipher Waqt's words. Then they heard a moan from the pillar behind them.

TWenty

olly turned to see a small, cross-legged figure, dressed in a grubby blue robe, sitting on the ground beside a water pot. He wore a pearl necklace and two gem-encrusted ankle bracelets. She guessed at once who he was. The man's circumstances were too like those of the maharaja at the Red Fort for him to be anyone other than the true owner of the Amber Palace.

The crooked man was hunched as though he'd been sitting there for years. His beard reached his lap and his unkempt white hair fell over his shoulders in an avalanche.

"Hello," Molly started.

The old man stared at the wall intently, as if he were watching an egg hatching.

Ojas put his hands together, dropped to his knees, and bowed. "This is the Maharaja of Jaipur. I recognize him from his portrait in Delhi. Word came two years ago that while out riding one day he was attacked by a mountain lion. All the time he's been sitting here in his fine jewelry but in filthy clothes!" Ojas shivered. "Waqt has a heart of ice. Can you do anything to help him?"

Molly shook her head and took the old man's hands. "I can't yet. He's been hypnotized and Waqt has probably locked his instructions in with a special time-travel lock or a time-stop lock. If I knew the password I could unlock it, but it could be any word in the entire universe."

Ojas tilted his head to one side. "Why don't you go back in time to when he was hypnotized and eavesdrop on Waqt," he suggested.

The idea was so simple that it shocked Molly. If the giant had done the final hypnosis in this room, then she could, in theory, listen in.

"The trouble is . . . ," she whispered to Ojas, "every time I time travel, my skin sort of scales up."

"Oh, I see. Oh, that is not good, is it, Mollee?" Ojas said, examining the flaky skin by Molly's ear.

"I don't want to end up with a scabby face, you see, like Waqt and . . ." Molly looked at the poor imprisoned maharaja, and faltered. "Okay, I'll try," she said.

She went over to the red tapestries, hoping that they always hung there. She peeled one away from the wall.

"Don't go anywhere," she said to Ojas. "I'll be back in a few seconds."

"A few seconds?"

"Hmm. Well, maybe I won't be able to plop myself in *exactly* the right time, so you must listen out for anyone coming. If I take too long, then you hide here, too. Okay?"

Ojas nodded and Molly disappeared behind the tapestry. She clasped the green crystal in her left hand and, after a few slow, concentrated breaths, when she thought again how amazing it was that she could actually time travel, she took off. As she whizzed backward through time, with the time winds caressing her, she extended her invisible date antennae and tried to locate a time two years back. She stopped and peered out from behind the curtain. As no one was in the room, she reckoned she must have gone back too far. She decided to spin forward in time as slowly as she could without her body becoming visible, so as to be able to see the moment when the Maharaja of Jaipur was first imprisoned in this room. She hoped she'd see the large and obvious form of Waqt hypnotizing him.

She gripped her red crystal.

Outside, night and day flashed by. Molly urged herself to slow down. Suddenly she became aware that a man was sitting cross-legged on the floor. She wanted to see him arrive in the room, so she concentrated on the green stone and went into reverse. Slowly. As slowly as she could. All at once, through a mist of moving time, she saw a giant man walking backward into the room. Of course, because *she* was moving backward in time, everything was back to front. The stooped Maharaja of Waqt paced up and down the room and then crouched on the floor. Then he walked *backward* out of the room with the Maharaja of Jaipur. It was as if Molly had just rewound a videotape and seen what was about to happen, in reverse. Molly stopped. The time-travel mist disappeared and she could see everything clearly.

She made completely sure that she was concealed behind the tapestry and waited.

Then she heard Waqt coming up the stairs. He was angry because, as usual, the space was too small for him.

He threw open the door and, dragging the maharaja behind him, entered the room. Molly hardly dared breathe. She listened intently and watched through a hole in the tapestry. She eyed Waqt's gun.

"And from now on, you will be under my power,"

Waqt said to the hypnotized maharaja.

Then Molly noticed that Waqt was fingering a red crystal. Without saying anything, he put his hand on the old prince's shoulder and clutched the stone. Molly couldn't believe her luck. Waqt was about to take the Maharaja of Jaipur on a little time trip—he was going to lift him a tiny bit forward and lock the hypnosis in with a password while they were floating in time. Without thinking, Molly felt for her red crystal, too.

Behind the tapestry, she zoned in and let her strange new antennae sense where Waqt was going. It was like following someone in the dark.

Waqt and the Maharaja of Jaipur hadn't changed place, yet they were moving slowly forward through time and Molly was following them. She could see their forms clearly through the gap in the tapestry, even though the rest of the room was flashing past—morning light, evening light, candlelight. Molly disengaged her mind and let her senses lead her. If she could just keep up, she would hear the password. She could hear snatches of what Waqt was saying, but if she erred at all from his exact time zone, her ears weren't in the same time as him speaking and then she missed the words. It was extremely difficult. It was like listening to someone talking on the phone with a bad connection, so that some of the words were lost.

"You will . . . under my . . . until . . . Now and . . . will be locked . . . the words . . . 'Pock' . . . I say it again . . . 'Key' . . . 'Pea' . . .'" Waqt stopped time flying, and Molly let herself shoot forward and away. She didn't want to tag Waqt anymore. Using her antennae like landing controls, she judged when she had left Ojas. She opened her eyes and peeped around the curtain.

"How long was I?" she asked, stepping out.

Ojas looked shocked. "You've only been gone two minutes!" He looked at her face and, by the way his eyebrows went up, Molly knew that the scaly skin must have got worse.

"Perfect timing," she said, ignoring his look.

The ceremony outside was still going on. The cloaked men were all on their knees, slapping one another with long green feathers.

Molly rushed to the old maharaja on the ground and seized his hand. She clung to the red crystal and took them both slightly forward into a time hover. For she suspected that only in this state could a time-travel lock be undone.

"You are now free and no longer under the Maharaja of Waqt's hypnotic command. I free you with the words 'Pock'! . . . 'Key'! . . ." Nothing happened. "With the words 'Pea'! . . . 'Key'!"

Molly hovered at her slowest time-traveling speed and thought hard. She'd obviously missed some of what Waqt had said.

"With the word 'Pocket'!" she guessed. "Pocket of Peas! . . . Pocket of Keys! . . . Pocket of Crystals!" Still nothing happened. Molly gave up. She would help the Maharaja of Jaipur later, but now she needed to conserve her energy. She landed them back in Ojas's time. He was looking worried.

"Well?"

"I can't do it."

Ojas shook his head sadly. "Don't worry. You tried. But now we must get back to the cart quickly, Mollee. Look, the ceremony's over." Indeed, the courtyard outside was empty.

Molly snatched a moment to touch the old man's cheek. Ojas stroked his feet and his gem-encrusted ankle bracelet.

"Just hold on," Molly said. "We'll be back to set you free. And we'll get rid of Waqt, don't you worry. He's not as alert as he thinks he is. We'll catch him off his guard." The maharaja blinked and sniffed. She hoped he could understand her. She knew that the bold promise she'd just made was as much to herself as to the maharaja. Deep inside, she felt about as confident as a mouse in the claws of an eagle.

Then she and Ojas sped down the stone helter-skelter-like staircase. They slipped surreptitiously back out through the door.

To their horror, the wagon had gone.

Twenty-one

Molly's stomach did a somersault. Had Rocky, Petula, and Forest been discovered? She looked up at the reddening evening sky as if the answer lay there.

"Psst."

With huge relief, Molly saw Rocky's dark face bob up behind steps that led to somewhere under the palace. She and Ojas hurried over.

"What happened?" Rocky asked. Petula jumped into Molly's arms and she hugged her.

"Waqt was performing some weird ceremony. We discovered the old man who *really* owns this place. I tried to help him, but it was no use. What happened to you?"

"Some kitchen workers came over and began talking

to the wagon man. They tipped a load of rubbish onto the cart and told him to drive the whole lot out of the palace. Of course, there was no way I could use my voice on them—I don't speak their language. We just jumped out without them seeing us."

"Man, that garbage stank," said Forest, picking green peelings off his head. "My dreads reek!"

Petula held her nose in the air, reading its smells. Ojas sniffed, too.

"This odor is very good," he said as if savoring a delicious soup.

"If you like rotten cabbage."

"No, there is something much lovelier. Can you not smell it? It is elephants!"

In the distance, deep drums were beating solemnly. Molly *felt* that her baby self was now fast asleep, obviously exhausted by her terrifying ordeal, but, oddly enough, she wasn't getting any memories from her ten-year-old self, or her six- or three-year-old selves about what happened after the ceremony. She wondered why.

"See!" said Ojas, pointing down the dark steps ahead of them. "This is the back entrance to the elephant stables." Like a hungry person trailing sizzling onions, he set off downward and the others, hearing voices approaching the courtyard, hurried after him.

"Where there are elephants, there is always hope," said Ojas.

"Where there are elephants, there are always piles of elephant dung," said Rocky under his breath. As they descended, the heavy, musky elephant smell grew stronger, until finally they were quietly lifting the latch of a wooden door.

Spread out before them was a grand, shady elephant stable, with a cobbled floor and high marble walls that divided the space up into twelve massive elephant stalls, six on either side, with a wide walkway in between. Beneath their feet was straw laid down on worn marble. Molly put Petula down.

"Stay close," she whispered to her.

Each stall had a stone gatepost crowned with a carved elephant's head. On each entrance pillar a copper placard had a name written on it.

"Ah, what fine stables!" Ojas sighed admiringly. "My father told me about this place." He walked down the aisle between the giant compartments. For a moment he looked sad and far away.

Molly looked around the elephant stables. Inside each stall were piles of straw and huge iron hoops set in the floor. There were water troughs at the back and enormous feeding baskets for elephant treats like bananas and mangoes. On the ground were large swathes of plants, branches of palm trees for the elephants to strip of their leaves and eat. Petula sniffed the ground, fascinated by the strong smells.

Molly glanced anxiously behind them, wondering whether anyone was coming. At the other end of the stable was a half-open door. Dusky light poured in through big, glassless windows.

They walked toward the view. As they did, a snoring sound echoed around the stables. Immediately they dived behind a post.

Molly whistled super softly to Petula and signaled silently to Ojas. She pointed at the wall and put her hands in a "Who do you think that is?" position. Ojas tilted his head as if listening to the tone of the snore.

"Is it a sleeping guard?" Molly whispered.

"I thought you weren't afraid of guards," said Ojas, smiling. Then he crept forward and peered around the post into the next stall. He came back with a wide grin on his face and beckoned them with his finger.

In the next cubicle was a magnificent sight—the very large posterior of an elephant. The elephant's bottom was painted so that it looked as if it were wearing colorful flowery trousers, and, since elephants have very loose skin over their bottoms and hind legs, its baggy, painted trousers looked as though they were slipping off. The elephant's front shoulder leaned against its stable wall and its giant back legs were crossed, throwing its hips at a jaunty angle. It wore huge silver bracelets on its ankles. A chain threaded through these hobbled it to the iron hoop on the stable floor. A soft, quilted red pad was slung over its back and on top of this was a *guddha,* or saddle, made of sacking stuffed with straw. On top of this *guddha* was a canopied boxlike carriage—a howdah. The whole contraption was strapped on with rope.

"Her name is Amrit," said Ojas, reading the plaque.

"And who's that dude?" asked Forest.

"Doood?"

"That man on the floor."

"Ah—that 'doood' is her mahout, but he sleeps now because he has been drinking too much."

"You mean he's drunk?" asked Molly.

"Yes, he is well and truly discombobulated!" agreed Ojas, waggling his head and laughing.

The thin brown man sprawled on the straw beside Amrit the elephant was fast asleep. His mouth hung open, emitting a soggy, guttural snore. A large bluebottle flew into his mouth and actually landed on his teeth before taking off again. Ojas tutted.

"A man like that should not be allowed to take care of a creature as lovely as this."

"Is his elephant asleep, too?" asked Molly.

As if in answer, the elephant opened her small twinkling eyes, leaned her body squarely onto her four legs, lifted her trunk toward her treat basket, and tossed a banana skin back toward her visitors. It hit Forest on the head.

"Man, what did I do?"

Ojas laughed. Then he approached Amrit and casually slipped along her right-hand side toward her silver-hooped tusks. He made some noises in his throat and gently clicked with his tongue and he patted her gray shoulder.

"Good girl." She in turn sent the pink speckled tip of her trunk to probe Ojas's head and face. He touched her headdress. "She was obviously supposed to go out with the other elephants. This mahout here has spoiled her day. Why don't we take her?"

"*Us?*" said Molly.

"Yes, riding her will be 'easy-peasy,' as you say."

"I never say that," said Rocky. "I say, a cinch."

"A cinch, then. Amrit means 'nectar' in Hindi. Sweet Nectar! I expect that means she is very good-natured. Amrit will be no problem at all for me."

"Man, that sounds mammoth!" exclaimed Forest, beaming at his own pun. "But will the lady take all of us?"

"Oh yes, this elephant could even take two more

with ease." With the lithe movements of an expert, Ojas began hopping about in the straw, undoing Amrit's tethers. "We must follow the other elephants." He picked up a long stick with a double hook at the end of it. "This is an *ankush*. Don't worry—it looks alarming, I know, but to an elephant being prodded with this is like you being prodded with a small fork. Sometimes it has to be used more strongly. Elephants can be dangerous if they behave badly, so it's important to have some form of control over them."

Molly watched as Ojas peeled the mahout's uniform turban off his head and put it on his own. The man made comforting *myum myum myum* noises before curling up like a baby and dropping into an even deeper sleep.

"Ojas is right," she said. "We must follow the other elephants. The elephants wouldn't be out all decorated like this for anyone else but Waqt. So, if we want to keep on his trail, this is the best way. We'll be well disguised."

Ojas took the drunk's jacket from a hook on the wall.

"I suppose you're right," said Rocky.

Ojas began pushing the elephant's massive chest so she moved backward out of her stall toward a mounting block. "*Peechay, peechay,*" he said, adding, "Besides, what else can you do? You can go forward in time and backward in time, but at some point, Mollee, you have to get close, very close, to Waqt. You will have to kill him, Mollee. You do realize that?"

Molly went cold. She stood in the straw in the musky-smelling stable and watched as Ojas kept pushing Amrit. She just watched as if he had said nothing. The impact of his words on her was huge.

The idea that the only way of truly sorting out this situation was to *kill* Waqt had only faintly suggested itself to her. And the idea was so horrible that she'd pushed it to the back of her mind. Because she wasn't a killer. She couldn't kill. How could she live with herself if she killed? But, perhaps, she thought now, unless she killed, she'd be killed herself.

By the time Molly came out of her daze, Rocky and Forest had mounted Amrit. Molly picked up Petula and climbed up, too. She frowned. A poisonous cocktail of feelings was fizzing away inside her.

Ojas clambered up and sat with his legs behind Amrit's ears. Behind him, a canopy covered his new friends, who sat, half hidden in the howdah, wrapped in warm royal blankets. For a moment Ojas was quiet. He shut his eyes and prayed to Ganesh, the elephant god, to ask for good luck on their journey. His father's last words before he died filled his mind.

I'll always be near, watching over you, Ojas. Always believe in yourself, and always remember that I'll love you forever.

Blinking back tears, Ojas made a clicking noise with his tongue.

Finally Amrit, hearing the voice of her new master— *"Agit! Agit!"*—stepped out of the stables.

Twenty-two

The view was magnificent and far-reaching. As Amrit walked majestically down the slope from the upper courtyard to the lower courtyard Molly could see the tops of soldiers' heads. She saw a couple of them horsing around, throwing small packets of Holi dye at each other, as if now that Waqt was away they could play. She saw palace staff hurrying about preparing for the night and she could see over the palace walls to the surrounding countryside.

Ojas was in front, the thick gray neck of Amrit beneath him. The elephant's ears had a lovely tinge of pink to them and were much softer than the other gray parts of her. She flapped them as she walked. Molly touched the gray leathery skin and discovered that it was covered with lots of coarse black hairs.

Flowery incense burned in the palace's Hindu temple and from inside they could hear the soft chanting of devotees. Amrit passed quietly under the giant arches, built to allow elephants through, and down the next cobbled slope.

Below them was the vast palace lake, its square shape shimmering with dusk light. In the distance they could make out the procession of Waqt's elephants as they walked along a ridge. Torchbearers carried beacons of fire in front of each elephant, so that the advancing party seemed lit by a giant chain of fairy lights.

Molly could make out that the largest elephant, the third along, carried the most enormous carriage. She expected this was Waqt's.

"Rocky," she whispered worriedly, "I'm not getting any memories of riding on an elephant when I was ten or six. Don't you think that's odd? That's the sort of memory that a person keeps forever. Why aren't I remembering an elephant ride? Maybe Waqt has left the other me's back at the palace."

"If he'd done that," Rocky pointed out, "wouldn't you remember being left at the palace?" He was quiet for a bit. "I think what's more likely is that Waqt has blocked your memories so that you don't know where he is."

Molly shut her eyes. "You're probably right." She sighed, realizing that the problem had just thickened.

And Amrit lumbered quietly on to the main road toward the others.

The journey was a long one. The swaying of Amrit's body and the chinking of her ankle bracelets as she walked sent Molly to sleep.

She awoke beneath a full moon. She sat up, rubbed her shoulders, and readjusted Petula, who was sitting on her leg.

They were on a tree-lined road, approaching some buildings half hidden by poplars.

"Where are they, Ojas?"

"Don't worry," said Ojas, gently prodding Amrit behind the ears with his feet. "You see those fires below? That is where Waqt is. I think he is performing another ceremony. That is Jaipur Observatory. It was built by a very, very clever prince. He wanted to be able to measure the distance of the earth from the sun and the stars. He built another observatory in Delhi. I have seen that one. They are very strange, beautiful places. Once Amrit gets close, you can climb down. You will find some good hiding places in the observatory. What will you do?"

Molly thought. "If I can, I'll steal Waqt's crystals. The whole lot. Maybe I'll get close enough to rescue my other selves."

"Yes. You will be all right, Mollee. It's dark and you

are dressed like an Indian girl. Waqt won't be expecting you. He seems obsessed by his peculiar ceremonies."

"So you haven't seen a ceremony like the one with the creepy purple men in it before?" questioned Molly.

Ojas laughed. "No, certainly not!"

"What religion do you think it is?" asked Rocky, stirring.

"A new one? One that Waqt made up? I don't know, Rocky!" Ojas laughed again. But Molly didn't find it funny. Who knew what strange beliefs Waqt held?

As Amrit walked on, the observatory gradually came into view. Over the wall they could see huge stone staircases that looked like slides without the slide parts. The tallest had a roof place at the top. Molly could see the other elephants close up now. Each had a mahout with his feet resting up on the elephant's head while the passengers were gone.

When Rocky stood up on Amrit he could see a group of the purple men standing around a fire, their ghostly faces lit up. Wild drumbeats filled the night air. He sat down.

"I'm not letting you go in there on your own," he said. Molly smiled and she and Rocky slipped down to the ground.

"We'll be back as soon as you can say 'curried purple man.'"

"Sounds tasty," murmured Forest in his sleep.

"If anything happens to us, Ojas, will you look after Forest and Petula?"

Ojas surveyed the sleeping man and wrinkled his nose. Then his eyes fell on Petula. He nodded.

Molly and Rocky crept through the observatory gate.

Petula watched. She didn't like them going at all.

To start with, she could smell the giant and the kidnaper man. But there was something more. Something ominous. For behind the strong odor of elephants and a bonfire, behind the innocent smells coming from ordinary people, of spices and baking and flowers, Petula could detect the scent of a very frightened animal. The animal was a goat. Petula didn't like it one bit.

Molly had been to a bonfire night when she was seven and the scene in front of her reminded her of that, although instead of sparklers in people's hands there were torches, and instead of fireworks, a full moon hung in the air like a ball of milk in the sky. They walked quickly through the crowds, past elephants and past one of the strange flights of stairs, to a place where they could watch the proceedings without being seen.

Standing around the crackling fire were Waqt's cronies in their purple robes, the flames casting demonic shadows on their whiskered faces.

On the right, a more compact circle of ghostly priests stood with their arms outstretched and joined at the fingertips. The material hanging down from their flowing sleeves made a wall of purple silk. The drums beat faster and faster. As the rhythm reached a frantic pace, the circle of men dropped to the ground, revealing Waqt, his face painted white, crouching on a low, cracked rock. Beside him sat the three hypnotized young Mollys. The baby Molly lay on a blanket on the rock. Waqt raised his hands to the moon and waved his arms about like long strands of seaweed. He looked like a devil from a horror film.

Then he picked up the hypnotized six-year-old. The hidden Molly stared in revulsion, hardly daring to think what he might be about to do. The fire raged to the side of him. He stepped toward it with the six-year-old Molly in his arms. Closer and closer and closer to the fire he walked until he turned and actually *stepped backward into it.* The audience gasped. Waqt had disappeared in the flames.

Molly knew where he was and what he was doing. In the next instant she experienced the most horrific memory.

A loud voice had shouted, "WAKE UP AND REMEMBER THIS! FOLLOW ME IF YOU CAN, MOLLY MOON!" Molly realized that these words were directed at her now.

She remembered being six and suddenly waking up to find the mammoth man she'd met before holding her at arm's length above him. His face was painted powdery white and he was laughing like a demented clown. She remembered screaming and crying, "I want to go home!" And the fear of the young Molly filled Molly now.

Waqt suddenly appeared out of the fire.

"How did he walk into the fire like that?" gasped Rocky.

The six-year-old Molly was crying loudly and the puppy Petula was howling. Waqt placed the small girl on the ground. The puppy Petula bounded up to her and the child clung to her black velvet form, sobbing.

"He just stepped out of time," Molly explained. "It looked like he was in the fire, but he wasn't. He was hovering out of the time of the flames, so the flames couldn't hurt him."

"His priests are impressed," said Rocky.

"Let's try to find his collection of crystals."

They crept closer, their eyes searching for a bag or a cushion or a box. Then Rocky pulled at Molly's sleeve and drew her attention to a low staircase near Waqt. Zackya slid out from behind it and sidled up to the giant. He was clutching his silver time-travel gadget. He stood on a block so that he could reach his master's ear and, panting, he whispered something and pointed to the crowd near to where Molly and Rocky were hiding.

Waqt cuffed Zackya around the head and laughed into the audience. Molly was sure that his laugh was directed at her. Then, as if testing her, Waqt turned to accept a long, bone-handled knife that a priest was offering him, and he steadily began mounting the tallest set of steps. The train of his green robe trailed behind him like long, iridescent peacock feathers and the blade of the knife flashed in the moonlight.

At the top of the steps a purple-robed man held a white goat. Its bleats could be heard above the beat of the drums. It was obvious now what Waqt was going to do. The drums reached a cacophony of rhythm, and his priests began to chant.

"Oohhhh Dahla . . . OOOhhhhlaa Deahliea."

Waqt crouched over the defenseless goat.

"Oohhhh Dahla . . . OOOhhhhlaallaa Deahliea."

Silently Waqt slit the animal's throat. The knife clattered down the steps.

A priest carrying a silver bowl scurried to Waqt's side. Blood splashed into the bowl.

Waqt descended the stairs and walked over to the flat, cracked rock. He picked up the sleeping baby Molly. He plucked a peacock feather from his cloak and solemnly dipped it into the bowl of blood. With great panache and a flourish of his hand he used the drenched feather to wipe the fresh blood on the peaceful baby's head. "Tonight, little Waqt, we shall see how many more crystals you can draw from the earth."

Molly and Rocky watched in horror. Neither knew that the cracked rock was a crystal fountain, nor that Waqt was using the baby to draw the gems from the earth. When Molly spied Zackya's familiar purple turban winding its way through the crowd toward them, she knew it was time for her and Rocky to disappear.

"That gadget seems to be giving him your exact location," Rocky said. Molly took his hand and gripped her red crystal. There was a BOOM.

Molly whisked them very, very slightly forward in time, but she didn't land. The warm time winds washed about them, and the world was a misty apparition moving in slow motion.

"This is too weird for words," Rocky said. "Look, there's Zackya walking about in the crowd looking for us, and Waqt doing his thing."

For a moment, they could think. Ojas's voice rang

in Molly's ears. *"You will have to kill him, Mollee. You do realize that?"*

If she wanted to, she could get really close to Waqt *now*. She could walk through the time-hover air toward the knife that lay on the ground. She could appear, take the knife, then disappear again. She could move through the time-hover air until she was right behind Waqt. And do what? Kill him? Molly could never kill a person. And, anyway, how could an eleven-year-old girl thrust a long carving knife into an old, sinewy giant like Waqt? Who was she kidding? She wouldn't have the first clue where to stick the blade. She'd make a mess of it. She'd just graze him. And then he'd turn around and chop her into little pieces.

"What shall we do, Rocky?"

Rocky frowned. "Go forward in time to *tomorrow,* when the observatory will be empty? We can go right to where the six-year-old Molly was left *tonight,* and then we can time travel back to *now.* When we arrive, we'll be near her. We can grab her and run to the others and the baby and, as soon as we're all touching, we can take off. We won't have his bag of crystals, but at least we'll have all of you!"

This sounded a far better plan than trying to kill Waqt. Molly concentrated on the red crystal. Like a well-fired arrow, she shot herself and Rocky to the next evening, just as the sun was going down.

A peaceful holy cow stood in the observatory beside the tallest staircase. It took a calm look at the visitors and continued grazing. Molly and Rocky ran over to the spot where the six-year-old had been dumped after her ordeal the night before.

Then Molly gripped her green crystal and held Rocky's shoulder.

"Are you ready?"

Cool time winds blew about them as Molly aimed them back to the night before. They hovered in time and surveyed the scene. Through the time mist they could make out Waqt's huge form. He was moving beside the cracked rock where the ten-year-old and the three-year-old and the baby Molly were. Molly nudged Rocky and herself forward in time a bit.

"There must be a moment when Waqt isn't near them all," she said. But every time they hovered, Waqt was there, like a limpet, sticking to the younger Mollys.

"Go back to the moment when the six-year-old is on her own," said Rocky. And so Molly did.

They landed and, running on adrenaline, Molly embraced the six-year-old. Rocky quickly caught the puppy and held Molly's shoulder tight. Focusing on the red crystal, Molly shot them forward and away. The little girl screamed.

With her arms around her younger self, Molly spoke in her ear. "Don't worry, Molly, I've come to save you. Everything's going to be better very soon." As Molly said these words she remembered a big person once saying them to her. It was a very odd sensation, but she ignored it, as she had to concentrate on escaping. She took them forward to the evening of the next day and they stopped in that time. Again, the cow looked up.

"Okay, Molly," she said, "are you all right?"

The six-year-old Molly wiped the tears from her eyes and looked around her, terrified.

"Has that nasty clown gone?"

"Yes." Molly hugged her younger self.

The puppy Petula wriggled and licked Rocky's face. Rocky touched his cheek to see how many scales had grown there, but his skin was smooth. Molly inspected the younger Molly's face and neck and pulled up her sleeves.

"Has she scaled up at all?" he asked.

"I don't think so," she said. "Her elbows are a bit dry, I suppose."

"Who are you?" the little Molly said, pulling her elbow away. "I don't really know you. And I don't like China. I want Mrs. Trinklebury."

"We'll take you home to her soon. And then you can see Rocky and that horrid old trout Miss Adderstone."

This made the small Molly laugh, and then, unfortunately, cry. Rocky stroked her head.

"You know, this is India," he said, "not China. And we can't stay here for too long or that nosy cow is going to come over and ask us what we're doing." The young Molly let out a small half-sob, half-laugh. "So," continued Rocky, "we have to go this way." He led the small girl toward the gate where the wall was. Now all they needed to do was remember where exactly Ojas had parked Amrit. Beads of sweat gathered on Molly's temples as she tried to judge the place.

"Okay, little Molly, now hold my hand tight. Rocky will hold the puppy. We're just going backward in time to rescue our other friends."

"But . . . ," objected the six-year-old. Before she could say any more, they were flying.

"This is nice," Molly assured the scruffy six-year-old as the world flashed by.

They landed in the warm, March full-moon night of 1870. A horrible sight greeted them.

Zackya was in front of Amrit. She pawed the ground with her great padded foot. Petula was barking madly.

When Molly appeared, he cackled.

"I knew you'd come back here, you fool! I knew you would have left your *friends* and your mode of transport out here."

Ojas gave a swift instruction to Amrit. "Baitho!" The elephant knelt down.

Molly thought quickly. She plunged toward Ojas, pulling the little girl with her.

"Take her," she shouted to Forest, and he helped little Molly clamber up. Rocky dived forward, still holding the puppy, and sprang onto the elephant, too. Molly clutched her colored crystals and grabbed the animal's trunk. Sweating, she sharpened her mind and, with an enormous effort of concentration, lifted the whole party out of 1870.

There was a thunderous BOOM as Amrit disappeared. Beneath this clamor was the noise of Petula's frenzied barking.

"Don't let her fall off!" Molly shouted up to Forest.

1890, 1900, 1930, 1950 . . . They shot forward. Molly clung to Amrit's trunk. Still, Petula barked.

Ojas whooped with excitement. Warm time winds enveloped them and the world reeled with color.

Molly shut her eyes and tried to judge how far they had traveled. She decided to put the brakes on.

The drone of cars filled the air.

They'd escaped. Molly let her hands drop in relief. But, as she did, a terrible thing happened. Two sets of taloned fingers scraped across her right palm, scooping out her two crystals. Petula's barking became louder and more frantic. Molly turned to see Zackya running toward the gates of the observatory, with Petula struggling under his arm, trying to bite him. He looked back. He was so ecstatic that he was practically dancing.

"You are a complete fool, Miss Moon!" he jibed, his eyes burning with mean triumph. "*I traveled with you.* So I now have your crystals *and* your dog!" He shoved Molly's crystals into his pocket and put his fist around Petula's nose. "All I needed to do was touch the elephant, too. The only one to notice was your dog. She jumped on me. Now you are easy meat for the maharaja!" He hopped about excitedly.

Molly could hardly bear to see Petula's big eyes blinking out at her from behind Zackya's fist. "Help me, Molly," they were pleading. "Help me." What Zackya planned to do with her, she dared not imagine. This was disastrous. They were all as good as dead if she couldn't time travel. Desperately she tried diplomacy.

"Zackya," she shouted, "please stop and listen! Don't take Petula. Please don't. And don't take my crystals! You already know Waqt doesn't appreciate you . . . as he *should.*" Zackya cocked his head to one side. For a moment Molly thought she might win him over. "Waqt has walked over your life. Taking Petula and my crystals to him won't make a difference. Why don't you stand up to him? Set yourself free! If you give Petula the crystals, you'll be doing something good. Join *us*. Together we can outwit him. Imagine that, Zackya. Imagine never being frightened that Waqt will hypnotize you or kill you ever again. Imagine being free! *Please*, Zackya." Molly longed to stare into his shifty eyes long enough to hypnotize him, but it was useless. Zackya shook his head and waggled his finger at Molly.

"You fool. You will never be able to help me in the way Waqt can. I *need* to get to the Bubble at the beginning of time. I *need* to be washed with the light of youth. Look at me. I'm scaly and old from all the time travel I've been forced to do. Soon my body will have aged so much that I will die. Before it does, I have to get to the light. You cannot help me, Moon. You are merely a child. As soon as we have enough crystals, Waqt will take me there." He gave a sideways, gap-toothed grimace and squeezed Petula.

In desperation, Molly froze the world. Everything went still—except for Zackya.

"Bad luck!" He laughed. "You're not with beginners now, Molly!"

Molly raised her hypnotic eyes to him, ready to bore through to the center of his brain. He dropped his gaze and reached for something in his pocket. When he looked up, he had donned a pair of swirly anti-hypnotism spectacles. Molly's hypnotic look bounced off them.

Holding Petula up tauntingly, and cackling as if he had just performed the funniest trick in the world, Zackya disappeared.

TWenty-three

Time winds swirled around Zackya and Petula. "This may take a while," he said, squinting at his silver time-travel gadget. "Between you and me, Petula, I am not the world's best time traveler. Let's stop here."

The world was bright with daylight. "Ah, you see, precisely my point—we need the night." He took off again, cursing his gadget. Petula growled, her mouth clamped shut with Zackya's fist. The next time they stopped, the moon was low and the sky was paling with the dawn. Zackya glanced into the observatory. The residues of Waqt's ceremony lay on the ground. Flower petals, dried blood, and a smoldering fire.

"This will do," said Zackya, and he set off toward the tree-lined avenue. "I shall take you to my quarters

in the palace. You'll be quite comfortable there."
Petula growled at him again.

"Oh, you'll get used to it. What shall I feed you with,
then?" He picked his way over stones to the small
observatory palace.

"Do you like chicken? Baked without spices? You'll
enjoy chasing the peacocks. Perhaps baked peacock
would be a delicacy for you! In my view, the more peacock pie, the better. They are such stupid, noisy birds."

Around them, morning crows squawked a dawn
chorus. Zackya rang the bell at the palace gate. While
waiting, he peered down at Petula. "I'll take my hand
away from your mouth if you promise not to bite."

Petula was tired. She'd never been a great one for
biting, anyway. When Zackya took his fist away, she was
still. She just looked at him with her big, dewy eyes.

"Good," said Zackya. He fondled her soft, floppy
ears. "So, Petula, would you like to be my pet?" Petula
shut her eyes. She was really upset. This man had just
stolen her from Molly and now he expected her to be
nice to him.

"Well, that's settled, then," said Zackya. The gate
creaked open. Petula's eyes filled with tears.

Whispering, so that the night watchman didn't hear
him, Zackya said, "And, you know, one of the first gifts
I will get you is an earring!"

Twenty-four

Molly's mouth hung open.

"He's just taken Petula to another time!" she cried disbelievingly, as if the others hadn't seen. "And there's no way we can get to her. He took the crystals. We're stuck!" She looked into the bushes as if by some miracle Zackya would step out of them with a changed heart. Molly was beside herself. "This is a nightmare!" she groaned.

"Don't worry about me!" said Ojas, admiring a motorbike as it blasted past. "I love it here. I don't ever need to go back to 1870. This is the future!"

"Ojas!" shot Rocky. "Petula is like a person to us. How can you go on about the motorbikes when Petula's just been taken by that lunatic?"

"Oh, I'm sorry. Yes, I'm sorry. My goodness, I'm so

sorry—I was distracted by those two-wheeled contraptions. Please accept my apologies."

Molly sank to the ground and put her head in her hands. "I've got parts of me stuck in the wrong time!"

"But, Molly," said Forest as the puppy Petula licked something turnipy from his ear, "can't you *remember* what happens to the other you's? I mean, they're all in 1870 India and that time is well past. Can't you remember how it all finished?"

"I can't!" cried Molly. "It's all a complete blur. Before, when I came forward in time, it was the same—it's as if there's a memory lag or something."

Molly glanced about at some tourists who were pointing at Amrit, and then she looked at the ruins of the observatory. The old staircases were battered and graffitied but the site sent a chill through her. The stairs reminded her that Zackya knew exactly where they were. He could easily lead Waqt to them. Part of her wanted to see Zackya again as there was a chance she'd be able to get the better of him and then rescue Petula and get the crystals back. But there was also a huge chance that if Zackya returned he would be coming with Waqt to kill her. Tears welled up in her eyes.

"We should get out of here," she said, hurriedly wiping them away.

"Baitho!" Ojas said, and Amrit dropped down on one knee. Ojas waited until Molly was safely up and then bid Amrit walk. He thought it best to head into the hustle and bustle of the main part of Jaipur town.

Molly sank down in the howdah and touched her cheek. The wrinkles were worse. The skin was bumpy with scales under her fingers. She felt desperately depressed.

Ojas was in front. Rocky and the little Molly sat behind. Forest was right at the back, with his eyes shut.

"I'm hungry for some meditation," he said, taking his glasses off. "All this time travel is screwing my head up so, man, I'm just gonna step out for a while, if that's okay with you. Hey, Rocky, watch the puppy, would ya? Call me if you need me." With that, he crossed his legs and shut his eyes.

"We'd better get some food for everyone," said Molly, talking on autopilot. "How, though, I don't know. I wouldn't know where to get food for Amrit." She tried not to cry. She wanted someone else to take control of the situation for a while.

"Leave the food to me," said Ojas, seeing her distress. He wiggled his right foot under Amrit's right ear so that she started walking, and added encouragingly, "You know, Mollee, Ganesh, the elephant god, may be looking down favorably on us." Molly shrugged. Ojas continued. "I really think so. And also, Mollee, I have something up my sleeve that is going to help us."

"You do?" Molly buried her face in her knees.

"Yes, but you have to promise not to be cross with me?"

Molly said nothing. She felt so miserable that nothing anyone did mattered to her now. She was consumed by the thought of Petula and her other selves stuck in the past with Waqt. She was drowning in fear and apprehension and sadness. And the scariest feeling, which sucked every other feeling toward it, was the huge gaping hole that was there because Petula had gone. Her Petula was gone. She swallowed a lump in her throat.

"*Agit!*" Ojas urged Amrit to walk on past a billboard advertising men's shirts. He glanced around them to see that no one on the ground was watching. Then, shiftily, he drew a shiny, hooped object from his sleeve.

"I took this from the Maharaja of Jaipur in 1870," he said, holding it out to Molly. "It is one of his ankle bracelets. I think in Jaipur in these modern days it will be considered a very extra-precious item!"

Molly looked up.

"Wow!" exclaimed Rocky, making the puppy in his arms jump and lick his chin. "That thing is studded with gems!"

"Exactly," agreed Ojas. "I thought we might need some paying power at some point. I decided that if the maharaja was wide awake, he would *definitely* say that we should take his ankle bracelet to help us defeat Waqt. It is all in a good cause, don't you think?"

Molly hid her face and cupped her knees with her arms. A terrible gloom was settling over her. A gloom that said she had reached a dead end. Even the bracelet couldn't help lift this sadness.

"Well done, Ojas," she said flatly.

"You must not be so sad, Mollee," Ojas said. "I know why you are sad and you are giving up hope, but there is something you don't know that you should."

Evening traffic puttered past. A man on a motor-bike, with a friend riding pillion, lobbed a packet of colored ink at another man who was speeding past them. Pink dye splattered across the back of his white jacket. "Good shot!" Ojas laughed.

"What should she know?" asked Rocky.

"Ah, yes. Well, you see, Jaipur is a very interesting town."

"Yes."

"You see it over there—we are heading toward its center now. Oh, my goodness, that whole family is orange with paint!"

"Yes. So what should we know?" Rocky pressed.

"It just so happens that in my time—in 1870—Jaipur was famous, very famous." A red motorbike zoomed past, and Ojas clapped his hands. "Now that is a beautiful beast!"

"For what, Ojas?" Rocky prodded impatiently. "What was it famous for?"

"Ah, yes. It was famous for its precious stones. The greatest of gem craftsmen lived and worked here. Their work was some of the best in India. It has struck me that perhaps these craftsmen's descendants are still cutting gems and making jewelry."

Molly raised her head.

"You mean that this town has lots of people who own precious gems?"

"If it is like it used to be—yes. There will be workshops that make jewelry from precious stones and shops that sell it."

"And you think that we might be able to find some time-travel crystals?" Suddenly, hope was on the horizon.

"I do. Yes."

Molly grinned and hugged Ojas. "Brilliant, Ojas, you're *brilliant.* I'm so glad you're here, Ojas. Isn't he clever, Rocky?"

"Hey, keep on this side of the road!" said Rocky.

And so Amrit plodded on. Ojas smiled and touched

his pocket. In it was the *other* ankle bracelet he'd taken from the hypnotized maharaja. It made him feel good. That bracelet meant that he'd never have to pickpocket again.

Back in 1870, it was ten o'clock in the morning.

Waqt was relaxing on a purple silk chaise longue in his silver-walled royal suite at the Amber Palace. Safe by his side was his velvet sack of crystals. Both his feet were up on padded stools. A small Indian woman massaged his right heel while another buffed his giant toenails. He let out a tired sigh and turned the page of his book. There was a knock at the door.

"Enter!"

Zackya stepped gingerly into the chamber.

"So," said Waqt, not bothering to look up, "did you get her?"

Twitching with excitement, Zackya said, "No, Your Highness, but I did get *these.*" He opened his hands to show Waqt Molly's red and green crystals. Waqt merely ran his finger down the page of his book as if still reading. He didn't look up. Undeterred, Zackya drove on. "And *this,* Your Highness!" He clicked his fingers. A servant entered the room, pulling Petula on a lead. Her claws scraped the floor as she refused to walk.

"You know, don't you, Zackya, that I'm *already* furious

with you?" growled Waqt, turning a page and not looking up. "I still had character tests for the six-year-old Molly. And she *might* have drawn some more stycrals from the earth for me . . . not that any of the older Mollys seem to magnetize them. . . . But that's peside the boint. The point is that because of *you*, she's gone. You aren't tasting my wime are you, Yackza?"

"N-n-no, sahib."

"If I am not tismaken, I can hear a dog."

"Yes, Your Highness."

"And what," said Waqt, in a slow, threatening tone, "is the point of daking the tog?"

"She will come back for the dog, Your Highness!"

Waqt raised his bloodshot eyes. "You fupid stool," he hissed hatefully. "You never did know how to play games. I *already* have bait for her. She will come back to save herselves! This is the second time you have stolen this animal. It is obvious that you want the dog for *yourself*! Guard! Take that animal and *kill it*!"

A tall, stiff man stepped out from the corner of the room, seized Petula, and removed her. Zackya looked nervously after her, waiting for the door to shut to obliterate the sound of Petula's barks, before he continued.

"And . . . and I have these crystals that she stole from you, Your Highness!"

A book came whizzing past his head, batting his ear as it went, and the tiny Indian women scurried toward the wall like two animals sheltering from lightning. Waqt got to his feet.

"YOU INADEQUATE IDIOT!" he exploded. "YOU'VE COMPLETELY RUINED THE GAME. NOW SHE IS STUCK IN THE FUTURE. YET AGAIN YOU—**YOU YACKZA**, *YOU BLITHERING FOOL FROM THE BOTTOM OF THE CESSPIT*—HAVE FUINED MY RUN. AAARGH!" Waqt hurled the two stools through the air. Zackya dodged them as if he were a moving duck in a fairground arcade.

"AAAAAAAAAARGH!" Waqt's yell filled the room, making the windows rattle. And then, as quickly as his temper had exploded, it stopped. For a moment he looked blank, then he observed, "She may well be lost in the future, but I suppose this will show us how good she is. Hmmm, yes, this will be interesting. *If* she is as good as I was when I learned the hypnotic arts, she will return. And we will leave a few clues for her. Clues to lead her to her death. You have done well, Yackza, my little rockcoach. No insecticide for you today." Then he said to the other guard, "Dollow the fog. When it is dead, take its body and wrap it up for a Ganges River burial." He picked at his eyebrow. "I'm tired of this observatory palace. Tomorrow I would like to spend the night at the Bobenoi Palace in Jaipur itself. There, the amenities are better." He looked at his toenails and scowled. "It's impossible to get a good pedicure these days. Zackya, get rid of them."

Zackya clapped his hands and bossily shooed the women away. When they'd gone, he knelt down to grovel at Waqt's feet.

"You are always so right," he simpered. "You have such style, Your Highness, such wisdom."

Traveling into modern Jaipur by elephant was quite an experience. Rocky sat right behind Ojas and explained how the flow of traffic worked. Amrit was as calm and as coolheaded as the camels and buffalo beside her, even when a paint bomb hit her side. Lots of people stared up at them, and one tanned couple with packs on their backs even took advantage of Amrit stopping at a traffic light.

"Excuse me," they asked Ojas, "but eez eet possible to book you and your elephant for a tour of zee city tomorrow?"

"I am sorry," Ojas apologized charmingly. "I would love to, but tomorrow I will be busy time traveling."

The tourists' eyes widened. They opened their phrase book to see what "time traveling" could really mean.

"You're optimistic," Molly observed.

"I find that is the best way to be," Ojas replied.

The streets became busier and more crowded. The roads and walls of buildings were all colors of the rainbow where splattered paint had dried, and the ground was stained with red marks from paan chewers spitting out their betel-nut leaves.

"I think Holi is nearly over," said Ojas. Amrit took them down the street, past the arcades of the bazaar, and Molly scrutinized the shop windows. Although many were selling leather sandals or cooking implements, most were selling jewelry. They passed a marketplace where men sat on the ground burning silver rope, collecting the silver that dripped off it in little piles. Flower sellers sat cross-legged in high stalls, piercing orange and yellow flowers with needles and threading them onto strings to make marigold and frangipani chains.

On the right-hand side the shops were beginning to look more special. Then something caught Molly's eye. "Look!" she said.

Farther up the road was a wide shop with glass-paneled doors along its front. Net curtains hid the interior of the shop from view. The sign above was very smart, painted in gold and red with curly letters.

THE RUBY KINGDOM

"You stay out here with Amrit and the puppy and Forest," suggested Molly. "I'll take little Molly and Rocky inside with me and see if I can find some time crystals."

"Yes, Mollee. I will look after the Man of Trees," agreed Ojas, looking over his shoulder at Forest, who was snoring. "Here is the bracelet, Rocky."

"And we'll get lots of money, too," said Molly, "so that we can get Amrit some food."

"Oh yes, Mollee, she is very hungry." Amrit bent down so that Molly, Rocky, and little Molly could climb down.

"So, what does an elephant like to eat?" Molly asked as Amrit batted her long eyelashes at her.

"Palm leaves, bamboo leaves, sugarcane stalks, bananas, rice, cakes, sweet dumplings and always *gur*."

"*Gur?*"

"*Gur* is unrefined molasses. Elephants love *gur*."

Molly nodded. "One *gur* and chips coming up."

Twenty-five

Molly knocked at the glass shop door. Eventually a man with a silky mustache pulled the net curtain aside.

"Can we come in, please?" Molly asked, mouthing the words very precisely so that he might read her lips.

The shopkeeper glanced at Amrit, who stood in the street behind, and then tapped his watch and shook his head. Molly prodded Rocky, who quickly revealed the antique bracelet. The shopkeeper's eyebrows did a little dance on his forehead; he said something to someone inside and then pointed to the side of the building.

At the side of the shop was a passage. This had a heavy metal gate and a big lock.

A ragged man sat on the floor beside the gate with a

bowl by his legs. One of his eyes was covered with a patch; the other was white, shrouded in cataract. The bowl was full of money. Molly reached in her pocket and put an 1870 coin into it.

"I'm sure the shopkeeper here will give you something for that," she said, hoping he understood English. "I haven't got any up-to-date money."

At the side of the shop a double-chinned security guard was waiting. He ushered them under an arch into a tiny lobby with green velvet seats.

The shop's walls were lined with glass cabinets filled with antique Indian objects: a gold chess set with the king and queen pieces on elephants and the pawns all men in turbans on camels; a silver ornamental ship decorated with filigree designs; a long snake made with gold links; a marble egg with colored stones inlaid in delicate patterns. There were shelves of black velvet boards from which hung fabulous necklaces made of diamonds and gems and pearls. In the middle of the room were glass-topped display cases full of rings and bracelets and precious stones.

And in the middle of the room stood the shopkeeper, in brown trousers and a crisp white shirt. He looked expectant. He indicated that the security guard could go.

"Good evening," he said. "So you have something

you would like me to see."

Molly was wondering whether she ought to hypnotize him. He looked kind-natured. But it was getting late and she didn't have time to make friends. He'd never believe in time travel, so to speed things along she smiled at him, and as soon as his eyes met hers she sent out a keen eye beam. The man stumbled backward and then caught his balance. When, shakily, he looked up, his eyes had glazed over and the girl in front of him seemed very important indeed.

"Well done," she said. "Now, Mr. um . . . what is your name?"

"Mr. Chengelpet," said the shopkeeper.

"Well, you, Mr. Chengelpet, are now completely under my command. I am going to explain something that I need and I want you to believe me completely. Then I want you to see whether you can help me."

The mild-faced man smiled. And so Molly began. She told him all about the crystals and time travel and she asked him whether he had any idea what the green and red crystals could be.

"I am—not sure—" the man said cooperatively. "I have—some crystals that—I could show—you that are of—these colors. Green emeralds—red rubies, garnets and—bloodstones. They are—in my safe in—the back room. They are—old gems that—my great-grandfather

246

bought. My—father wouldn't sell them—and neither will—I. They are—very—special."

Molly's eyes lit up.

"Okay, they sound good." She shot a look at Rocky, who stood beside the small Molly making sure she didn't break anything. "Show us them, please."

The man led them all through a carved door and down a short flight of steps into a small, cluttered, windowless office. It had two large safes at the back of the room and a desk with chairs on either side of it. The desk was covered in trays full of important-looking papers, with scales and weights and an assortment of magnifying glasses. While Mr. Chengelpet fiddled with one of the dials on the safe, Molly sat in a chair and looked at the framed family photographs of him and his wife and two small boys.

"I have—these red—gems," he said, pulling leather boxes out of the safe and opening them.

"Cor! Those are nice!" said the little Molly.

Unsure, the older Molly picked up a gem. It was tiny and, what was more, when she shut her eyes she could feel it had no power to it.

"What sort of stone is it?" she asked.

"A—ruby. That one—is *big*—but this one—is even—*bigger.*" The jeweler unlaced a small suede pouch, prized out a pea-sized ruby, and passed it to her.

Molly held it hopefully, but again there was no power to it. Her heart sank. Rocky looked inquiringly at her. She shook her head.

"The red gem that I used before was eight times bigger than this."

"I cannot help—you with—a ruby—that big," said Mr. Chengelpet. "There are big ones—like the eighteen-thousand-carat—*Heracles*—in Thailand. The ruby—I have—shown you is, by all standards, big—I—won't sell it, because—it is so—rare and large."

"Looks titchy to me," said the little Molly.

"Hey, shhh, Molly," said Rocky. "Big Molly's trying to concentrate."

Molly wondered whether the time-travel crystals were amazing rubies or different gems completely.

"Do you have any other red crystals?"

"I have these gems—they are—tourmaline—and these—pieces of topaz," declared the shopkeeper. The beautiful red stones he handed her were completely life-less, too.

Molly felt frantic desperation rising up inside her. "What about green crystals?"

"Some—emeralds—yes. I have some—very fine—emeralds that I rarely show—anyone!—And some—green sapphires and—green opals." Molly plucked up some optimism and watched as more gem-laden trays came out of the fat safes. Inside these were more small crystals.

"Ooooh, those are really pretty," said the little Molly, unable to contain herself.

Molly touched the small gemstones. One by one, her finger passed over them. All were beautiful, but none held any power.

"This is useless!" she whispered to Rocky. Then, just as she leaned forward to push the trays away, the little Molly exclaimed, "Uuurgh! Look at that horrid dirty one at the back!"

All eyes fell upon a lychee-sized muddy green crystal lying camouflaged on the faded velvet. It looked very shoddy, with a strange scar the shape a boomerang along the side of it.

"What's this?" Molly asked, picking it up. She shut her eyes and before she even concentrated on the crystal she noticed a current of energy coming from it.

"I'm not sure. It's an—odd stone. A form of quartz—perhaps. Not precious, but odd. That is—why I keep it."

Molly nodded to Rocky. He pulled the bracelet out from his sleeve.

"What do you think of this?" he asked.

The jeweler waggled his head and took the heavy object in his hand. He turned it over and in a hypnotized way admired the blue sapphires and white pearls that were studded into it.

"This—is a—marvelous example of—jewelry from the—1750s. I have—seen—pieces like—this only in—the museum collections."

So the ankle bracelet was even older than they had thought.

"Would you like to buy it? What is the right price?"

"Two million rupees. If I wanted to—make some profit—I would buy it—for one and a half million—rupees."

"Do you know what that is in pounds or dollars?"

"Eighteen thousand—pounds, or thirty-five—thousand dollars."

"That's lots of money!" exclaimed the small Molly.

"And how much would you sell that scarred green stone for?"

"That dirty green stone?" the small Molly piped up. "Don't buy *that* stone!"

"Shh, Molly."

"It is not—really—for sale," the jeweler continued, ignoring the little girl, "because I like it—very much, I have—never thought—about its price. I don't think—it is—very sellable."

"Hmm." Molly picked up the scarred crystal. "All right then, the deal is this: We will sell you this ankle bracelet for seven hundred thousand rupees, so you are getting it really cheap, and in return you will give us your scarred crystal."

The shopkeeper nodded, his head bobbing like the branch of a tree in a breeze. Molly pushed the ankle bracelet toward him and put the muddy green crystal in her pocket.

"That is a really bad deal," muttered the younger Molly and, exasperated by the apparent stupidity of her companions, she turned her back and stomped up the steps of the office.

"Do you have the rupees here?" Rocky asked.

"Of—course." Mr. Chengelpet turned and opened a briefcase. He took out fourteen wads of bank notes, each secured with an elastic band. Rocky took them and put them in Molly's bag. He indicated to Molly that they should get going.

"It was very nice doing business with you," said Molly, once they were back in the cozy shop. "In a minute I will bring you out of your trance. You will think that you just made a deal with a French man, who has gone now, who sold you the ankle bracelet for such a good price that you gave him your green crystal. You will *forget* that we had anything to do with the ankle bracelet. Instead, you'll think that we are just some nice kids who wanted to look around your shop."

"And once we're gone, you'll forget about us and the elephant outside," added Rocky.

Molly clapped her hands. Mr. Chengelpet woke up. It took a few seconds for him to rejig his thoughts so that Molly and Rocky's instructions sank in, and then he began to look really happy.

"Oh, children, children, it's been lovely having you here," he said, "but I really must be going home. I have a bit of celebrating to do!"

"A birthday?" asked Molly.

"Oh, no. I have just had an extremely good day of business!"

"Yes, you *have!*" said the little Molly. Rocky tugged at her to be quiet.

Molly felt the crystal in her pocket and hoped that she hadn't been imagining its worth.

"I hope you and your sons have a great evening!" she said.

"How did you know I had sons?" The man laughed, showing them to the door.

Ojas was waiting for them outside. People were crowding around Amrit, who was dozily resting, her back legs crossed like those of a person leaning against a fence.

They pushed the small Molly up onto her.

"That was the worst shopping I ever saw," she said

disgustedly once they were all up.

Ojas was bursting with curiosity. "Did you get what you needed?"

"I hope so," said Molly. "Well, I got part of it—this green crystal. Look."

"Not a red crystal?"

"No."

"So you can only go backward in time?" Ojas whispered. "Still, if you go back to the right place, you can find a red crystal there, don't you think?"

"Exactly—as long as this one works. I'll try it in a minute. It has a different feeling from the ones before. But I've got some hope now. Thank you, Ojas. It was really nice of you to give us the bracelet. You could have kept it for yourself."

"That's my pleasure!"

"I don't think we should try the crystal now, Molly," said Rocky. "We've got to have a break. We need some sleep and a good meal before we face Waqt again."

"And food for Amrit." Ojas added, backing the elephant in her parking space.

"I suppose you're right," said Molly. "There's tons of money in my pocket now. We can go to the smartest hotel in town. They'll be able to find her something to eat."

"If you can pay, they will surely find." Ojas called

down to a man below. The old fellow pointed toward the center of Jaipur and said something in Hindi.

"The best hotel in town is in what used to be a palace!" Ojas exclaimed. "This should be very, very nice," he added, waggling his head from side to side in the typical Indian way.

Twenty-Six

The Bobenoi Palace sat in the middle of Jaipur. It was a small, beautifully kept palace belonging to a very rich Indian family. As soon as word reached them that Waqt was making his way there, the father of the household had horses harnessed and his wife arranged for picnics to be hurriedly made. Waqt's temper was legendary, as was his power, and the family had no desire to meet him. Taking only the basics for travel, they, their six children, and their helpers piled into their biggest carriages and set off for a country house in the hills.

When Waqt arrived, there was no one in residence. But the servants in the palace welcomed him. They moved furniture out of the high-ceilinged drawing room and put a large bed in it so that he didn't have to go to the low rooms upstairs to sleep. They emptied the pond of goldfish, cleaned it thoroughly, and prepared to bring buckets and buckets of hot water out to it should Waqt want a bath.

The servants watched as two skinny, messy-haired girls, aged about ten and three and looking like sisters, got down from an elephant and went inside. One of them carried a baby. There was no sign of their mother.

Waqt, carrying his velvet sack of crystals, led his captives through the hall and out into the ornamental gardens. He ordered that a cushion and rugs be brought outside. Soon he was reclining lazily, having a betel-nut leaf rolled for him. He popped the paan into his mouth, patted his bag of crystals, and eyed his trophies. Then he picked up his notebook and clicked his fingers. "Three-year-old Molly, wake up!" The small child came to.

In her trance, she'd registered the swing at the bottom of the palace gardens. She blinked and spotted it again. And immediately sprang up to run down the lawn.

"COME BACK HERE!" Waqt yelled. But the little Molly didn't hear him. The whole of her mind was filled with the idea of the swing. "Oh, I give up," said Waqt in disgust. He turned to the other Molly.

"Ten-year-old Molly! Awaken and remember!"

The ten-year-old Molly was now completely aware of her surroundings. The last time she'd been allowed out of her trance she'd been at the Red Fort, being tested. She'd been very confused then, but now she felt clearheaded. For, since then, she'd absorbed their journey and what had happened. Molly had worked out some basic things.

The first was that she'd been hypnotized, the second that they were in India, the third that they'd traveled backward in time. She knew that the crystals around the maharaja's neck were for time traveling. She'd deduced that the small girl and the baby with her were both herself. And she was sure that the maharaja was bad and that the big girl who looked like her, who'd appeared by the fire and taken the six-year-old, was on her side. For she remembered as a six-year-old being saved by the older girl and being taken to an elephant and being looked after. Molly knew that she must help this older Molly if she possibly could.

"Right," said Waqt, stretching his legs out, "today I want to find out how good your hypnotic skills were before you found out about hypnotism. When the baby Waqta is grown, I want to teach her, so today I'll practice on you." Molly stared at the three-year-old dangling from the swing. "In a minute you will look into my eyes," said Waqt, "and when you do, you will try to protect yourself from the strong hypnotic look that I give you. Look up."

Molly reran in her head what Waqt had just said. *". . . I want to find out how good your hypnotic skills were before you found out about hypnotism . . ."* This sounded as though one day she would know a lot about hypnotism. Was the older girl a brilliant hypnotist? Was that girl her future? Molly looked at the giant and was reminded of all the nasty people she'd met in her life: Miss Adderstone, Edna, and Mrs. Toadley, her mean teacher at school. Molly was often getting into trouble with her, and the way she dealt with it was to let her mind float away as though she were dreaming. So this is exactly what she did now. When she looked up into the giant's eyes it was as if the eyes in her skull didn't belong to her. She felt herself looking as if from behind them, at a safe distance. The maharaja's outline was blurred.

"Look into my eyes!" Waqt's voice sounded as though it were coming up a drainpipe.

Molly held herself in this suspended state, not letting herself properly interact. Her technique proved very successful. For as Waqt stared at the girl, he found that her eyes weren't engaging. He couldn't penetrate the pupils. They were shielded. How she'd done this, he wasn't sure. Part of him was admiring and full of excitement for his adopted baby's future. The other part of him was uneasy, for how would he ever be able to put this girl back into a trance? Then he relaxed. He could always go ten minutes back in time and sort it out. Anyway, he concluded, she wasn't a threat, even unhypnotized—he'd just have her guarded. So that she didn't leave any big clues for the older Molly, he would keep her blindfolded.

And so the ten-year-old found, to her great surprise, that Waqt was no longer interested in keeping her in a trance. Cautiously she let herself come down from her cloud. But before she had an opportunity to look at her surroundings, she found a blindfold being tied over her.

This is why ten-year-old Molly never saw how beautiful the Bobenoi Palace was. But she could taste, smell, feel, and hear.

Blindfolded, she ate a delicious Indian lunch and listened to the birds singing. She heard soothing Indian music and the three-year-old telling the maharaja that she wanted some sweets. As she sat with her pink blotchy legs stretched out in front of her it struck her that, apart from not having her friend Rocky and Mrs. Trinklebury to talk to, this place was pretty good—better than the orphanage. The only problem was the mad maharaja and not knowing his plans. She wondered how long she'd have to wear the blindfold. She wondered where the older Molly was. She might appear out of thin air again soon and save her and the three-year-old and the baby. Perhaps she needed help. Molly felt she had never been much use to anyone so far in her life. She set her mind to thinking how she could help the older girl.

In the year 2000 the best hotel in Jaipur was the Bobenoi Palace Hotel. It hadn't always been a hotel. It had once belonged to a smart Indian family.

Ojas steered Amrit to a pretty, blossom-filled courtyard and everyone dismounted.

"I wish I hadn't swallowed that purple capsule," Molly said quietly to Rocky and Forest as they straightened their clothes. "I don't like the way Zackya and Waqt can track me. They could pop up any moment. But we don't know where they are. They could be anywhere. I mean, how are we going to ever track *them*?"

"Waqt won't be able to resist teasing you," said Rocky. "I bet he'll leave some sort of clue. He likes playing with you, Molly. As soon as we go back to 1870, we'll find clues. As soon as you're back in the same time zone as the younger Mollys, and there isn't the memory-lag thing, I'm sure you'll remember exactly where they went—and where they are."

"But I've only got this green crystal. I can only go one way—*back* in time. *I* might get stuck back there."

"Not if you get a red crystal once you're there."

"What if I don't?"

"Well, then, you're stuck as a duck in muck," said Forest.

"Forest!" said Rocky. "That is not what you should have just said."

"Er, sorry, man." Rocky put his hand on Molly's shoulder. "Forget it for now. We're all tired; let's just get a good night's sleep."

And so, leaving the others with Amrit, Molly and Rocky stepped up to the ornate entrance of the Bobenoi Palace Hotel. A huge Sikh with a turban and a bushy mustache emerged, looking more like a warrior than a doorman. Molly covered her scaly face with a scarf. The man smiled and bowed deeply. Molly bowed.

"Namaskar."

Inside, the hotel was cool and peaceful and very fine, with a brown and white marble checkered floor and a high ceiling. Some Japanese tourists sat around a glass table looking reverently at a heavy antique book with signatures in it. It seemed to be some sort of visitors' book. An Indian woman in a sari that matched the bronze columns around her was standing behind a desk.

"Welcome to the Bobenoi Palace Hotel." She smiled. "Can I help you?"

Molly's experience was that adults never did business with children, and she'd expected a tricky hotel receptionist; so she was taken aback by the woman's helpfulness.

"We're not with an adult," she said. "Well, we are but he's not like a normal adult. I mean, he's not mental or anything, he's just . . . um . . . outside meditating on an elephant. . . ."

Rocky shot Molly a have-you-lost-your-marbles look.

The woman smiled. "What can I do for you?"

"We'd like to book three rooms, please," said Rocky. "We can pay up front. And we've got a hungry elephant that needs a bed, too . . . obviously not in the hotel, but might you have a place in the garden where she could sleep . . . ? The most urgent thing is that she's very hungry. We can pay what you like for getting her some food . . . palm leaves, that sort of thing. I don't suppose you keep them in the kitchen?" he added weakly.

"Well, what a tall order!" said the lady, whose teeth were like two rows of shiny pearls in her lovely smiling face. Molly and Rocky were amazed by how easygoing she was.

"Our motto here is, 'Where we can help, we will, and where we *can't*, we will, too.' See, there it is, written on the wall." She pointed to a notice.

> *Where we can help*
> *we will,*
> *and where we can't*
> *we will too.*

"Oh!" said Molly. "So is this a case where you can't help but you will nevertheless try—or where you *can* help, so you definitely will?"

"Oh, indeed we can help! We *love* having elephants to stay. It is *our* privilege. Thank you for choosing us! Your elephant will bring us all sorts of good luck!"

"Wow—well, that's settled then," said Molly. She was amazed. She couldn't imagine the hotel in Briersville accepting an elephant as a guest.

For ten minutes the lady made some phone calls and then apparently everything was under way.

"The bellboy is telling your friends to walk the elephant through to the gardens and down to the bottom where the cottages are. I will meet you down there and show you your rooms. Your elephant's supper is on the way."

And so they stepped out.

263

The hotel's gardens were very exotic, with green parrots flapping about over the lawns and fawn monkeys hopping around in the trees. There was a large, turquoise swimming pool with statues of elephants that spouted fountains of water from their trunks. There was a bowling green and a temple-like place for yoga and a beautiful garden restaurant where people were eating under red patterned gazebos. They pointed in delight at Amrit as she plodded behind Ojas across the grass and at the puppy Petula who tripped as she tried to keep up. Ojas led Amrit to a frangipani tree, where a porter said she could be tethered.

The cottage rooms were very fine, with four-poster beds draped with colored silk. The baths were sunken, with steps down into them, and the outdoor showers were surrounded by bougainvillea-covered walls and roofed with jungly leaves. A sign said:

> *Please keep the windows shut while you are out of the room.*

Molly put the new crystal very carefully down in a golden bowl on the table and threw herself onto a bed.

Little Molly did the same. Both were exhausted.

"How about this? Nice, isn't it?"

"It's like a fairy-tale place," said the six-year-old.

"Hey, this is grrrrreat," said Forest. Then, opening the minibar and pouring himself a pineapple juice, he added, "Molly, I've been meditatin' on what sorta yoga poses you need to get Zackya's silicon chips out of ya. There's a few potions I know that will help shift that purple pill from your insides. I'm gonna talk to the chef about the ingredients. You're gonna have a 'shift the purple pill' supper."

"I was thinking of having a ketchup sandwich and a glass of concentrated orange squash," Molly admitted.

"No delicacies like that tonight. If you wanna slosh that thing out, you have to eat what I say."

Later that evening, as the puppy gnawed on a bone, Molly began chewing on a tough and chewy, bitter-tasting stick. A tray of decanters containing dark liquids lay beside her.

The little Molly was put to bed and Ojas settled down in the room he was sharing with Rocky. He was mesmerized by the television. Rocky left him sitting wide-eyed watching a colorful Bollywood movie. Molly meanwhile was given a very intense yoga lesson from Forest. Rocky laughed as Forest twisted and prodded

Molly's body into circuslike contortions.

"You'll be glad you did this," Forest said as Molly stood on her head with her legs crossed. "This combination of treatments always works. It flushes everything out. So tomorrow you won't have that trackin' pip inside you. Just make sure that in the morning you can get to the bathroom quick."

"Great. Thanks," Molly said as her stomach gurgled. "I hope you're right."

That night, with a fan blowing in the room, Molly slept badly. She tossed and turned as her whirling mind tackled the problems she faced.

She dreamed she'd turned into a bent old woman, scaly and dry from time travel. In the dream she was trudging through a muddy wood, following a trail of children's footprints. There were paw-prints alongside them and yeti-sized tracks led the way. In the nightmare, Molly was led deeper and deeper into the forest. As she walked the trees about her became thicker and thicker until the wood was pitch dark and she could no longer see the ground. And then the mud began to gurgle and move and swallow her up. As she sank down into it she saw the green, scarred crystal disappearing into slime.

Molly woke up, frightened and shivering and terrified that she had lost the scarred stone. She got up and found it at once, lying in the golden bowl on the table. Relieved, but still reeling from the nightmare, she picked it up and went to get a drink of water. In the mirrored bathroom she switched on the light and stared at her reflection. It looked as though a Bollywood makeup artist had started work on her face, covering her cheeks in scales, and then had gone for a tea break. But her face hardly bothered her now. She'd sacrifice her whole body to scales if the reward was getting Petula and her younger selves back. And that, she realized, was the price she might have to pay.

Molly went back to bed, putting the scarred stone under her pillow with her clear crystal. In the darkness she thought again about why Waqt wanted to adopt her baby self and not an older Molly. She thought again of her mother, Lucy, and how she'd seemed so gloomy and disappointed in Molly.

Feeling sad and useless, Molly slipped into a deep, dreamless sleep.

At seven o'clock, her stomach woke her up.

She had a terrible cramp. It felt as if there were monsters inside her, gripping and pinching her intestines. She flew out of bed and spent the next hour in the bathroom.

"I'll get you, Forest!" she shouted from in there.

However, by the time she came out, she felt fantastic. And the purple capsule was now gone. Flushed away, shooting down the sewage pipes of Jaipur.

Forest had not fared so well. After a dawn shower, he'd forgotten to shut his bathroom door. As a result, while he'd been off at the yoga platform, saluting the rising sun, monkeys had let themselves into his bedroom. When he got back, his room looked as if a bomb planted on his breakfast tray had exploded. Food was everywhere. The monkeys hadn't *quietly* helped themselves to the breakfast—they'd decided to play catch with it or something, because the windows were splattered with green curry, and three fried eggs were stuck to the ceiling. And the ten different fruit juices that Forest had lavishly ordered now dripped down the walls and dribbled through the canopy of the four-poster bed. Pillows had been ripped apart so that feathers floated about, and the books in the room had been torn up. The bathroom was even more of a disaster. The monkeys had helped themselves to toothpaste and bubble bath, and the floor was all wet and slippery from their splashing around in the toilet, which was now blocked with two rolls of paper. A third roll had been unraveled and was draped around the place. But Forest's biggest grievance was that the monkeys had popped every single one of his super-duper, specially designed, will-make-you-feel-relaxed pills out of their packet and eaten them.

"Man, those were my herbal remedies, specially prescribed for me by my pressure-point therapist," he moaned.

Outside the cottages things were equally chaotic. Amrit, who was hobbled for the night, tied to the hundred-year-old frangipani tree, had pulled it up from where it was growing beside a wall, and so released herself. The ancient plant lay prostrate and dying on the lawn. Then the elephant had waded into the swimming pool, where she now sat squirting water, happy as could be. Nearby, under parasols, aping the lazy humans they so often saw sunbathing, four brown monkeys sprawled on lounges, soaking up the sun.

Amazingly enough the hotel staff did not seem very bothered by the turn of events. Despite their signs, monkeys often came into the bedrooms. They found Amrit's paddle really funny and kept saying what good luck the hotel would now have. They apologized for suggesting Ojas should tie her to the old frangipani tree, insisting that it was their fault. They decided to let the monkeys move on in their own time, as no one wanted to risk getting bitten.

Rocky had slept well. He'd gone to sleep wondering

why his skin wasn't affected by time travel, but in the morning he'd realized that maybe it was. The area behind his knees was very dry and flaky. The effects of time travel certainly weren't as bad for him as they were for Molly. Maybe it was because *she* was actually *making* the time travel happen, while he was only going along for the ride. Mulling on these thoughts, he finished his breakfast and went to the hotel reception to pay their bill. As he crossed the lawn, the large wad of bank notes in his pocket bumped against his leg. Rocky intended to make sure the hotel wasn't out of pocket from all the damage that Amrit and Forest had caused.

In the hotel foyer, the Japanese tourists were also leaving. They stood by the desk with their wallets out, so for the moment the cashier was busy. Rocky cast his eyes around the room, admiring the splendid domed ceiling. Then his gaze fell upon the antique book that the other guests had been looking at the evening before. Approaching the glass table it lay on, he noticed how battered and charred it was. A label beside it read:

> This was the original Bobenoi Palace Visitors' Book. Please handle carefully, as it was damaged in the fire of 1903 and is very fragile.

Rocky gently tipped the cover open. Inside, the first entry was September 1862. There was a signature in black ink. Rocky turned. The next page held three entries, added in October 1862. At once Rocky wondered about 1870. He wondered if the true Maharaja of Jaipur or the fallen Maharaja of the Red Fort, had ever stayed here, and he delicately leafed through the book through 1863, 1865, 1867, 1868 . . . Among the signatures of foreigners and local dignitaries he saw no names that he knew. Eventually he came to entries for the year 1870. January, February, and then March. Suddenly, there on the yellowing page, in a great curling scrawl, was written:

The Maharaja of Waqt
13th March 1870. How Time Flies! The crystal fountains flow! March, July, August, November! Jaipur, Agra, Udaipur, and on by boat to

The bottom of the page was charred, and so the rest of the sentence was a mystery. But it was enough for Rocky. Quickly he scanned the rest of the book to check whether Waqt had returned, which he hadn't. Then, seeing the counter empty, Rocky bounced over to the receptionist and paid the bill.

Ojas was down by the pool, coaxing Amrit out with a large bunch of bananas. Molly sat down on the grass and watched as Amrit waded out and greedily stuffed the sixty small bananas into her mouth, skin and all. Some, half munched, spilled out onto the ground. Then she playfully knocked the puppy Petula with her trunk. Molly pulled the scarred green crystal out of her pocket and turned it over in her hand.

"Can't we stay here?" little Molly asked, as Forest and Rocky held her hands and led her toward Amrit. Molly knew how she felt, for this was the loveliest place the young Molly had ever been.

Rocky tapped her on the shoulder. "Guess what!" he said.

Molly smiled. "Um, Zackya's been shrunk to the size of a cockroach and he's tap dancing in the hotel kitchen?"

"I've found out something really useful!" As soon as Rocky said this, everyone was listening. "There's an old visitors' book in the hotel!" He told them about the entries and then about Waqt's particular addition. "He says that time is flying and the crystal fountains are flowing."

"What does that mean?" asked Molly.

"Don't ask me. But, listen to this. He says he's been to Jaipur and he's going to Agra and Udaipur and then he's going on a boat somewhere, but that bit was burned off. Then he mentions months. March, July, August, November. He *was* in Jaipur in March, so maybe he's in Agra in July, Udaipur in August, and wherever he's going to on a boat in November!"

"Amazin'," said Forest, "You know, Agra is really close to here. Why don't we just go there, zing back to July 1870, and *ambush* him!"

"Or go back to March 1870 and ambush him right here in the Bobenoi Palace," suggested Rocky.

"Do you think the entry in the book is a trick?" asked Molly.

"Put it like this," considered Rocky. "We've got no other leads. If he wrote in that book without knowing that we'd find it, then we really are one step ahead of him, because we now know where he's going."

"*Pukka!*" exclaimed Ojas, and he began performing a small *puja* prayer ceremony in preparation for their trip.

Then he led Amrit over to a quiet glade. There, with great effort, he, Forest, and Rocky tied the howdah onto her back. Soon everyone was sitting in it. Before the hotel staff noticed them, Molly shut her eyes.

"Good luck," said Rocky.

"So, March 1870, you think?"

"Yes."

"Hang on tight, everyone," Molly said. She held the muddy gem lightly and took herself into a trance. She was really nervous, as it was critical that she land in roughly the same time as her younger selves. If she shot back a hundred years too far, that was it. They were doomed. Trying not to think of this, she concentrated on the scarred crystal. At once she heard a BOOM and felt them lift. They were off, whizzing backward through time. The seasons rushed past. Rain, sun, storms, and winds were momentary flashes. Backward through the elements they flew. But the travel wasn't like before. Molly didn't feel as in control. It was as if the crystals she'd used before were high-tech versions and this one in comparison was rusty and broken. Their movements were jerky. They'd go at only five years a second then they'd suddenly cover *fifty* years in a second. The crystal wasn't in proper working order. But it was at least taking them back.

Molly tried to gauge when to stop, but this crystal moved so erratically that she didn't feel confident of where they were. She looked at the dirty stone and decided it was muddy because it was broken.

* * *

Waqt lay back on his bed, his hands behind his head. A pile of red, green, and clear crystals lay on the quilt beside him. For him these were the best treasure in the world. And he felt good—better than he'd felt for years.

His recent crystal-fountain ceremonies had been excellent. At Jaipur *and* Agra *and* Udaipur, the crystals had flowed from the earth. They'd burst through the rocks, glistening like pomegranate seeds, drawn by the baby Molly Moon. She was the perfect magnet for them. Even the older Mollys seemed to draw the crystals sometimes. He had high hopes for the ceremony in Benares in November—surely the crystal harvest coinciding with Diwali, the Hindu festival of lights, would be auspicious.

On top of this, he'd enjoyed playing his game with the older Molly Moon. It had actually been fun leaving clues for her. Fun! As much fun as hunting! He wondered how many of the clues she would find.

He'd graffitied trees, he'd had flower beds planted so that the shrubs spelled out words. Flags had been made with his whereabouts embroidered on them. He'd even sent some twenty-fifth-century devices over the cities at night, lighting up the dark skies with sentences that told exactly where he was. He'd let the three-year-old Molly remember things. And yet the eleven-year-old hadn't yet turned up. He could always send Zackya with his machine to track her, of course, but that would spoil the game.

He must lure her. Tempt her. Reel her in. Then the trap would snap shut.

Twenty-Seven

Molly decided to stop. Were they in March 1870, or had they traveled too far back? The world materialized around them and at once they were surrounded by water. The puppy yelped as a torrent hit her nose, and she burrowed into the material of Rocky's jacket. Molly had never seen a place so wet. The rain was pelting down and obviously had been for days. The old hotel building was still behind them. But it wasn't a hotel. Now it was a functioning palace with ornamental gardens. The dry ground where they had been standing was so flooded that the water was up to Amrit's knees.

The elephant was delighted and immediately began stamping and splashing. She put her trunk in the water, sucked up a trunkful of it, and happily squirted it up in the air and over her head. It showered down on Ojas's legs.

"NO. Bad girl!" he shouted angrily, jumping down and picking a large banana leaf, which he held over his head as an umbrella.

"Man, she's only havin' some fun!" said Forest from the howdah.

"It won't be fun if she drenches you." Ojas sternly retorted, getting back up. "With monsoon rain like this, where will you get dry if she soaks you? Huh?" He was now dripping.

Molly tucked her legs into the howdah. Even under its cover they still got wet. The canopy above them sagged with water. Ojas poked it with the wooden end of his ankush and the water flooded down the back and down Amrit's bottom.

"Cats and dogs! We will have to push this water out continuously," he commented, "or the canopy will break." The puppy barked at the sky.

"I'm cold!" said little Molly, squeezing Rocky's arm for warmth.

"This isn't March. Is this December weather?" Rocky asked Ojas.

"Oh no, Rocky. This is July or August. Monsoon time."

"Sorry," said Molly. "I misjudged it. This crystal

doesn't work properly."

"Are you getting any memories now that we're near the other you's, Molly?"

Molly nodded, feeling the strange vibrations emanating from her younger selves. She remembered being ten and being let out of her trance by Waqt.

"He's blindfolded the ten-year-old me, though, so that I can't remember seeing where they are. But I can feel them. They're somewhere over there." Molly pointed southwest. "Oh, I wish I were picking up memories of Petula!"

"That's kind of where Udaipur is," said Forest. "But it's quite a ways away. After Udaipur, where did the visitors' book say they were going?"

"On a boat," said Rocky, "but we don't know where to or on which river."

"I do," shouted the six-year-old Molly, evidently delighted by some thought that had struck her. She slapped her knees and bellowed with laughter. "Guess what sort of river they're going to. Guess!"

Everyone looked at the small, scruffy girl suddenly laughing from under the howdah canopy in the rain.

"What's so funny?" asked Forest.

"The name, the name! The name, of course! Guess it!"

Everyone looked blank.

"How do you know the name of the river?" Molly asked.

"I remember!"

"Waqt's let the three-year-old you remember!" said Rocky. "It's a clue."

"The six-year-old remembers the three-year-old Molly's memories, but you've forgotten them," said Forest.

"Why don't you just tell us the name?" asked Molly, slightly embarrassed that this younger version of herself was holding everyone to ransom.

"Oh, she wants to play a game," said Ojas, water dripping down his nose. "So why don't you give us a clue, little Mollee," he coaxed.

"Well, it's what you put on your toast in the mornings," said the six-year-old, clapping her hands with glee.

"Ketchup," said Molly.

"Butter," said Rocky.

"Ghee," guessed Ojas.

"Turnip paste," said Forest.

The rain fell down, making their teeth chatter.

"No!" exclaimed the little Molly.

"Okay, we give up. Just tell us," said Forest.

"No, it's a secret," said the six-year-old.

"Marmalade?"

"Marmite?"

"Baked beans?"

"Egg?"

"Mashed-up Molly," said Molly.

"Cheese?"

"I don't like cheese on toast," said little Molly.

"What *do* you like on toast?" asked Rocky slyly.

"Well, mostly ketchup, if I'm allowed, or butter and jam," admitted the little girl.

"Is the name of the river 'Jam'?" asked Rocky.

"Yes! Yes! Jam! Isn't that the funniest name for a river? Just think of being in a boat on a river of Jam!" She laughed as if it were the funniest joke in the world. Rocky laughed to humor the little girl. Then he turned to Ojas and Forest.

"Ever heard of this river?"

"Well," said Forest, wrinkling his brow, "there is a river called the Yamuna. Some people say Jamuna . . . like jam. It rises in the Himalaya Mountains and runs down through central India. It passes through Agra. Then it joins the Ganges River. And after that, the *very* important, mystical place that it washes past, that I am *sure* Waqt will be interested in, is Benares—the *City of Light*. Yeah, man. That is one off-the-end-of-the-scale place. In our time it's called Varanasi. That crazy dude will definitely want to go *there*."

"Varanasi must be where Waqt's going to be in *November*," said Rocky. "*That's* where he's going by boat."

"Will Waqt have to go back to Agra to get on the Jamuna River?" asked Molly.

"Yeah," said Forest. "I suppose so."

"Well," said Molly, "let's get to Agra. Then we stand a chance of catching up with him."

"Agra is to the east, about one hundred and thirty-five miles away," said Ojas. "I asked the hotel porter. At four miles an hour, and that is a steady pace for an elephant, that will take about hmm. . . ." Ojas was quiet for a moment.

"Thirty-four hours," calculated Rocky. "So what's that? Three days' walking." He paused as Ojas poked his ankush up into the canopy and more water emptied out onto Amrit's bottom. "The way I see it is this: we either go to Agra now, and get there before Waqt does, or we could whiz back and ambush him here in Jaipur, in March, like I said."

"With this crystal," said Molly, "I can't be sure of landing in exactly the right time. This crystal doesn't work very well, remember. It's safer to go to Agra."

"I suppose," said Ojas, prodding Amrit with his foot. "We should get moving, then. Anyway, those children at the window are looking at us. We're in their garden."

And so off they set through this new, watery world.

Amrit waded through the flooded green gardens and under the stone arch to the street. And when they got there, what a sight they beheld!

The road had become a river.

"Everything's soaked!" said Molly.

"This is normal," said Ojas. "The monsoon rains last for ten weeks in this part of India. People are grateful for them because it gets very hot in May and June and July. If there is a bad drought, all the crops fail. Then people starve. So when the heavens open up, everyone is very, very happy indeed."

Ten minutes later the rain stopped. People came out of their houses and got on with their business as if going to school or work by river-road was the most normal thing in the world. Four children splashed happily past, shouting up at Ojas and pointing at the puppy. A tailor ventured out of his premises with a roll of material on his shoulder; a mother pushed two tiny boats, each made out of a halved barrel and containing a small, laughing toddler, down the river-road. A dog paddled past, his tail wagging even as he swam.

Soon they were out in the countryside and on the open road, where the water was shallower. Sun burst through the brooding clouds and, for a while, everyone dried out. They slid down from Amrit and collected their own big umbrella leaves. It wasn't long before the skies blackened once more. The clouds descended as though they wanted to smother the earth, and again it began to rain. The fields on either side were submerged in water, and silver raindrops danced off their gray surfaces. The noise of the rain was cacophonous. It thudded into the pool in the canopy above them. Every so often the skies thundered, a deep rumbling as the elements in the air above grumbled and burped.

"Look," said Ojas. "The rains must be nearly over because those purple flowers are growing. And those yellow ones and those mushrooms. It must be late August."

Molly thought of Petula.

"Molly," she said to her six-year-old self, "do you remember a dog, a black dog, being there when you were with the giant when you were little?" The young girl's face darkened. The eleven-year-old Molly realized that there were probably only a few clear memories in the six-year-old's head from when she was three and traveling with Waqt. Still, she hoped Petula would be one of them.

The little Molly screwed up her face trying to remember things from her short life. "I remember going to a big place with a top like a cloud meringue."

"Sounds like Agra," said Forest.

"And I remember going to a big house in the

middle of a sea and there were lots of purple men all hopping about. And it was raining and the baby got all wet, but there wasn't a dog."

"Sounds like the city of Udaipur. The palace is on a lake."

Suddenly a clever thought struck Molly. If she could remember the ten-year-old's experiences, and the six-year-old could recall the three-year-old's memories, then surely the *ten*-year-old would get memories of being *six*. Her six-year-old self might be able to send a message to her ten-year-old self. It was worth a go. Molly quickly explained her thoughts to the others.

And so they began to teach the six-year-old a rhyme. It wasn't melodic. In fact, it was quite irritating. But it was the sort of rhyme that a six-year-old will sing over and over and over again. It went:

We are coming to rescue you, Mollys,
Rescue you, Mollys,
Rescue you, Mollys.
We are coming to rescue you, Mollys,
And when we come we need your help!

Twenty-eight

Molly and her entourage made their way at an elephant's pace to the town of Agra and the Jamuna River. As Amrit plodded on they sang the rescue rhyme so that it became well and truly ingrained in the six-year-old Molly's mind. And Molly put some other memories there, too. One afternoon, when Forest was asleep and she was walking down the puddle-filled road with little Molly, she made her laugh. She did a funky-chicken act, then a constipated camel dance, and finally a Forest impersonation. When she did the whole lot at once, little Molly was in stitches. Molly knew exactly how to make her younger self giggle. And the nice thing was that after they had settled down to walking again, she was filled with a strange, distorted memory of a big girl called Molly once making her laugh. Some of the details were confused but it was one of her strongest memories and the warm feeling generated by the moment was still intact.

Molly was amazed how that one giggling moment injected so much positive energy into her. She looked at her friends and it struck her how important it was for people to have happy times—for positive feelings of happy times will stay in a person's heart and mind forever.

Waqt sat in his grand barge, sprawled on lavish, tasseled cushions. A very dark Indian man dressed in white was clipping the hair in his ear, catching the remnants that fell in a gold dish. When the man replaced the maharaja's feathered turban, Waqt sat up and clapped his hands.

The ten-year-old Molly was brought before him. He nodded to the guards, and they removed her blindfold.

Molly rubbed her eyes as they adjusted to the light. While she'd been cooped up she'd received all sorts of memories from when she'd been about six. Most of all, she remembered a rhyme that she'd sung over and over. She looked at the giant in front of her and wondered whether the big Molly was going to rescue her now.

Servants came scurrying into the room carrying dishes with silver lids. The food inside them smelled irresistibly delicious.

"Eat! This melicious deal is all for you, Lommy!"

The ten-year-old faltered. Why was the maharaja being so nice? Suspiciously, she began to eat.

At the first mouthful Molly realized what torture was being inflicted upon her. The food was fiery hot with chili. She coughed and reached for a napkin to spit the food into.

"I said, EAT IT!" Molly tried again. She had never tasted anything so hot. Her mouth began to feel like a burning inferno.

"I can't!" she said.

"You will." Waqt's face loomed up close. "You will eat it, or you die," he said, smiling.

So Molly ate. Her mouth went numb. She drank three jugs of water, but still her mouth was a roaring fire.

"Nicey spicy! Spicy nicey!" Waqt taunted. It was torture. And the more she spluttered and drank, the more the cruel giant laughed.

"Do you merember this?" he laughed. "Can you merember this?" was the strange question he kept asking her. Molly didn't know what he meant.

* * *

Molly woke sweating from a late afternoon nap. While she'd been asleep in the howdah, the memories from her younger self had materialized. Waqt's "Do you merember this?" was directed at her *now*. He was talking to her now through her ten-year-old self.

She remembered that eventually she'd eaten the food and gone to the room where the three-year-old and the baby slept. After two hours the feeling had returned to her tongue.

Molly cuddled the puppy Petula and thought how much she smelled like her own Petula. This made her smile, because of course they were the same.

If Petula was alive, perhaps she would remember this cuddle, Molly thought. She plunged her nose into the puppy's velvety fur and shut her eyes.

Twenty-nine

That evening, as the sky turned golden, they arrived in Agra.

"I told you I'd been here," said the six-year-old Molly, pointing. The Taj Mahal was as little Molly had described it—its marble roof, towering on elegant columns, was just like a meringue.

"Awesome, ain't it?" said Forest.

Ojas prodded Amrit to turn right and they proceeded to the docks on the river. The Jamuna River.

It wasn't a sophisticated dock. In fact, it was more of a soggy muddy bank because of the rains. But there was a short wooden landing jetty and some wooden boats were tethered to the shore. Two girls sat on their haunches beside their crop of melons nested in straw. The other side of the river was a bare, grassy flood plain. They all dismounted.

"So," said Ojas, pointing down the gray expanse of river, "Benares, the City of Light, is that way." Molly followed his finger and something bright caught her eye, making her jump.

"What are those things burning?" she asked, stepping toward the river's edge.

For there, beside the jetty, bobbing about in the water, were what looked like handmade dolls, wrapped in white and yellow silk. The dolls' faces were uncovered. And each doll, it was perfectly clear, represented one of her party. There was Forest, Rocky, herself, Ojas, little Molly, and the puppy. Each doll was set alight and the flames licked at their features.

"They're like voodoo dolls!" Molly gasped.

"I don't believe in voodoo," said Rocky, staring with revulsion at the effigies in the water.

"It's a clue," yelped Ojas. "The City of Light is where people go to die. When they are dead, their bodies are wrapped in silk and burned! Waqt has left this clue for you to find, so that you know to go to the City of Light."

"But I don't want to be wrapped up like a birthday present and burned!" shrieked the six-year-old Molly.

"No, no, of course you won't be," Rocky consoled her. "This is just a . . . just a joke."

"A joke? Oh." Satisfied with this answer, the little girl sat down on a rock and began playing with the puppy.

"The guy is seriously sick," said Rocky. "Needs to be put in a top-security loony bin."

Molly looked up the river and spotted a large wooden vessel with a hooped bamboo roof. The prow of the boat was pointed, with a small deck at the front. The long, middle part was totally enclosed, but the back ledge before the stern of the boat was an open, cargo-carrying platform. "Ojas," she said, "can you go and ask that man whether we can hire his boat?" She pulled out her purse full of money from the clothes shopkeeper.

Ojas nodded. "Good idea, Mollee." He put two fingers to his mouth and whistled.

The captain, a swarthy man with a flat, broken nose, poked his head out from under a tarpaulin where he'd been napping.

That was how Molly and her friends found themselves aboard a traditional Indian boat with an elephant.

The captain raised a small grubby sail and they were off. Steering the boat with a tiller oar, he took them away from Agra. Carried on the fast currents of the Jamuna, they headed for the Ganges and Varanasi, the City of Light.

* * *

Days and nights unfurled and rolled along. The river curled under them.

There wasn't much to do on the river. Molly and her friends spent hours watching the world go by: watching birds and the people who lived along the riverbank.

The rains had subsided. Morning and afternoon, they washed the dung off Amrit's end of the boat, and every evening they moored the vessel and all went for a swim. Amrit would lie on her side in the shallows and someone would stand on her and scrub her with a broom. When they all dived in the water, she would immerse herself completely, swimming in the river like a huge hippo.

Mealtimes punctuated the day, with delicious dishes cooked by the captain's mate.

Molly played with the puppy Petula. Although life on the boat was perfect, in a way, all the time, she was tortured by anxiety as she wondered whether her big Petula was being well cared for.

One night Rocky and Molly lay on the deck of the boat, staring at the stars.

"I'm sorry I haven't been able to help you more," Rocky suddenly said.

"What are you talking about?"

"Well, you know, my voice hypnosis hasn't come in very useful."

"That's not your fault. People here don't speak the same language as you. And, anyway, you do help so much, Rocky. You always have the right advice. You found the visitors' book, and you keep us all calm. You're wise, Rocky."

"Yeah, well. But I can't do the really starry action stuff."

"What—you think the starry action stuff is more important than what you do?"

"Well, you know, I'm not exactly Mr. Key-Mover."

"Rocky! You are Mr. Cool-Cucumber-Everyone-Loves-You-and-You-Make-Them-Feel-Good. I'd rather be that than Miss Key-Mover. If your real mother ever found you she would really like you, I know it. You're just so *likable.* You're so calm and reassuring. Rocky, without you, the six-year-old Molly would have been freaking out."

"Really?"

"Yes. She loves you. She loves you more than she loves me!" Molly laughed. "She ought to love me best because I'm *her.* But she doesn't! She loves you best!" Rocky smiled. "You have a special talent for making people feel good. If that isn't something special, I don't know what is. You're going to be a star doctor in our hypnotic hospital when we get home."

"Thanks, Molly."

The next evening, as the sun set, they passed a small white temple on the riverbank. In front of it was an old man whom Ojas was very excited to see. He explained that the man was a legendary saddhu. Both the man's arms stuck straight up in the air and he was standing on one foot. His fingernails were so long that they curled back on themselves. Apparently he'd been in this position for *forty-three years.*

"Is he mad?" asked Molly as the boat drifted past.

"No, he is *devout,*" said Ojas in awe. "He is doing this to show the gods how much he loves them. If he makes this kind of sacrifice, then there is a better chance of him not being born again after he dies. Instead, he will go to heaven."

"Let's hope the gods notice!" Rocky commented drily. "Or he's been stiff as a post all his life for nothing!"

"So Hindus believe that after you die you are born again?" asked Molly.

"Yes," said Ojas. "Born again as a bee or a mosquito or a lovely elephant or a brilliant hypnotist! Depending on how good you have been!"

"Do you believe that?"

hordes of holy people bathing in the river, dipping themselves in it like biscuits being dunked in a river of tea. They did this because they believed that if they dipped themselves into the holiest river in India they would be forgiven their sins and filled with holy spirit.

"YOU SHOULD WORSHIP ME," he called, but his words were carried away on the wind. "Maybe you will," he added quietly. "Yackza!"

As quick as a bad allergic rash, Zackya was by his side.

"Bring me the young Mollys."

Zackya bowed low and soon returned with the hypnotized three-year-old and the blindfolded ten-year-old, who was holding the baby.

"So," said Waqt, taking the child from her. It wriggled in his arms and made a gurgling noise. "Yes. Hmm. You are the one, my little Waqta," he said. "I'll get you a fleet of noper prannies soon—just one more stycral-fountain ceremony and you will have been properly initiated." He glanced at the older girls. "Then it will be over and we can get on with your life." He handed the baby back to the blindfolded Molly.

"They are on the Ganges now, aren't they?" he said to her. "I've received word that they are traveling with an elephant. Ha!"

Molly said nothing. She had lovely memories of

being six and playing with an elephant and a puppy on a boat. The rhyme that she'd sung so much was still etched in her mind.

"Fiercely loyal, I see. That's good." Waqt cracked his knuckles. "It seems that Molly has found herself some trime-tavel stycrals. Cunning! I don't suppose you would fill me in on how?"

Still, the ten-year-old stayed quiet.

"I'm glad to know Waqta will be cunning. You can go," said Waqt, giving up, and they were removed by guards.

"YACKZA!"

"Yes, sahib?"

"The game goes well. Molly Moon has stycrals, so she can follow me. But she's getting a little bit big for her boots. She needs to be shown her place. I want to give her a faste of the tuture. The dead pug—you have prepared it for burial?"

"Yes, sahib," said Zackya, bowing low.

Thirty

The scruffy boat finally arrived at Benares. The green Ganges River swung around a bend and suddenly there it was. Benares, or Varanasi—the holiest city in India. Molly put her antennae out to try to sense where her younger selves were. They were near, somewhere a little way inland.

The captain drove the boat close to the water's edge. There they saw women in saris dipping in the river, men in *lungis* going under the water, and saddhus in loincloths praying. And floating on the Ganges were hundreds of flowers and lit candles—offerings to the gods. Holy cows stood or walked along the steps and platforms of the *ghats* and monkeys hopped from building to building above. They passed a place where bonfires were burning on the shore. Nearby were huge piles of wood to build more fires. The puppy and Amrit sniffed the air. The others sat at the side of the boat looking out.

"Those are funeral pyres," explained Ojas. "Soon you will see a procession."

Sure enough, the next minute a group of people emerged from the streets above the *ghats*. Six of them were carrying a body wrapped in yellow material. They brought it down to the fires at the river's edge and set it down on the shore.

"Burning in fire is a very fine way to go," Ojas went on. "Remember, it is just a body. Dead as a dead insect. It burns and the smoke rises to heaven. A body wrapped in yellow is a man. Women are wrapped in white."

A small boat with seven white clad men rowed out past them and into deeper water. They had a wrapped and weighted body on board. They pushed it into the river, where it floated for a second before sinking.

"Ah, now that body was the body of a very, very holy saddhu or a priest. Only they are allowed to be dropped into the Ganges like that!" Ojas leaned over, dipped a cup into the green water, and drank from it.

"Yuck," said Rocky. "How can you do that? Have you stopped to think what kinds of bacteria are in this river?"

"I don't know what you mean by 'bacteria,'" laughed Ojas, "but I do know that you people have very weak systems. My stomach is like iron. I never get sick."

Then Molly saw something else wrapped in white bandages burning on the water. It was coming toward them, carried on the current.

"And what's that?" she asked Ojas, realizing that the burning parcel was the size of a dog or cat.

Ojas studied the bobbing object. He looked about and his eyes widened. "There's no funeral party with it."

"Are dead pets always burned on the water?" asked Molly.

"This . . ." Ojas found it difficult to find the words. "This is not normal, Mollee."

The small burning dolls that they had seen in Agra flashed through Molly's mind and at once she knew what the burning parcel was.

"It can't be Petula! It can't be!" Molly watched the orange flames curl about the white bandages, blackening them. As the bound body drifted closer, six brown letters painted on its bandages leaped out at her. PETULA, they read. Ojas knelt down and began nodding in prayer.

"That's horrible," Rocky gasped.

Molly's head spun and a terrible misery flooded her. Her skin prickled as sadness sprang through her.

Without Petula, she didn't feel whole. Petula, who'd been by her side, who'd shared her life. To see Petula's body burning on the water now, it didn't seem possible. But it was real. A pain that stabbed at the pit of her heart shot through Molly, making her quake. She heard herself shouting, "YOU MURDERER, WAQT. YOU TWISTED, FOUL MURDERER." Then she crumpled up.

As she lay sobbing, she felt a small wet nose dab at her cheek. It was the puppy Petula and it was as if she were saying, "Don't worry, Molly. I'm still here." Molly hugged the puppy, but she didn't feel better. For she knew that, if ever they got back to the future, this puppy would have to be returned to her correct time. The Petula that Molly knew was dead. Molly buried her face in the puppy's fur.

The boat ferried them up alongside the Benares riverbank until they were away from the burning *ghats*. Molly had never felt so sad. More than ever, she knew that Waqt was perfectly capable of killing the younger Mollys. She sat up and tried to pull herself together. As she did, she realized with sudden horror that while she'd been crying about Petula, the younger Mollys had moved from this time. What was more, the feeling of them was getting fainter and fainter—like characters on a train leaving a station, they were becoming more and more distant. But they weren't on a train. Waqt was carrying her younger selves away, away into the future.

"Waqt's taking the other me's forward in time!" she gasped. "They were here, but he's just taken them *forward*."

"Just *now*?" asked Rocky.

"Yes. It feels like they're months ahead now. They've stopped *months* ahead. And I can't move *forward* in time. This means that we'll have to wait here for *months* just to get into the same time zone as them! What's more, Waqt might move in time *again*. But I don't care. Nothing matters now that Petula's dead." Molly put her head in her hands and massaged her forehead. She was starting to feel really tired, like an exhausted climber stuck on the side of a vast mountain.

"I wish I could help," Forest sympathized. He was quiet for a moment, then he said, "Maybe I can help."

Molly shook her head. She doubted it.

For a while they listened to the sounds of Benares. The hollow chimes of copper temple bells drifted over the water, and wooden bells on cows made a *CLOCK-CLOCK* noise as the animals wandered the *ghats*. Pilgrims chanted, somewhere someone chopped wood, washerwomen chattered, and oars splashed in the river.

"You know, this time traveling has got me thinkin',"

Forest said. "Thinkin' about the years I spent with Buddhist monks. There's this word they have—*kalachakra*. It means 'wheel of time.' A Hindu priest once told me that the Hindu word for 'time' is *kaal*. Hindus also believe that time turns like a wheel and there are scientists who think time goes around in a wheel, too. Interesting, eh?" Everyone watched the shoreline, as if no one was paying attention to Forest. But Molly listened. She wiped her eyes.

"A wheel of time?" she said slowly. "If time *is* a wheel, then that would mean that the end joins the beginning."

"Yeah, but in, like, a big, spacey weird way."

Molly tilted her head as if letting a strange new idea pour into her ear. And then her eyes began to light up.

"So if time *is* like a wheel, and the end of time is joined to the beginning of time, then if I go back in time far enough, back to the beginning of time, and keep going, then I'll automatically travel through to the *end* of time. You're saying all I'd have to do is go backward through time from there. Eventually, I'd go past the year 3000, then 2000, and keep going backward in time until I got to November 1870 and arrived at where Waqt is *now*—"

"That's crazy, Molly," Rocky interrupted, turning around. "You don't *know* that the beginning of time

305

joins on to the end of time. It's a harebrained theory. What if it doesn't? There might not *be* a beginning of time. And then you'll just be stuck somewhere horrible, trillions of years ago. Don't be stupid, Molly."

"I don't know," said Forest. "No one believed that the world was round. It sounds real dumb that the world might be round, like we should all fall off, like bugs fallin' off a ball. Maybe time *is* like a wheel."

Rocky suddenly shouted, "Forest, stop it! It's *really* irresponsible of you to tell Molly that time is like a wheel. No one knows what's at the beginning of time. And you certainly don't!"

"Man, sorry. I was just trying to help."

"I've got a feeling," Molly said suddenly, "that time *is* like a wheel."

Rocky's face darkened. "Molly, don't be stupid. You're not stupid. Don't go by a hunch. We'll wait for the future to come in a normal, human way. Then you get better time-travel crystals. You don't need to time travel backward to get to the future. And, anyway, who knows how that sort of time travel would affect your skin? It might scale up your insides as well as your outsides, Molly. It might age you so much that you die!"

"Rocky," said Molly slowly, "I *have* to try to find a way of chasing Waqt to the future to catch him out before he kills the younger me's."

Molly saw that the boat was almost at the edge of the water and that the captain was set to dock. On shore, a crowd was gathering. Quietly, she reached into her pocket for her muddy green stone.

Rocky saw her hand moving.

"Don't do it, Molly!"

"I'll see you soon," Molly said and, shutting her eyes, she vanished from his time.

Thirty-one

As soon as Molly was reversing through time she
realized what a crazy decision she'd made. Her
task felt as hopeless and impossible as an
attempt to fly across a huge ocean in a tiny microlight
with a lawnmower engine. For the green crystal made
her time travel jerky and it didn't always respond to
her. She demanded that it take her backward through
time as fast as possible. She squeezed it and concentrated on moving into top gear because she knew that
to get to the *beginning of time* she had a giant distance to
travel. But traveling with this crystal felt as if she were
in a rusty old vehicle with a jammed transmission and
a broken accelerator.

She reckoned that she had gone back three hundred
years. And then a ghastly mathematical thought occurred

to her: At this rate, she'd be an old lady before she reached the beginning of time. Molly felt the years flash past and decided she was probably now in about the eleventh century. But this was as fast as she was going to move with this crystal.

She realized that she'd made a dreadful misjudgment. Numb from the news of Petula's death, she hadn't been thinking properly. She felt as if she was traveling at about a hundred years a minute, six thousand years in an hour. In twelve hours she would have gone back . . . Molly did some math in her head . . . seventy-two thousand years—that was all. And she would need to sleep and eat and drink. She hadn't considered that problem. What should she do? Stop and sleep?

Molly couldn't believe what a horrifically stupid mistake she'd made. As she shut her eyes a lesson from long ago wriggled up from the bottom of her mind. She remembered her bad-tempered teacher Mrs. Toadley making the class recite a rhyme about time. The rhyme rang in her head like a horrible teasing song.

Three hundred and fifty thousand years ago,
Humans were first on show,
Sixty-five million years ago, I think,

Dinosaurs became extinct,
Two hundred million years before today,
The dinosaurs first came to play,
Three and a half billion years back,
One-celled life popped out of the sack,
Four and a half billion years ago, it's charted,
The world started,
Fourteen billion years ago, *it's said,*
Time went "BANG" and started her thread.

Molly gulped as she did more sums. Her calculations took a while. At the rate she was traveling, if she did stop to sleep, she'd be lucky to travel ninety-six thousand years a day. It would take her a whole year to travel thirty-five million years back in time. In ten years she'd go back three hundred and fifty million years. That was nowhere near *fourteen billion* years. Molly started to panic and her hands grew very clammy. The world whizzed past her. She had no idea where in time she was now. She squeezed the crystal and implored, "You MUST go faster. You must. You have to or we'll never get to the beginning of time. Please. Please."

Molly understood that she was doomed, and her eyes filled with tears. She knew now that she was going to die somewhere thousands of years away from everyone and everything she loved. She would have to stop, and where she stopped was where she would have to live, forever, until she grew old and died. She realized then that if it was impossible to go to the beginning of time, she should of course stop, as soon as she could, and so she slowly brought herself to a hovering position until she could see that the Ganges River was below her and the shore a yard away.

She stopped and at the same time jumped so that she landed in the mud on the banks of the river. When she looked up she saw there was a man close by. He held a begging bowl and was sitting cross-legged in front of her. He was old and blind. One of his eyes was shut; the other was white with cataracts. As she landed he raised his head. Molly glanced about. Benares was smaller and more primitive. Maybe she was in the first or second century.

Molly collapsed in the mud.

"I can't live here!" she sobbed out loud. "What have I done?" She looked down at the crystal in her hand and turned it over.

"You stupid, lame lump of muck!" she spat at it. Then she glanced out at the river, where the sun's first rays of the day were spreading out like fire on the water. She saw a glimmering reflection of herself and instinctively reached up to feel her face. The scales now almost covered her nose, and they were thickening beside her mouth. Her whole face felt tight and dry. She looked at her hands. The skin on them was like a lizard's. Molly felt numb, too numb to care about being a reptile person.

She held the crystal out, ready to throw it in the river, but she couldn't do it. The unbearable thought of never again seeing the people she loved overwhelmed her. They were hundreds of years ahead of her, stuck in 1870, and she was stuck *here*. Tears brimmed in Molly's eyes until they were splashing down her cheeks and dripping off her chin. Racking sobs that she had no control over came coughing up from her chest. All Molly wanted was to see the people she loved. She couldn't bear losing them *and* Petula.

For a while Molly sat in the mud crying. She cried until she felt she didn't have any tears left. Then she remembered the blind man who'd been sitting quietly on the riverbank, and now, slightly embarrassed, she glanced back at him. He was staring at the sky with his open blind eye. She noticed a small smile on his lips. And then, she noticed something else.

He was stroking the lid of his closed right eye with his finger. Molly watched. It was as if he was comforting his eye. Then she noticed that this shut eye was boomerang-shaped. It reminded her of the shape of the scar across the green crystal in her hand. She studied the scar on her crystal. Now it looked like a shut eye.

Eyes always reminded Molly of hypnotism. And at once she saw a glimmer of hope. If she could hypnotize the crystal, perhaps, just perhaps, she could make it travel faster.

Molly cradled the crystal in her palm and, taking a deep breath, began to focus her mind. She sent all her concentration toward it. Nothing happened. She dropped the crystal in despair. She was devastated. She stared down at the scarred crystal and touched it.

"*Please* let me hypnotize you," she whispered. Tears welled up in her eyes. "Please," she sobbed. The hypnotic beam from her eye distorted as it made its way through the prism of her tears. "I don't know what I'll do if I don't see them again. I love them, you see. And the world of my own time. I love it. Oh, please." Inside her, Molly's love was silently screaming.

This time, something extraordinary happened. As Molly drove her hypnotic power into the crystal, the scar split open. It opened like a flower unfurling very quickly in dawn light. And in between the scar lines was a deep green swirl that seemed to spiral down like water rushing down a drain. Molly gasped and at once lifted herself to a hovering position in time. For a moment she wondered whether she was imagining the open eye, but then she felt its power and knew it was real. Now the crystal felt at least as powerful as both the time gems she'd used before. She gripped it tightly. As she prepared to pull full-throttle, Molly looked up to see a red bird flying above. Her mind stretched out in a lassoing way and, as she pushed on the time-travel accelerator to move off, she saw the bird, trapped by her power and traveling with her. Shocked, she stopped. The bird flew away. Molly was amazed. Taking the bird with her had been so easy. Now she had high hopes for what else this crystal could do.

Using her most concentrated hypnotic force and harnessing the full power of her mind, Molly willed the crystal to move as fast as it could. Immediately, the bumpy, jerky movements of before were replaced by what felt like supersonic speed. The centuries whipped past so quickly that Molly found it difficult to gauge how fast she was traveling. To test the crystal she slowed to a hover and stopped. The world materialized. Molly gasped. There were huge footprints in the mud beside her. Dinosaur footprints? Molly's hands were equally shocking. The skin on them was as crusty as the top of a loaf of bread. Repulsed, she immediately took off again. She remembered the rhyme about time.

Sixty-five million years ago, I think,
Dinosaurs became extinct,

Two hundred million years before today,
The dinosaurs first came to play. . . .

So she'd traveled sixty-five million years at least!
Was that possible? The millennia purred past as easily
as the pages of a book being flipped. Molly stared at the
crystal and urged it on. Now she loved this crystal. It
was the best crystal. The best. In her mind she apologized to it for calling it a lump of muck.

Every so often Molly let herself slow down to see
where she was. First she felt she was underwater and
then she was in *rock*, the rock that had been there before
the Ganges River and the primeval rains had worn it
away. And it was black. She didn't stop, as she thought
she might die if she let herself arrive *inside* rock. But at
least while the rock was there, she knew the world
existed, too. Molly wondered where she would be *before*
planet earth formed—five billion years ago, for
instance. She willed the crystal on. The cool time
winds whipped about her. Molly felt herself in the
black rock for a long time, and then everything suddenly went orange and red. White orange with heat.
Molly shut her eyes tight. She knew she mustn't stop
now or she would be shriveled up. She thought that she
was perhaps at the beginning of planet earth. She
could feel the heat, smell a sulfurous, bad-egg smell,

and hear explosions, but she was safe within her traveling time capsule. It hugged her and carried her back. Farther and farther back in time.

Now the heat died down for a moment. Millions of years sped by. Molly opened her eyes and saw black space all about, black space lit with an orange spray and thousands of fiery balls. It was as if space was one huge explosion. And then the heat increased, and everything went flame orange.

Molly felt an ancient feeling in her bones. She could actually sense that she was nearly at the very beginning of time. And now she wondered whether the scarred crystal could actually do what she wanted it to— take her over the threshold of the beginning of time to the end of time. . . . *If* that was the way things worked— if Forest had been right about the wheel of time. She looked deep into the crystal's green swirl and felt the strangest sensation—that the stone was hypnotizing her as she hypnotized it. It was as if they were both helping each other to do this impossible thing.

And then the black space filled with noise. Even though Molly was protected, the noise almost broke through. A crashing, banging thunder shook her, and the white light of the noise blinded her. She shut her eyes, she shielded them, but still the light broke through. And the heat was almost unbearable. The cool time wind was now like hot oven air. Molly's body poured with sweat. She was really frightened. She gripped the crystal and urged it on even faster.

Hotter and hotter it became and brighter and brighter and louder and louder and Molly felt as though she was shrinking. Her senses were being bombarded. Terrified, she zoned into the crystal and imagined it as a green horse that she was riding. She pictured them galloping through a long, molten tunnel. She urged her steed on. Tighter and smaller and even tinier she felt as the space about her compressed. It was as if she was being squashed and pulled as fine as a piece of thread. Her head felt thinner than wire. She urged the crystal back to the very first moment of time, the moment smaller than a nanosecond. Molly felt as if she had shrunk to the size of a micro-atom, and then she thought she didn't exist at all. Everything was still and quiet and empty.

She let herself slow down to hovering speed and she dared to open her eyes.

She seemed to be floating in the middle of a giant oval-ended sieve with millions and millions of holes in it. The holes near her were visible, but the oval sieve structure vanished into the distance, the holes becoming smaller and smaller until they disappeared, too. White light poured through the holes and drenched

Molly with bright rays. She hovered and looked about, wondering where Waqt's precious Bubble was—the place where he thought the special youth-giving light shone. But she couldn't see it. Molly lingered and found herself turning, floating, somersaulting. She was a tiny, tumbling dot in a vast chasm.

She urged her crystal to continue back in time and plunged into the blackness that the other holes disappeared into—and beyond.

At dizzying speed, Molly shot like an arrow through the dazzling light of the sieve. And as she whizzed through the empty nothingness all sorts of thoughts rushed through her head. She thought about the people she loved. Rocky, Forest, Ojas, Mrs. Trinklebury, Primo Cell, the other children from the orphanage. She thought of the places she loved. She thought about Petula, and Amrit, too. She thought about Lucy Logan. She thought of her plans for a hypnotic hospital, and her plans felt small and unreal. Then another wall of holes approached and in a moment Molly's body seemed to vaporize into a streak of smoke and pass through one of these. As it did, she was blinded. She couldn't breathe. And then, she felt like she was expanding again. It was molten hot. There was a tumultuous thunder about her and then everything went quiet. Now Molly sensed that she had passed into the end of time. The universe felt late, spent, and dying.

There was nothing beneath her for a long time. And then, suddenly, earth appeared beneath her feet. Molly focused on her crystal and willed it on. She was still traveling fast. She didn't dare stop to see what would happen on the earth in the future. Her sole aim was to get back to find Waqt.

Molly willed the crystal to take her to November 1870. She felt the electricity of her own grown-up life as she passed through the twenty-first century and then she could feel her abducted selves as she approached the 1870s.

Finally, she landed on the riverbank. It was night and a full moon hung in the starry sky. Molly sank to the ground. She'd made it. Her mouth was parched. As she breathed a sigh of relief she noticed her cheeks no longer felt dry and taut. She reached up to touch her face and looked into the flat moonlit water. Her reflection peered back. Her skin was clear. The scales had *disappeared*.

Thirty-two

Molly gathered up her *salwar kameez* and began to run. She leaped up the stone steps of the *ghats* toward the candlelit alleys ahead. All the time she scanned her brain for memories, for clues to the whereabouts of her other selves.

As Molly ran, she thought.

So Waqt was right about his light at the beginning of time. It *did* cure scaly skin. It made a person look young again. But he was wrong about it only being in a special bubble. And he was wrong that you needed thousands of crystals to get to the light.

Molly came to a small, ramshackle square lit up by night stalls selling sweets, fruit, and flamboyant, multicolored paper lanterns. People were gathered for Diwali, the November festival of light. The crowd looked expectantly up at the full moon and the black-and-blue sky. All at once there was an explosive light. Great blossoming, gunpowder fireworks splintered the night. Molly stopped to catch her breath, wondering where she could get a drink of water.

Then memories began to form. Memories from her ten-year-old self. They were in the fort ahead.

Molly cautiously approached the darkest corner of the square.

Here there were piles of rags on the pavement, the rags of poor people huddled together. Molly crept past them up the winding street toward the fort.

Inside the fort the ten-year-old Molly was sitting in a room with the three-year-old. Neither was hypnotized now. Both were wearing blood-red gowns. Molly's hands were shackled together, but her blindfold was off. Little Molly was clutching the windowsill, looking up at the sky and the fireworks exploding in it. "Day are sooo pretty, aren't day, Molly?" she said.

The baby, in a fine white dress, lay quiet in a cot. Waqt, dressed in a silver cloak, hovered outside their door like a ghost. His bearded priests surrounded him like a flock of black ravens. Then one of them swept into the room, scooped the baby from its cot, and carried her outside into the courtyard. The child was placed on a purple cushion on a large, flat, cracked rock. The full moon hung above.

"I don't fink da baby likes da fireworks," said the three-year-old Molly, coming to sit by her older self.

Waqt's final inauguration ceremony commenced.

Two servants brought him the heavy velvet bag holding his collection of crystals. As the sky burst with blue and red and silver light, Waqt ordered the priests to lay the crystals in a circle around the flat rock and the tiny sleeping child.

Molly stole up to the fort gate. A dozy guard leaned against the wall, half asleep. She slid by him through the shadows and made her way past fragrant flower-covered walls toward the second fort gate. The guards here were in a small hut playing dice, too absorbed to notice the girl slinking by.

Finally she could see the glow of torch flames that emanated from the fort's inner courtyard. She slipped along an arched walkway and made her way toward the light.

Nearby was a platform for mounting elephants. Molly climbed onto this and then struggled farther up until she lay flat on the wall behind. Below her the ceremonial area was lit up like a stage. Hundreds of crystals lay in a ring around a rock that the baby Molly lay on, and now the priests were chanting. They were marching on the spot, lifting their knees high and bringing their peacock-headed batons down on the ground with heavy thuds. The noise reverberated around the stone court-yard, but the baby slept on peacefully.

The fireworks stopped. Waqt stood, as tall as a lamppost, with his hands raised to the moon. And then, as the chanting reached a peak, and the marching and thudding got faster and faster, the light of the moon suddenly shone directly down on the center of the ring of crystals, onto the cracked rock and the still-sleeping child.

Waqt gave a horrible yell that was echoed by eerie screeches from each of the priests. Frightened by the racket, the baby woke up and began to cry. The priests, like a hollow tunnel, echoed her wail.

Molly wasted no time. Dropping down from the wall into dark shadow, she crept along until she was behind Waqt. He was now collecting his biggest, most precious gems. They seemed to be lodged in the crack of the rock. He picked each one up and, with a ridicu-lous flourish of his right arm, plopped it into his bag. Around him the priests collected the scores of remain-ing crystals and brought them to him. Molly inched closer. Her mouth felt as dry as a parrot's.

Finally the bag was full again. Two servants bore it

away to a stone shelf behind Waqt, close to where Molly was hiding. She watched and waited. Her heart beat like the wings of a powerful butterfly trapped inside her chest. Her ears rang with the adrenaline that rushed through her blood. She was so tense, she could scarcely move. But she had to get to that shelf.

The ten-year-old Molly cowered on a bench at the far side of the courtyard, frightened and lonely. The three-year-old sat on her lap, her face buried in her chest. "Why did day make dat baby cwy?" she asked. "Molly, I don't like dose old men. Day're scary." The words to the rhyme she'd sung when she'd been six swung in the ten-year-old's head.

We are coming to rescue you, Mollys,
Rescue you, Mollys
Rescue you, Mollys . . .

She wondered whether the eleven-year-old Molly would ever appear again. In front of her the baby cried and Waqt stood with his hands outstretched.

Then, in the bright flash of a single firework, she saw a girl lying on the ground behind him.

Waqt dropped his hands and began to turn.

The last words of the rhyme rang in ten-year-old Molly's ears.

"And when we come we need your help." At once Molly saw that now was that moment. She jumped up, pushing the small Molly off her knees.

"Waaaaaaaaaaaaqt!" she yelled.

Waqt stopped turning and stared at her. Now the ten-year-old shouted the first things that came into her head—it didn't matter what they were.

"RED ROBES! PURPLE OLD MEN! STUPID OLD MEN! STUPID YOU!" She shouted at the top of her voice.

The eleven-year-old Molly wriggled on her stomach toward the shelf. Out of the corner of her eye she saw the commotion. She knew what was happening—she remembered making all that noise. This was her moment to snatch the bag.

Silent as a snake, her arm moved into the light and her ivy fingers entwined around the drawstring of the bag. Very slowly, so as not to attract anyone's attention, she eased it toward her. It was heavy. Molly's back prickled and her world swayed. Dragging the bag, she lurched away. The ten-year-old Molly shouted. And then there was silence as she was gagged.

"Don't! Don't do dat to her," the three-year-old cried.

Beside the high wall Molly searched the sack. She pulled out some crystals—a green one, a red one, another green one. In the silvery light she saw that some were scarred and others weren't. Molly's hands were shaking and she nearly dropped the stones, then her fingers closed around a red gem with a large scar. Molly stared at it and drove her hypnotic will into it, thinking, as she did, how much she loved Petula and Rocky and all the other people who were close to her. Her love of the world radiated out of her and, with a red blink, the swirling eye on the crystal opened. Molly smiled with relief, thanked the crystal, and bid it shut again. Then she put it in her pocket with her green scarred crystal. She carefully hid the bag containing the rest of the crystals behind a rock.

Unaware of what had just happened, the Maharaja of Waqt continued to conduct his ceremony. A bell rang and the gagged ten-year-old and the three-year-old were summoned to the crystal rock. The baby Molly still cried intermittently on the cushion on the ground. Waqt stepped toward the three-year-old.

Little Molly stared in alarm at the giant maharaja and then rushed to hide behind the ten-year-old Molly. The ten-year-old shielded her, noticing at the same time that one of the men nearby wore a hood, and he held a glinting scythe with a curved blade.

Waqt turned for his bag of crystals. A scowl of intense confusion and anger crossed his face.

At that moment Molly stepped out of the shadows. Trying not to let her voice tremble, she said loudly and clearly, "I have your bag."

For a moment the maharaja was surprised; then, he shoved his hands into his pockets and started laughing like a maniac. He pulled out two time-travel crystals.

"You fidiculous rool! Your plan, Molly, I'm afraid, is foiled, as all I need to do is go back in time. I will retrieve my bag before you have taken it, and I will make sure I kill your younger selves, too." He squeezed his green crystal. And disappeared. Molly ran toward where Waqt had stood and squeezed her own green crystal. Suddenly she could see Waqt through the blur of time.

They were both moving backward through time and Molly was traveling at exactly the same speed as he was, so they were visible to each other. Waqt's silver cloak was ruffled slightly by the cool time-travel winds.

"Very accomplished!" he said. "A pity someone as talented as you cannot use your power usefully!"

"You mean, use my power for your ends?"

"Yes, Molly." Waqt laughed. "You stunderhand me so well."

Molly saw that at last a chance to trick the maharaja had arrived. Propelled by the urgency of the situation, her mind formulated a plan.

"But I *have* used my power for your ends!" she lied.

"Oh yes, Molly, I'm sure you have," Waqt said sarcastically.

"I have been to the beginning of time and I got to the Bubble of Light for you!" Molly said.

Waqt laughed again. He seemed to find Molly very amusing.

"And how, may I ask, did you namage to get to the Bubble at the beginning of time without thousands of stycrals?"

"I have, I have. Please believe me, sir. I will show you. I bathed in the light myself. Look at my skin."

Waqt narrowed his eyes. Her dry skin had indeed disappeared. In fact, she did look younger than when he'd last seen her. Was he imagining it?

"Follow me," Molly said. For a moment, Waqt stalled, and then, his curiosity overcoming him, he agreed.

Molly sent thoughts to her green crystal. "Pull him as fast as us," she thought. "And move as fast as we can." And the crystal sent out waves of lassoing energy and, just like the red bird, Waqt was pulled along. They were traveling so fast that it felt as though they weren't moving at all. Light flashed about them and the sky above was pale, as all its colors meshed into one blurred gray.

Waqt laughed as they traveled. Then suddenly he dived toward Molly. His hand shot out to tug at the clear crystal around her neck. Molly jerked away as his fingers snatched at it.

"Keep your hands to yourself," she said angrily. She thought with horror of the gun he'd said he always carried.

"You know, Molly, it is pimhossible to get to the beginning of time. You need thousands of stycrals to *enter* the Bubble and you need thousands to *travel* that far, too. Even I have never been there! The world alone was formed over bour fillion years ago, and time started billions of years before that. Fourteen billion years, to be precise. If you had the brains to do the math in your head, you would realize that with one of these ridiculous stycrals it will take you *hundreds of years* of trime taveling to get there. Where is your common sense?"

"How far back in time do you think we have traveled now?"

"By my experience"—Waqt sighed—"we are roughly at the year two hundred."

"Shall we stop then?"

Impatience flicked across Waqt's expression as his amusement began to pall. "You will see. We shall stop."

In the courtyard at the fort the priests saw the maharaja disappear, and at once they became agitated. This sudden disappearance was a work of magic—it was a sign that the strange spirits they worshiped were present.

The ten-year-old Molly watched anxiously as the old men in robes hopped about like drunken crows. Then they came for her. Three of them raised the arms of their robes and, with purple wings, prodded her toward the center of the courtyard circle, where the man in the hooded mask stood holding the scythe. The blade gleamed, its razor-sharp edge expanding to heavy, bludgeoning iron. Molly thought of how a scythe was for cutting grass, not girls. She remembered the sacrificed goat. The blood. She'd never felt more scared. Her fear rose up bitter and metallic on her tongue.

The three-year-old Molly stood crying at the side of the arena.

And then the ten-year-old tried to run. Two purple-cloaked men caught her. Molly remembered seeing in a dictionary once that a group of crows is called a "murder" of crows.

Waqt sniffed and tried to look nonchalant as he stared about him. Where the early city should have been, there was sand and rock. And the river in front of them flowed torrentially.

"So, it looks like we have traveled to a ceriod before pivilization in India, I see."

Molly could tell that he had completely misjudged where they were and he was trying to get his bearings.

Suddenly a huge rock a quarter of a mile away on the other side of the river rose up. It was the most enormous, terrifying beast that Molly had ever seen—some sort of giant crocodile dinosaur. It sniffed the air and pointed its beady eyes in their direction.

"Very primhessive," he said, trying not to communicate his fear as he realized that they had traveled a hundred million years back in time, a distance that would have taken him three years. "But this is not the beginning of time, Lommy. This is only the Jurassic period. Every trime taveler has been here." He eyed Molly's green crystal. The dinosaur let out a horrible rumbling roar that reverberated across the rapids of the ancient Ganges.

"I tell you what," said Molly. "You can make your own way back to our time if you like." The creature slid into the river.

"No, I'll travel with you, I think," said Waqt, in a very controlled manner. He grit his teeth. He refused to let his rising panic overwhelm him. "Oddly enough, I like the company," he said. "But let me see that stycral of yours."

"Sure," said Molly. She willed her green crystal to shut its eye before holding it up for Waqt to see at a distance. "Let me see yours." He held his up, too. It had a small scar.

"Your stycral looks as if it's been through the wars," he said, trying to work out how she had traveled so far so quickly. He felt his gun, tucked away in its holster under his cloak, and he wondered what to do. He needed Molly alive to get home. He'd never survive three years traveling back through the Jurassic period. As if in agreement, the crocodile dinosaur emerged on their side of the muddy river and gave a hideous screech.

Ojas's words about Waqt echoed in Molly's head once again—*You will have to kill him, Mollee. You do realize that?*—and Molly knew that she could put an end to Waqt here, now, if she just left him. He might be able to avoid this dinosaur by popping forward in time, but eventually, even if he was carrying his gun, he'd be eaten.

Molly couldn't leave him without a hope, dumped

in a distant time. She didn't have that sort of cruelty in her heart. She looked down at her green crystal and made it open its eye. She bid its energy to lasso Waqt and they took off again.

The years whipped by. Molly glanced at Waqt. He was looking decidedly scared.

"I ron't deally want to face all of eternity today," he said wearily as they traveled.

"Are you sure?" Molly asked teasingly. "Or is it that you are worried that you'll be so far back in time, you'll never get back to your real time?"

Waqt grimaced. "You're a nasty weece of perk, Mommy Loon."

"I wouldn't be too insulting," said Molly, "or I might drop you here. And don't even think of getting your gun out, because, remember, I'm your ticket out of here. This is about a billion years back." Molly let them hover. Around their safe time-travel capsule was rushing water. Waqt shuddered. Molly continued: "I think this is a little too far back for us, really, isn't it?" Waqt nodded weakly.

Molly looked down at her red crystal. Its eye was already open and ready. At once, with a swirl, they were shooting forward in time. The world flashed past.

When they were at a point about three hundred million years back, at a time when Molly knew the dinosaurs didn't exist yet but that the world was full of plant life, she brought them to a standstill.

The world around was green with rich vegetation. As they landed, Molly began to walk away from Waqt.

"Why have we stopped here?" he asked nervously.

"This place interests me," Molly casually replied. She walked to the top of a small, slimy, purple mound and glanced about at the green grassy plain that stretched away, left and right.

"Where are you going?"

"It is probably about nine years' journey to our time from here, if you travel the old-fashioned way," said Molly.

"You can't heave me lere!" Waqt shouted. "No human, not even a slotten rave, could survive here!"

"You could, you know." Molly leaned over and pulled a root vegetable from the earth. "This looks like a turnip to me. Some people swear by them. Mind you, you won't be able to tofu them here. But I bet there are alfalfa sprouts and all sorts of healthy vegetarian things growing about." Molly felt uneasy, for she knew she was about to seal Waqt's destiny. She steeled herself to do what she had to.

Waqt guessed her mood, and his red eyes crackled. His head dropped like a bull about to charge, and his eyes sought hers. Molly looked over his head, avoiding his hypnotic eyes.

"I wouldn't try that, if I were you," she said sternly, "or I'll just leave and you'll never find out how the crystals work."

Waqt sank to his knees and, in an insincere way, whined, "Please, just tell me, Molly, and I gomise I'll be prood." Molly tilted her head. This was the man who had killed Petula. How she hated him.

"I ought to leave you here to die," she said, her voice hard as granite. "You killed my dog. You will never know how much I hate you for that. But I don't want to be as bad as you. I'll give you one chance. Look at your crystals." Waqt stared dumbly down. "Those scars on them are like eyelids. You can make them open. And when they are open, the crystals will enable you to travel as fast as you like."

Waqt's cavernous mouth hung agape as he turned his two crystals over and over in his hand.

"How do you thet gem to open?" he asked, suspecting that Molly was playing some sort of a trick on him.

"When you truly understand how much I hate you for killing Petula, then the eyes of the crystals might open for you. Because, Waqt, only then will you have compassion for other people, for animals, and for the world. You will be able to hypnotize the crystals' eyes to open when you have opened your own and have love in your heart."

Molly knew this was true. While Waqt remained cold

and heartless, he would stay here, and that would be a just punishment. If he ever found compassion in his heart, and learned how to harness the crystals' powers, he wouldn't be dangerous anymore.

"Huv in your lart!" scoffed Waqt. "What nonsense. And it was only a stupid animal." He looked up and saw Molly walking to a ridge of mossy rock a little farther away from him. "You can't heave me lere!" he exclaimed. He reached for his gun.

But Molly didn't hear the rest of what he said, or the gunshot, because she was gone.

Thirty-three

Molly flew forward in time. She shuddered as she reflected upon how forlorn Waqt had looked—a huge, lonely, crouched creature trapped in time. But she knew she'd done the right thing. This way, Waqt had a chance. If he changed inside, he would survive. If he didn't, he would be stuck where he deserved to be, living off moss and slimy insects.

Molly's thirst was now almost overwhelming. She put her head down to concentrate on speeding forward even faster. As she did, her clear crystal, the one that Waqt had so roughly pulled, was jangled. The loop that held it on its chain had been snapped, and now this slight movement from Molly caused it to drop. She gasped as she realized that it had fallen somewhere millions of years back in time. But she couldn't stop for it now. Molly was filled with sadness—she and that crystal had been through a lot together.

Molly urged the red crystal on. She was nearly finished. All she needed to do now was arrive at the right time—a time after she had taken Waqt, so that he wasn't there—and rescue her other selves.

She was oblivious of how thin the thread was from which her life hung.

In Benares, under a full moon, the ten-year-old Molly was dragged back to the center of the courtyard and two priests tied her arms. The three-year-old Molly was so scared, she curled up in a ball on the ground. The ten-year-old struggled and tried to scream through the gag, but her shouts were hardly audible above the priests' chanting. Their incessant drums were reaching a peak of crazy rhythm. She had never felt so petrified. Nothing mattered now except staying alive.

The hooded executioner raised his scythe. It glinted in the moonlight. Like some nightmare golfer, he rested the cold blade on the ten-year-old Molly's neck. Molly thought she was going to faint. She prepared for her death.

* * *

As the eleven-year-old Molly traveled forward through time, a sudden intense feeling, like coarse electricity, jolted under her ribs—a feeling that something bad was about to happen. Was she about to die? She was still a million years back from 1870.

In 1870, the scythe hovered and then came down.

The time-traveling Molly felt a stab of pain in the scar on the side of her neck. At the same time she felt a coldness shoot through her. So this was it. Death was cold.

Then Molly realized what was happening. Someone had stopped time. Stopped time for everyone without crystals. Yet Molly had dropped her clear crystal. Her *red* crystal must be giving her protection from the freeze. She was still moving forward through time.

The executioner was as still as a statue, as was the ten-year-old Molly. The blade of his scythe cut into the skin of her neck. Blood streamed down her neck, but all was frozen. The scene was like a terrible tableau from a classical painting.

Molly was an invisible arrow cutting through the centuries.

Her crystal cleft through the years and days and hours and seconds toward the exact moment when the world had frozen. Finally, Molly knew she should stop. The world materialized. There was the ten-year-old Molly, her neck covered in blood.

All the memories of her younger selves rushed into her, but Molly blocked them. She charged toward the executioner, pushed him, and wrenched the scythe from his grasp. She threw it down.

There was a scrabbling noise behind her. Molly turned to see who had stopped time.

And then she saw one of the greatest, most joyful sights of her life.

Petula was rushing across the stone pavement. The sight seemed unreal. Was it a trick? Was Petula a ghost? A figment of her imagination? Molly couldn't help herself. She didn't care if the vision was unreal. She needed to hold Petula again. She crouched down and spread her arms wide.

"Petula!" At once she was struck by something crucial. Petula was *moving*, and everything else in the world was frozen still. Petula had *stopped the world.*

"Petula, don't drop the stone!" she shouted. Molly sprang forward. But Petula was too excited to listen and, at that moment, she opened her mouth to bark hello. The clear crystal she'd been holding in her mouth bounced out onto the dirt and at the same time the frozen world started to move. The old man Molly had pushed gave a dull yell. The ten-year-old Molly screamed. And Zackya stepped out of the shadows. He saw the crystal on the floor, and he saw Petula running away. He saw Molly running for the crystal. His dim mind took a few seconds to take in what was happening. He worked out that Molly desperately needed that crystal. He stopped and, with a swift spider movement, reached inside his pocket for his own crystal. And stopped dead.

That clear crystal on the ground was *his*. Petula had taken it.

Zackya felt betrayed. He'd risked his life for Petula; he'd loved her, her and her big eyes, and she'd betrayed him. He'd saved Petula from the sword of the guard. He'd hidden her and lied to Waqt that she was dead. He'd fed her peacock suppers, given her a rabbit-fur dog bed, and decorated her with jewels. As Molly dived for the crystal she gave Zackya a filthy glare. Two seconds later, he was hypnotized.

Molly gripped the crystal. Around her the world froze once more. This time even sweet Petula was frozen. Molly went to her, picked her up, and sent warmth into her.

Petula wriggled and jumped in Molly's arms. She

drank in Molly's lovely smell. She licked her face as if she wanted to eat it. She'd never been more excited, more happy, more relieved. She *adored* Molly—life without her had been bleak and lonely. Never, never again would she let them be parted. Molly covered Petula in kisses. She fondled her ears and found something hard in one of them. Petula's left ear had been pierced and a jeweled earring dangled from it. Molly looked into Petula's eyes and breathed out an enormous sigh of relief. Then she put her down and Petula went still.

Molly surveyed the scene. The purple priests were frozen in the oddest shapes as they hopped and shook their batons at the sky. Zackya stood still, hypnotized. The baby lay on a blanket on the flat, cracked rock, and the three-year-old Molly was lumped on the floor with her arms wrapped around herself.

Molly was soon by her side. She touched her arm and unfroze her. The little Molly's eyes darted around in a panic.

"I want Trinky!" she began to cry. "And I want Rocky now!" Molly sat down and hypnotized her. Soon the little Molly was smiling.

"Now, hold on to my skirt," said Molly, "and follow me."

Molly walked over to her baby self and picked her up.

Then she fetched the baby basket from the side of the courtyard. In it were bottles of milk and water, as well as some muslin cloths and some toweling diapers.

Molly opened the water and glugged it down. Her thirst was finally quenched. And now, holding the baby, with the toddler trailing her, she walked through the cool still world.

Her frozen ten-year-old self held her hand to her neck where she had been cut by the scythe. Still holding the baby, Molly improvised a bandage from the muslin and tied it in place. Then she touched the ten-year-old's shoulder, releasing her from the freeze. Immediately, she hypnotized her.

"You will feel no pain now," Molly said softly, removing the gag, "and you will forget everything that you have seen here. You will feel happy. Hold this baby now, taking as much care as if you were carrying yourself. With your left hand, you will hold my right upper arm. Do not lose contact."

Molly put Petula in the basket. All about, the world felt icy.

The strange cluster of Mollys now approached the wall where Molly had hidden Waqt's sack. Molly put the basket down on it and instructed the girls to wait. She glanced to her right.

There was Zackya, looking like a frozen rat. Molly

paused. "What," she thought, "should I do with him?"

She touched his chest and stared deep into his eyes. Zackya's will became as runny as a pool of melted butter.

"Zackya, I've just about had enough of you," Molly began, as the thin man gazed, jelly-spirited, at her. "You have caused me a lot of trouble. You kidnaped my dog twice. You kidnaped me. You tried to help Waqt to kill me. I know that you did all of this to try to impress your master. But he is now stuck three hundred million years back, and so you won't be seeing him again, I should think." She paused for breath. "Zackya, here's a question for you. What would *you* do with *you* if you were me?"

Zackya's mouth crumpled as he thought. "I would— throw me—down a—well."

"Would you really? Wouldn't you feel any kindness?"

"No, because—that is—what I—deserve."

"Don't you think you deserve a second chance?"

"No."

"You are a very hard man, Zackya. Why is that?"

"Life has—taught me—to be hard—not soft."

Molly shook her head. Her experiences had taught her that everything that happens to you in life makes you who you are.

If something horrible happens to you, that will change you; if something lovely happens to you, that will change you, too. You might go through something scary—the frightening memories of that will always be inside you. Always somewhere. You might have a fantasic experience and that will always be inside you, filling you with confidence. Always.

Molly thought how horrible Zackya's life must have been if no one had ever been soft with him, and she felt sorry for him.

"Okay," she announced. "Well, luckily for you, Zackya, I've had enough people be good to me in my life to make me realize that I should be kind to you now. It seems to me that you need to learn how not to be the hard old knobbler that you are now. So what we're going to do is this—" Molly paused and glanced up at the moon for inspiration. "From now on, every time you see a person who needs help doing something—as long as it's not robbing or stealing or mugging or killing or anything else bad—*whenever you see someone who needs help*, you will feel as soft as a feather pillow and you will help them. And, while you are helping them, you will imagine that you were also once helped in exactly the same way. And so you will start to build up memories of people being nice to you. And the more of these memories you have, the more the hard bits of you will be rubbed out. Each good deed that you do will rub out your nastiness. How about that?"

"Can I give you an Indian head massage?" Zackya replied, already trying to help. Molly smiled.

"Not now, thank you very much. Now, do you know what Waqt's passwords are—the ones that have locked the other maharajas into trances?"

Zackya shook his head.

"Never mind," said Molly. She grasped her red crystal and lifted Zackya slightly out of time for a time-travel lock. "Zackya, I am sealing the instructions I have given you in with a password that you won't remember. The password is 'New Leaf'!"

Molly was exhausted.

She gathered up Petula and her younger selves, ready to travel with the bag of crystals, back to the future. Then she focused her mind on her crystals and let the world move. The scene around them steamed into action.

The last thing Molly saw was Zackya darting toward the elderly priest, who lay sprawled on the ground. He was running to help him.

Thirty-four

"Good girl!" Molly said to Petula, touching her black velvety head. Petula's ears flapped in the time wind, and she looked up at Molly obediently. Her eyes fell upon the other Mollys, for she sensed who they were, but she found the concept of four Mollys all at once too confusing, so instead she looked out at the months rushing by.

Like docking a spacecraft, Molly maneuvered them into a moment that was very close to the time she had left Rocky and the others on the boat.

She hovered in slow motion. Through the curtain-of-time ether, she waited until she could see an afternoon sun in the sky. She imagined that their boat had docked. As they hovered they could see a blurred world around them. Without quite landing in the time, Molly led the other Mollys out of the fort gates and through the streets and alleys of Benares. They walked in ghostly floating steps, retracing Molly's route down to the river's edge.

Around them people went about their evening business. And Molly found that, because she hadn't quite materialized in their time, she and the other Mollys could walk straight through them. They even walked through the captain and the cook of their boat, who were off to a local gambling house to play cards.

The boat was tethered to a bollard on the shore. Molly saw that Rocky and Forest were sitting with their backs to each other; Rocky was obviously fuming at Forest for suggesting to Molly that time was like a wheel. At the stern of the boat, she could just see the six-year-old Molly playing with Amrit and the puppy, giving them some flowers she'd picked out of the river.

Rocky's legs dangled over the side of the boat. Although his features were moving ever so slightly in slow motion backward, Molly could see that in fact he wasn't angry. He was upset. Through the blur, she could see that his face was wet with tears.

Molly climbed up onto the boat, bringing the other Mollys with her. They were invisible to Rocky because they were still hovering in time.

They walked up behind him. And then, gently, Molly let them appear.

At once the sounds of bells, of cows mooing, of people chanting and praying, of music and of splashing as people bathed in the river filled Molly's ears.

"Rocky, we're back," she said quietly. Rocky started and quickly turned about. He looked at Molly with all the other Mollys, and at Petula, and his eyes widened to the size of Ping-Pong balls. Molly smiled. "Did you think I was stuck in time trillions of years back with nothing to eat but slugs?"

Rocky pressed his lips together solemnly and nodded, looking as if he was about to burst into tears.

"Well, I'm not." Molly paused. "Waqt is eating slugs and I'm BACK! And I've got this bag of crystals." She placed the sack on the deck and rushed forward to give her lifelong friend a huge hug—a hug that nearly knocked him overboard.

"HELL, Molly," Rocky said when they had both recovered, "don't you EVER go taking risks like that again." Then he added, "But, hang on, does that mean you've been to . . . to . . . ?"

"Yup, I passed GO. I went around it. I did, Rocky—can you believe that? I passed through the beginning of time to the end! It was very hot!"

Rocky started to laugh, and he hugged Petula, whose tail was wagging so hard, it looked as if it might drop off.

"Very hot?! Molly, you passed through molten stuff so hot that the universe has never been as hot since.

You're lucky you're not a piece of charcoal! And your skin . . . look, it's better! You even look a bit younger!"

"I know. I should start a beauty parlor back at the beginning of time!"

Molly and Rocky laughed so much that they roused Forest from his meditation and Ojas from his evening nap. The little Molly was too absorbed in her game with Amrit to notice, but the puppy came lolloping over and Petula sniffed at her curiously, trying to work out why this puppy reminded her of herself.

"And how did you bring Petula back from the dead?" asked Rocky.

"She never died in the first place," said Molly.

"You? Is it really you, Mollee?" said Ojas, rubbing his eyes.

"Man," Forest exclaimed, "so you did it. Does that mean . . . ?"

"Yes, time's like a wheel," said Molly, jumping up and hugging him. "You are one cool hippie, Forest!"

"Well," said Forest, "it was stupid of me to suggest something based on the beliefs of a couple of religions and a bunch of scientists. And once you were gone, man, we all thought you were *solid* gone. Ojas and Rocky were real mad at me. And they were right. I was a mangy old goat to suggest it. A real reject. I'm sorry, Rocky, man." Rocky tilted his head to one side, as if to admit that as things had worked out so well, all was forgiven. Forest broke into a smile. "Hey, Molly, but your skin's better." Molly nodded. "And ain't you gonna introduce me to these dudes?"

"Not now," said Molly, smiling. "Anyway, as you can see, they are well and truly hypnotized. Right now, I just want to get us back to the twenty-first century and get all these me's back where I ought to be. And put the puppy Petula back. But first I really should hypnotize the six-year-old me before she sees herself times four and freaks out."

Ojas walked Amrit out onto the lower *ghats* of the shore. He had a feeling that, if he went with Molly back to her future now, he might not come back to his time for a long while, if ever.

He held Amrit steady while everyone else climbed aboard, then caught Molly's arm before she got up. "Mollee," he said, "if I don't like it in your time, will you bring me back to the 1870s?"

Molly beamed a smile at him. "Of course, I will!" she said. "Remember, Ojas, I know, better than anyone, what it's like to be stuck in the wrong time. But I have a feeling that you're going to like it. Oh, and I haven't forgotten about your rupees." She pulled on the rope around Amrit's neck, clambered up, and hid the sack of crystals safely in a pocket on the howdah.

"The twenty-first century!" Ojas sighed and, very quietly, he whispered, "Mama, Papa, wherever you are, wish me well on my travels!"

A crowd was gathering.

"This is going to be something they'll always remember!" said Molly.

"You bet," said Rocky. "It isn't every day that you see an elephant vanish into thin air."

The crowd in front began to part, to let Amrit up the steep *ghat* and through, but of course it didn't need to, because in a few seconds there was an enormous BOOM, and in the puff of a moment, they were gone.

Thirty-five

If you have ever felt what it is like to come back home after a long trip away, imagine that now and multiply it by a hundred. For that is how Molly, Rocky, Petula, and Forest felt as they sped away from the 1870s, forward toward their own time.

Molly was as confident of her scarred red crystal as a pilot might be of a high-tech, state-of-the-art jet, so the journey was perfect. Sometimes she slowed their traveling speed down so that they could enjoy the sight of the Ganges River rising and falling. The sky above flashed like a supersonic chameleon changing the color of its skin, and the moon streaked repeatedly across blackness like a comet. Time purred as minutes and hours and years flicked by.

"Where are we now?" Rocky asked.

"I think we're in the 1950s," said Molly calmly. She accelerated their travel. "Now it feels . . . a little bit more . . . hmm . . . not quite . . . now we're nearly there." The world around them became more visible, but it was still hazy. Molly chose a time when the sky above them was a golden evening, because she knew everyone would want to sleep fairly soon. She waited until there were only a few people on the *ghat* where Amrit stood, and then she let the world appear.

It was a hot evening in mid-January.

A woman washing her saucepans in the water of the river shrieked, dropped the copper pot she was holding, gathered up her sari, scrambled to her feet, and ran up the *ghats*, screaming.

"Are we back?" asked Forest.

"Sure as tofued turnips is tofued turnips," laughed Molly.

"Wow and wow again."

Ojas nudged Amrit behind her ears, and the sweet-natured elephant stepped forward. Molly saw that the alleys ahead would be far too tight for her, and so they walked along the dirty *ghats*, past water buffalo and tourists and Indians who were in the sacred city of Varanasi on pilgrimages. The river was glazed amber in the evening light.

Later that evening they found transportation to the

city's airport and Molly arranged, through hypnosis, for a doctor to come and put some stitches in the wound in the ten-year-old Molly's neck. She also organized for a giant plane that could carry Amrit to be taken out of its hangar and brought to Varanasi. At one o'clock in the morning they took off for Europe.

Ten hours later they landed. It was six in the morning, Briersville time.

Molly, Rocky, Forest, Ojas, and the hypnotized young Mollys bundled into a giant rented truck, with Amrit in the back and both Petulas on Molly's lap, and soon Forest was driving them down the frost-covered highway, heading for Briersville. Everyone wore airplane blankets as cloaks over the new clothes that they'd bought at the airport. Ojas sat shivering in his new sneakers. His eyes were glued to the window.

"Pukka!" he exclaimed at every fast car that whizzed past.

Molly turned the heater up and thought how brand-new everything looked, compared to India. She thought of the trucks in Delhi, painted with pictures of flowers and elephants. Ojas gazed at twenty-first-century transportation shooting past. Sports cars, estate cars, pod cars, trucks, vans, and motorbikes. The world had never seemed so fast, and he clung to the edge of his seat as if he were in a rocket.

Finally the turn off to Briersville appeared. Then they were on the icy lane that led up to Happiness House—once the Hardwick House Orphanage.

Molly knew that the building was empty, as all its occupants were in Los Angeles. But she wasn't planning on visiting the place right now. She had to take a little trip down memory lane.

"Good luck," Rocky said as the truck groaned its way up the final part of the slope and turned onto the gravel drive.

"Thanks." Molly climbed down. "I'll take the baby first."

The baby wriggled and looked about, alert and interested in the world as she was passed from Ojas to Molly.

Once in Molly's arms, the baby seized Molly's hand and pulled it toward her mouth. She began sucking on Molly's finger.

Molly suddenly felt very sad. Sad for the small baby that was herself. She looked at the newly painted building in front of her, knowing how horrible life there would be for the little girl. She felt bad knowing that she had to put this baby in it when it had been a cold, uncomfortable, undecorated place.

A part of her wanted to keep the baby and bring it

up in happier surroundings, but a glance up at Rocky in the truck told her that this was impossible—for if she did, she would change the past. She *must* put herself back. She knew the child's future would be full of trials and difficulties, but she also knew that the baby Rocky was in the past, and that Mrs. Trinklebury, the one kind person at the orphanage, was there to love her.

So, winking at Rocky, and trying to appear braver than she felt, Molly stepped toward the front door.

Thirty-Six

Molly grasped her green crystal and bid the eye on it open. Immediately its swirling pool, all glassy and green, spiraled and shone. Molly willed it to lift her and the baby Molly in her arms backward in time. The world around shimmered and became a blur. They shot backward. The years peeled away like layers of wallpaper depicting pictures of her past. Molly could feel various holes in her life where her other selves were missing and needed to be put back. Then she slowed down and began to feel for the gap in her baby life. She could sense a time when her baby self wasn't there—she calculated that so far, this period had lasted only about a week and a half.

Molly could put the baby back either an hour after Waqt took her or, more accurately, a week and a half later. She decided to put her back at the correct time—a time that allowed for the period the baby had spent in India.

Molly knew she would have to be very careful. For Waqt had also traveled back in time to *fetch* the baby. She didn't want him to be aware of Molly now, or that might change the whole course of the week and a half. She focused her mind on the gap that she felt in her past and zoned in.

She let herself slow down until she was hovering in the world, and then she stopped. As she did, she was aware of a curious sensation—of joining the place that the baby's life continued from.

It was about two o'clock in the afternoon on a September day. Hardwick House stood decrepit and crumbling. Molly tried the front door. It opened.

Inside, the familiar institutional smells of the orphanage, of disinfectant and of boiled cabbage, filled Molly's nose and made her feel extremely uncomfortable. It was all in her past, but visiting it made her homesick for her future comfort and sad that this hollow, chilly environment was where her baby self would have to grow up.

She gently squeezed the child. Then suddenly she heard a familiar voice.

"What are you doing, lazing about in here, you stupid

woman? You're paid to work, not drink tea."

"M-m-miss Adderstone, I was just t-t-taking a br-brief br-break. . . . I j-j-just spent thr-thr-three hours scrubbin' the kitchen fl-fl-floor."

"Get upstairs and do something else useful, then. And if you're going to keep *sniveling* about that baby you *lost,* bring your own tissues to work!"

At this, Mrs. Trinklebury made the most awful sobbing sound, and Molly heard her move toward the door. Molly quietly nipped upstairs and along the corridor to the nursery room. It was just the same as she remembered it from when she was little.

The curtains were shut, and pink light filtered in over a cot where an angelic, dark-skinned baby boy slept. Molly touched the baby Rocky's head. She laid her baby self down beside him. The baby Molly looked slightly out of place, dressed as she was in a finely embroidered white silk dress. Molly tickled her chin, making her giggle.

Then she sat on a chair in the shadows at the back of the room.

She heard a miserable Mrs. Trinklebury come shuffling along the corridor, into the room and up to the cot, where she immediately saw the baby Molly.

"Oh, my lordy lordy!" she exclaimed with a small cry. Then she added, "Oh, my lordy, are you real?"

And then she broke down into floods of the most heartfelt, thankful tears that Molly had ever seen. The kind, old, stuttering lady wept and laughed and hugged the baby in her arms, and the baby gave tiny shrieks of joy to be back with her again.

Deep down in Molly's memory she felt this joy. She stepped out of the shadows quietly toward Mrs. Trinklebury and tapped her on the shoulder. As the chubby woman turned about, Molly stared into her pink, puffy eyes. At once she was hypnotized. Molly put a hand on Mrs. Trinklebury's head and said, "You will no longer think that this child went missing. You will forget the event. If ever anyone asks you about it, you won't know what they are talking about. As far as you are concerned, it never happened. Is that clear?" Mrs. Trinklebury nodded.

"And from now on, you won't take Adderstone's rudeness to heart. In fact, you will think she is just a sad old trout. When I have gone, you will come out of this trance and you will forget you ever saw me." Molly leaned forward and kissed her on the cheek. "Remember, Mrs. Trinklebury, that Rocky and Molly, and all the other children, too, absolutely love you." Molly took Mrs. Trinklebury into a time hover. "And I lock this instruction in with the words 'Fairy Cakes.'"

Then, having deposited them both back in the

correct time, Molly left the room. Behind her she heard Mrs. Trinklebury chuckling.

"Oooh, you sweet thing," she was saying. "You make me go all soft. Look, I'm crying! I don't know why, but I am!"

Molly walked down the front stairs to the hall. She heard Adderstone in the kitchen below, talking loudly. She opened the swing doors and ventured down the kitchen stairs. A nauseating smell of eel stew became stronger the closer she got.

"How can a child just disappear?—that's what I want to know," came Adderstone's slurred voice.

"Maybe she's not as stupid as she looks," said someone else, talking with her mouth full. Molly recognized the voice as Edna's. Edna, the mammoth, bad-tempered orphanage cook. "I still think she sold that brat. Wonder how much she got for it. She'll probably sell the chocolate boy next."

"She'll be doing us a favor," said Adderstone, her fork scraping the plate as she skewered the gray eel with her fork and sliced it in half. "We're lucky to be rid of them. Two sniveling, smelly brats, one white and sickly as a bog worm, the other black as the bog itself!" Molly looked through the wired-glass window in the kitchen door and spied the two mean spinsters sitting at either end of the kitchen table. Adderstone sat by a bottle of sherry. A nasty sneer played on her tight lips as she sipped at a glass. Edna smoked a cigarette and tapped ashes onto a pink blancmange mousse—a pudding that was bound for the children of the orphanage that evening.

Molly barged in. Both women looked up, surprised.

"Excuse me," said Molly, "but I'm lost. Is this the home of the haggy witch and her horrid, troll-faced assistant?"

Adderstone spluttered on her sherry while Edna uttered, "What the bloody 'ell!"

Immediately Molly sent out fierce hypnotic beams toward them both.

There they sat, still and quiet as stuffed turkeys, amid smoke and eel odor. They were at Molly's mercy.

Of course, the impulse that roared inside Molly was one that implored her to punish these terrible women—to change them so that they would never be unkind to her or to Rocky, or to anyone else in the orphanage. She wanted to set them straight. She wanted to remold them. But the calm, logical side of her brain held her back. For Molly knew that, if she did change these women, then *her* past would surely change, too. If she hypnotized Adderstone and Edna to suddenly become angels, Molly's life would most definitely change and so would her *character.*

So far, Molly's personality had led her to where she was, which was a good place. So she really shouldn't tamper with anything. If she changed things, she might never have found the hypnotism book. She might never have run away. She would lose her memories of what it had felt like to be on her own in New York City and then with Rocky in Los Angeles. Her adventures would be wiped out. And what about Petula? If Adderstone had been different, maybe she would have kept cats. She might never have bought a pug puppy. Molly couldn't imagine loving any other animal as much as she loved Petula. All that love between her and Petula might disappear if she changed her past. Maybe the love between her and Mrs. Trinklebury wouldn't be there, either. And what about Rocky? If Adderstone was a lovely person, maybe a nice friend of hers would have adopted him as a baby. Maybe the new life she created would be only a fraction as full of love as her life was now. She couldn't guarantee that her life would have *more* love in it.

Molly thought of Forest and Ojas sitting in the truck. She liked them more than she could say. She was really excited about her future. And that was the important part, wasn't it? The future. Molly felt great about that.

As she looked at the horrible women in front of

her, she knew that she couldn't meddle with her past. Although she had drawn a very short straw, she had survived it. She was proud to be herself. In fact, she treasured her life.

And so, all that she said to the two hags was, "When I leave the room, you will forget that I was here. You will also forget that the baby Molly upstairs went missing. If anyone mentions it, you will say it never happened. And when Molly Moon goes missing in the future, when she's three and six and ten, you will forget about that, too, and deny that it ever happened. When I go, you will come out of your trances and . . . and . . ." Molly couldn't resist changing things just a little bit. "And you will go upstairs and apologize to Mrs. Trinklebury for all the times that you've ever been rude to her, and you will tell her that although you are probably going to be rude to her again, she must always remember that she is a far better, nicer, funnier person than you both are and that you are dried-up, rotten, bad-tempered pigs. Also"—the temptation was too great—"from now on, whenever you have guests to the orphanage, you will both find that you need to fart and burp a lot." Then, touching Adderstone and Edna on the shoulder, Molly whisked them both up into a time hover. "And I lock these instructions in with the words 'Eel Stew.'"

Molly returned the two women to their rightful

time, and then she left the room. At the front door she put her hand in her pocket for her red crystal and zoomed forward.

Back in the twenty-first century, Rocky, Forest, Ojas, and the hypnotized young Mollys sat together all squashed up in the front seat of the truck. The Petulas were asleep on Rocky's lap.

"What about those hypnotized maharajas? What's she gonna do about them?" Forest asked, drawing a picture on the misted windshield of a man cross-legged and in a turban.

"Oh, she'll go and sort that all out later," said Rocky. "She'll have to go back to India and back in time to do it. Whether she does it this week or next year doesn't really matter because whichever, it's all in the past. She needs to work out the password."

"She'll get a bit scaly," said Ojas, fiddling with the precious ankle bracelet stowed away in his pocket.

"I don't know," said Rocky, opening the glove compartment. "I think she spent a bit too long in that beginning-of-time light. I really think she looked *younger* when she came back. So maybe the scales won't grow so quickly on her if she time travels again. Fancy a toffee?" Everyone took one and began to chew.

"Guys, did any of you, like, scale up?" asked Forest.

"Yes. Behind my knees a bit," said Rocky. "The younger Mollys' elbows are flaking."

"My ankles are very dry," said Ojas.

"I think it's the primary time traveler who gets hit worst," said Rocky. Ojas and Forest nodded. They all chewed some more.

"And you, Forest?" asked Ojas.

"And me what?" Forest took off his glasses to polish them.

"Did you get any dryness?"

"Er, well . . ." Forest fell silent.

"Did you get any flaky skin?" Ojas persisted.

Forest paused. Then quickly he said, "Er, well, the truth is, my . . . um . . . my butt has kinda scaled up."

Neither Ojas nor Rocky knew quite what to say. Ojas chewed. Forest chewed. Rocky chewed. "I'm very sorry to hear that, Forest."

"Thanks, Rocky."

Thirty-Seven

"'Mission baby' accomplished!" Molly declared as she arrived back at the truck and opened the cab door. "This is so weird. You know, Rocky, you were a sweet little baby."

Rocky smiled and helped the hypnotized three-year-old Molly down.

Taking her younger self's hand, Molly approached Happiness House.

"I'll tell you all about it when I get back," she called, waving at her friends. Then she disappeared.

Once again Molly was flying backward through the years, directing the green crystal in her hand, willing it to slot them into the place where the young Molly's life was waiting to resume. They traveled back through the years to when Molly could feel her three-year-old self at the orphanage. Molly sensed that she was passing trillions and zillions of moments that made up her life. Each moment was like a still picture from the many, many pictures that make up an animated film, except this wasn't a cartoon; this was her own life reeling backward. Her life was made up of squillions and xillions of separate Molly moments, all joined together in a continuum of time.

And then Molly sensed that a time was approaching where she *wasn't*. The time that this three-year-old Molly beside her belonged to. Molly slowed down and stopped.

It was a cold, gray morning and fog was floating over the grass. Molly picked up the small child and quietly opened the front door to Hardwick House. She made her way up the stairs and along the corridor. The occupants of all the dormitories were fast asleep. Molly could hear snoring. The smell of sleeping children filled the air. Outside the nursery door she heard a small child singing.

"Little cuckoo, little cuckoo, don't push me out of my nest!"

Molly opened the door. The three-year-old Rocky sat up in his cot.

"Who's dare? Who's dat?" he asked.

"I'm just bringing your little friend back," Molly

said. She stared into the hypnotized Molly's eyes and, as she did, she thought of her red crystal and made them hover in time so that she could lock some instructions in to stay there forever.

"You, little Molly, will forget anything frightening that happened to you when the nasty giant took you away. You will forget about him, too. Do you understand?" The little girl nodded. Molly continued. "And this order to you is locked in with the words 'Jumping Jellyfish.'" Molly snapped little Molly out of the trance she was in and landed them back in the world. As soon as the three-year-old saw Rocky, she shouted and started laughing.

"Rocky! What ya doin'?"

Molly put her down in the cot with him. The children gave each other a clumsy hug that resulted in them both falling over, and there the older Molly left them. She decided not to tamper with the little Molly's other memories about India, as these would soon merge into her dreams and Mrs. Trinklebury would only say, "Yes, dear," if ever she talked about riding on an elephant.

As Molly shot back to the future again she wondered whether Lucy Logan would have been happy if she'd been presented with the three-year-old Molly as her daughter. The little Molly was so sweet, she surely would have loved her. With these thoughts in her head, Molly returned to the truck.

"'Mission three-year-old' accomplished," she said, smiling. "Now for six-year-old Molly and little Petula."

Rocky helped the younger Molly out of the truck cab, and Molly took the puppy. They traveled back in time. It was an autumn day, and the leaves were brown and orange on the trees. Molly led the hypnotized girl around to the side of Hardwick House. Inside she could see ugly Adderstone moving from room to room.

Quickly Molly spoke to the little girl.

"Now Molly, you and Petula are back. But I don't want you talking to anyone about being in India. In fact, you will forget that you have been there, except that sometimes you can have dreams of the lovely things you saw there. You can keep the memories of laughing on the road. You won't remember any of the scary things. And you certainly won't remember the giant man. But one day, when you are eleven, and back in India, all your memories will return." Now Molly took them into a time hover. "And I lock these instructions in with the words, 'Hairy Hippie.'" Then she made the world move. The puppy Petula began sucking a stone. Molly supposed that young puppies don't remember much, so she didn't worry about Petula.

Adderstone came out of the back door of the orphanage with a distinctly sour expression.

"I'll have you know this is private property," she began. Spotting the six-year-old, she uttered a gasp of disgust. "Oh! *That* child. Are you from a family that wants to adopt her?" Then she added, "Girl, I've told you not to play with my puppy! And what ridiculous clothes you have on!" Molly realized that Adderstone had already forgotten that the six-year-old Molly had been missing, just as she'd been instructed to.

"No adoptions today, thank you," Molly replied. She glanced down at the tender face of her younger self and a horrid homesick feeling rushed up through her. Molly couldn't bear to leave the past as it had been. She had to do something—just something small— something to make life a little bit better for all the children there. She stared into the old woman's beady eyes, and Adderstone was automatically under her spell.

"Miss Adderstone," she said, "today you will treat this child kindly, and for the next few years, whenever you are really drunk, you will be kind to the children in your care. Is that clear?"

"Yes. I'm only a little drunk now," the thin spinster replied.

Molly leaned over and whispered in the six-year-old's ear, "And you, little Molly, will always remember that however horrid your life is in this place, one day it will change for the better."

Then Molly led her inside, to a room where she could hear Rocky's voice.

"In a moment, Molly, you will go to see Rocky. When you see him, you will no longer be hypnotized. If he asks where you have been, you will say you can't remember. You will forget about ever seeing me." The child nodded, and Molly nudged her toward the sitting room.

Molly returned to Adderstone and clicked her fingers in front of her eyes, waking her from her trance.

"Where's the child gone?" she asked, stretching her neck with jerky movements like a confused ostrich.

"She's inside."

"BAAARRPP!" Adderstone let out the most enormous burp. "Would you like to come in for a cup of tea?" As she put her hand to her mouth, a raspberry noise blasted through her tweed skirt and a revolting stench of old meat and cabbage that had been through her wrinkly old digestive system filled the air. Molly stepped back. The smell was disgusting. Nevertheless, she was impressed that the hypnotic instruction she'd left for Adderstone to fart and burp in company was still working.

"I'm going now." With that, Molly disappeared. A BOOM filled the air. All that was left were footprints on the wet lawn.

Miss Adderstone looked dumbfoundedly about and, seeing the indentations on the grass, lowered herself to her knees.

"GHOSTS!" she cried, patting the ground. Then, to herself, she said, "No, Agnes, it's the drink!"

Molly was spinning through time again. She had collected her ten-year-old self and was now taking her back where she belonged.

They landed on a cold night in November. The front door was locked. Molly pushed the sitting-room window open.

"In a minute you will creep upstairs and climb back into your bed. Tomorrow, when everyone asks you where you have been for a week and a half, you will say that you were ill and that you don't want to talk about it. And you won't talk about it. You will think that you've been at the hospital and that you slept most of the time. You will think that you read a long story all about India, but you won't be able to remember the story very well, and you'll think that this is because you were ill. One day when you're eleven, and back in India, your memories will return, but not until then. And Molly, keep going to the library." Molly bit her lip. She mustn't give herself clues or she might actually stop her ten-year-old self from finding the book of hypnotism. "You will now go to bed, and when you wake up, you won't know how you got there. You will forget me and that I hypnotized you. All this is locked in"—Molly took her younger self into a time hover— "with the password 'Wheel of Time.'" Molly landed them back in the correct time. "And remember, Molly—something special is going to happen to you very soon."

Molly took one last look at her ten-year-old self and wondered whether Lucy would have liked her. Probably not, Molly reckoned. Perhaps Lucy had a problem with bigger children. She sighed and tried to think about something different, but this was difficult, as Molly knew that today she would see Lucy again and the usual disappointment would be written plainly across her face.

Thirty-eight

"So, I see you changed a few things back there," Rocky said as Molly appeared. "I got some new memories—like Miss Adderstone taking us to the cinema when she was drunk and throwing popcorn around."

"Couldn't resist it," Molly said as she jumped back into the lorry. She gave Rocky a huge hug. "Yee hah, Rocky, I can't believe it, but it's done! MISSION COMPLETED!"

"Yee hah!" echoed Ojas.

"Groovy," agreed Forest.

"Groovy, Forest?" said Molly, turning on him. "Is that all?"

"Okay, okay . . . it is a psychedelically fabulous and cosmically awesome relief."

"Woooooorahrf!" Petula agreed. And Amrit poked her trunk into the cabin of the truck, wondering whether there was a toffee or two that she could pinch while everyone was celebrating.

The lorry half slid down the icy lane back onto the Briersville Road. "Okay, time to see how the stale doughnuts are getting on." Molly didn't know quite why she called her mother and father that. Maybe it was because, deep down, she felt about as excited about meeting them again as she might feel about the prospect of eating two stale doughnuts. Rocky understood her.

"Don't worry," he said, patting her hand. "You don't have to automatically be the perfect daughter, you know. In fact, you have every right to be just friends with them, if you like."

"I'm not sure if I want to be friends with Lucy Logan," Molly said as Forest put on the brakes to avoid hitting a pheasant. "She wasn't exactly happy to discover I was her daughter. I was disappointing. But you know, Rocky, I can't help it if I'm not automatically, obviously nice, like you."

"Molly, you shouldn't take it to heart. There's probably a good reason she behaved like that."

"Yes, she didn't like me."

Forest drove the lorry onto the main road that passed through Briersville town.

"It's strange not having the little Mollys with us. I miss them. I hope they're all right," Molly said.

"Man, that is the craziest thing you have ever said." Forest began laughing like a hyena. "Of course, they're all right. They're *in you*, Molly!"

"I guess they are."

Ojas's nose was still glued to the window. "So this is the future!" he gasped as they passed a farm with big corrugated barns in its yard.

"That's just a farm," said Rocky. "You wait till you play a computer game. That is going to blow your mind!"

"Blow my mind . . ." Ojas experimented with the new phrase.

Petula sat up and tried to see out. She could smell the llamas of Briersville Park. She began to twitch with excitement. She couldn't wait to run around the lawns there. She wondered whether her special stones were still all safely buried in the places she'd left them.

She shivered and for a moment thought of the lovely heat in India. It had been quite a trip, she thought. That peacock pie had been delicious, and the beauticians at the palace had been very nice. Her claws were still pink with nail polish. Still, she couldn't wait to chase some rabbits.

"And what about your parents? What are they like?" said Ojas.

"They're not really my parents," said Molly.

"No?"

"No. I mean, their parents were my grandparents, but I've only just met them. They don't know me, and I don't know them."

"Do you like them?"

Molly thought. "Well, they're a bit weird. You'll see. They're both a bit muddled, I suppose. But they're not scary or anything."

The truck rumbled on along frosty country lanes and finally came to the black gates of Briersville Park. Soon they were driving up the long, winding driveway, past pastures of grazing llamas, with animal-shaped bushes in the fields.

"Oh, I'm sure they'll like Amrit," Ojas said. He pointed at an elephant-shaped bush.

"Well," Molly explained, "those bushes were actually all put here by my uncle. His name is Cornelius. By the way, at the moment he thinks he's a lamb. Look, there he is!" Forest slowed the lorry down.

Cornelius Logan, dressed in a ski outfit, was standing

in a meadow with a flock of sheep.

"I suppose," said Rocky, "Cornelius was hypnotized by Waqt to behave the way he did."

"Poor Cornelius," agreed Molly. "Waqt got to him a long, long time ago. I remember Cornelius said he was jealous of his twin sister Lucy *all his life*. Waqt must have hypnotized him when he was a small boy. Poor, poor Cornelius. I mean, to be hypnotized *all* your life, starting when you were three or something—that's freaky. If I unlock Waqt's hypnosis, Cornelius might go mad from the shock. He looks so happy there, nibbling that grass."

"Yes, but he's in prison. He's in a hypnotic prison," Rocky said. "He has the right to know his real life." The engine of the truck grumbled as it idled.

"One day you'll discover Waqt's password," Forest reckoned, changing gear and driving on. "Then you can go back and free Cornelius and those maharajas."

"I'm going to do it—well, probably next week," said Molly. "But the password is going to be a problem. 'Pock,' 'key,' and 'pea' don't work. There must be other words. It's like some mad gobbledygook spell. All I know is that it ended or started in 'pock' or 'key' or 'pea.' It'll be practically impossible to guess the rest."

Forest pulled into the graveled forecourt of Briersville Park. As he did so, Ojas slipped into the back of the truck to prepare Amrit for her arrival.

The tall, mahogany front doors opened wide. Primo Cell put the palm of his hand to his forehead and squinted in the cold sunlight, wondering why a huge truck was pulling up in front of Briersville Park.

"Molly, Rocky, Forest," he shouted worriedly, "is that you?"

Petula jumped out of the cabin. She was extremely excited to be back. As she bowled up the steps, Molly, Rocky, and Forest stepped down from the truck.

"Um, we're back!" said Molly, as calmly as if she'd just been out to the shops for a pint of milk.

"Lucy!" Primo shouted. "They're back. *They're all back.*" He ran down the steps and seized Molly and Rocky. "God, we thought we'd never see you again!" he said, hugging them both, one with each arm. "We thought you were . . . were . . ."

"Dead? No way, man. Death courted us but it didn't date us," quipped Forest.

"Oh, thank goodness." Primo Cell buried his face in Molly's and Rocky's shoulders. Rocky winked at Molly as if to say, "I think he likes us."

And then Lucy Logan came rushing out of the house. She faltered at the top of the steps and then came running down. She didn't hug Molly and Rocky. Instead, she smiled and smiled and her forehead was a mass of surprised horizontal lines. Molly avoided catching her eye.

Primo laughed. "So where have you been?"

"It's a long story," Molly began. Slightly embarrassed, she edged her eyes toward Lucy. Primo noticed.

"Lucy is much better now," he said. "We've talked a lot and got to the bottom of why she was sad."

Molly's heart gave a jolt. Had they talked about all the reasons why Lucy found Molly so disappointing?

"Oh, Molly!" gasped Lucy, shocked to see nervousness written all over her daughter's face. "You were probably dreading seeing me!" She clasped her hands together and implored her. "Don't worry. I promise I won't be the washed-up person I was again." Then she exploded. "I'm *so* sorry, Molly. I was like a sad, wet biscuit! When we found each other I should have been really happy, but I couldn't help turning over and over in my mind what I had lost. I just couldn't accept my past. I kept wishing that it had been different. I kept wishing that you and . . . and . . . hadn't been taken from me." Molly was half listening. She was buzzing with a mixture of anger and fear of what Lucy was going to say next.

"Lucy," said Primo, twisting his mouth awkwardly, "I think we should wait to tell Molly. She'll be as shocked as I was. Here on the drive doesn't seem—"

"Yes, sorry, it just slipped out. Later."

"Later for what?" Molly asked, ignoring Petula, who was jumping up at her. She reran in her head what Lucy had just said. "You kept wishing that me and *what* hadn't been taken from you?"

"I kept wishing that you and . . . and . . ."

"Cornelius?" Molly guessed. "We know that Waqt took him. That isn't news. We know."

"Waqt? Who's he?"

"You don't know Waqt?"

Lucy shook her head.

"He's the man who had taken Petula," said Molly.

"A man called Waqt *took* Cornelius? What do you mean? How?" Molly found herself in a sticky situation. She had decided not to tell Lucy about Waqt hypnotizing Cornelius as a little boy. She glanced at Forest and Rocky. Both were looking uncomfortable, staring at their feet. They'd all thought it best not to tell Lucy yet, because the news would be so distressing for her. But now half of it had slipped out. Which was what Lucy had just done—let something slip out.

Molly tried to change the subject. "You first. You tell me what else was taken from you," she said, biding her time.

Lucy shook her head and looked at Primo for guidance.

"Tell her," said Primo.

There was a long silence as Lucy plucked up the courage to tell Molly why she had been so very sad. Molly began to see that this other thing was something fairly big. And now she really began to wonder what it was.

"You know, Molly," Lucy began, tears welling up in her blue eyes, "that Cornelius is my twin."

"Yes," said Molly, frowning as she tried to guess what Lucy was trying to say.

"Yes, well, as you know, I was a twin—and twins run in families—and . . . and . . . and so . . ." Lucy put her hands over her face.

"And so were you, is what she's trying to say," said Primo. "So were you."

"So was I what?"

"A twin."

"What? I have a twin?" Molly said dumbly. "A twin? But where is she?"

"He."

"He? He? Where is he?"

"We don't know, Molly," said Primo. Lucy beside him was wiping her eyes with a yellow hankie.

"I'm sorry," she said. "I thought I'd finished crying about this, but it's difficult to . . . to accept without being overwhelmed with . . ." She stifled a sob. ". . . with tea-aa-ars!"

Molly stared at her. "A brother?" was all she could say.

Suddenly images of a boy a bit taller than her, standing there with her, filled her head. She looked at Rocky. "Did you ever see him?" Molly asked Lucy.

"Yes, before . . . before someone came and took him."

"Cornelius really doesn't know what happened to the child," Primo said. "It's been a terrible blow to us both not knowing where he went, or whether he is alive or not. We just don't know what happened to him." Primo looked more serious than Molly had ever seen him before. His lower lip quivered. "Oh dear, this was really the wrong time and place to tell you this," he said, running his foot along the step.

"No, it wasn't!" said Molly. At once, all her paranoia about not being good enough lifted. A new confidence filled her. To Molly, the bad news felt good, because it made her see that Lucy hadn't been disappointed that Molly was her daughter. She'd been sad for a completely different reason. A reason that Molly had no power over. But now Molly could help. Once again, she found herself in the position of being calm while her wobbly parents were riding roller-coasters of emotion. She tried to reassure them. "You mustn't worry. I know things now that mean I can find out what happened to him. I really can! Not today," she added hastily, "because I'm really, really tired, and I'd quite like to spend at least one day in my right here-and-now before I whiz off again to another one."

"What do you mean?" asked Primo.

"She's a time traveler, man," explained Forest. "Molly here can zing about in time. She'll find your son."

"Yes, I will," said Molly. She walked up to Lucy and squeezed her hand. "So stop being sad, Lucy. There *is* some hope." Molly wondered where her brother could be. Was he in another country, in another time? Or was he in the next town, in another orphanage? "I'll track him down. And I'll do my best to bring him back."

"Can you really do that, Molly?" Lucy pinched her cheek. "Oh my, am I dreaming?"

At this point, Ojas, clad in three blankets, stepped out from behind the lorry.

"You are not dreaming, memsahib," he said, shivering. "Mollee here is a wonderful time traveler."

"This is Ojas," said Molly. Lucy smiled bewilderedly and shook his hand. Ojas then shook Primo's hand.

"I am very delighted to meet you," he said. "And it is a privilege for me to be in your century!"

Primo and Lucy looked at Ojas. Primo asked, "So, er, what time are you from?"

"Oh, 1870. I come from Delhi, India, 1870. It never gets this cold in Delhi! Amrit is from there, too. She must have a *coat* made if she is to live here!"

"Amrit?"

Rocky was already unbolting the back of the lorry. He swung the tailgate down. Amrit didn't need enticing. She was keen to investigate her new surroundings and began edging her huge gray body backward down the metal gangplank. Then she approached Primo and Lucy, sniffing the air with her long trunk.

"My goodness!" exclaimed Lucy. "I've always loved elephants. Oh, how fantastic—she can live in the pavilion by the swimming pool."

"She will like that," said Ojas, patting Amrit's trunk. "She is very keen on swimming."

"Would you like to ride her?" asked Molly.

"Ride her? I'd love that!" said Lucy. And at last Molly heard something that she'd long been wanting to hear. She heard Lucy laugh.

So Ojas bid Amrit kneel down, and soon Lucy was up. But before they set off, Ojas did something else. He put an object into Amrit's trunk and gave a little whistle. Amrit's trunk obediently followed his order.

"What's this?" Lucy asked as the end of Amrit's trunk passed her a package. She undid the paper wrapping to discover a large, gem-encrusted bracelet.

"It is a present for you," said Ojas. "For you to wear. Next week it has to go back to its rightful owner, but until then, you can make the most of it." He gave Molly a cheeky smile.

"Oh, thank you, Ojas," said Lucy, slipping it onto her wrist and finding it much too big. "It must have belonged to a very large woman!"

Everyone laughed.

"Oh no, Lucy, it is not for your arm. You must wear it around your ankle!"

Primo handed Ojas his padded coat.

"Why don't we go and see whether Amrit likes her new home?" he said, grinning broadly.

And so, reunited, everyone set off across the lawn to the swimming pool.

"You must have had some amazing adventures," Primo said, fondly patting Molly's and Rocky's shoulders as they walked. "We've been worried sick ever since you all disappeared. When you've had some food and sleep I'll be extremely interested to hear what happened and to find out how time travel works."

"Oh, there's plenty of time," Molly said, smiling up at him.

Amrit walked along, her great bottom swinging as she plodded after Ojas.

"I must say," said Primo, "now Amrit is here, I realize that what this place *really* needed was an elephant! A house is always best filled with children and elephants!"

"And funny grown-ups," said Rocky, smiling as Forest did a cartwheel on the lawn. Petula rushed past them.

"And pets!" added Molly. "Especially Petula-shaped ones!" She crouched down to retie her damp shoelaces. "I'll catch up with you," she said.

The ground in front of her was wet with dew and covered with footprints: Amrit's, Ojas's, Rocky's, Primo's, and Petula's. Molly glanced back at her own.

The past was made up of the prints and impressions of life, Molly thought. She wondered where life was leading her now. She'd intended to start a hypnotic hospital, but yet again it looked like her plans were to be interrupted. Now she had to find her twin brother. Half of her wasn't sure if she wanted a brother; the other half had a burning desire to meet him.

Ahead, Rocky whistled. The tune was from a song he'd once made up. Molly knew its words well, and now they sang in her head:

There's no time like the present,
No present like time.
And life can be over in the space of a rhyme.
There's no gift like friendship
And no love like mine.
Give me your love to treasure through time.

Molly smiled. She loved her friends and her life, too. From now on, whether she was at the beginning of time or the end of time or slap-bang in the middle of it, she would make the most of every moment.

M eanwhile, a couple of thousand miles away, on the outskirts of Jaipur, on a piece of land that served as a sewage pit, a huge worm slithered through the slime. An equally slippery character picked his way across the sludge.

Zackya's silver tracking device was switched on. He put his scarf to his nose and tried to ignore the sulfurous stench in the air.

"I'll find her, wherever she is," he muttered dumbly, bringing his bleeping machine down to the stinking mud. The brown water squelched between his toes. "I KNOW YOU'RE DOWN THERE, MOLLY MOON!" he shouted madly. "I CAN HELP YOU!"

Throwing the silver gadget onto the bank, he began to scoop up the filth with his bare hands.

All night he dug, and the moon and stars came out to watch him. At the bottom of the muck, a battered purple metal pip sent out its last signal. Then it switched itself off and began to rust.